CAROUSEL

T0282046

First published 2015 by
FREMANTLE PRESS

This edition first published 2024.

Fremantle Press Inc. trading as Fremantle Press
PO Box 158, North Fremantle, Western Australia, 6159
fremantlepress.com.au

Designed by Carolyn Brown, tendeersigh.com.au
Printed and bound by IPG

 A catalogue record for this
book is available from the
National Library of Australia

ISBN 9781760993337 (paperback)
ISBN 9781760994532 (ebook)

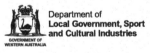

Fremantle Press is supported by the State Government through the
Department of Local Government, Sport and Cultural Industries.

Fremantle Press respectfully acknowledges the Whadjuk people of the
Noongar nation as the Traditional Owners and Custodians of the land
where we work in Walyalup.

CAROUSEL

BRENDAN RITCHIE

 FREMANTLE PRESS

To J & P

1

It was definitely Taylor and Lizzy. They were sitting on one of those island-type lounges you find in the middle of most shopping centres. The ones filling space between juice bars and mobile phone stores. This one was curved and black and might have worked better in a hotel lobby.

They were looking at their mobiles and talking. Well, Taylor was. Her hair was a bit longer than Lizzy's, and chopped up on the sides. Lizzy's was bobbed like a helmet in some fifties sci-fi movie. Their hair was always awesome.

Taylor was throwing snatches of speech at Lizzy, who was letting most of it fly. Only occasionally chiming in to answer before her sister had finished the question. Both of them were pretty preoccupied with their phones.

What the hell were they doing here?

I knew they were touring. Wedging in some dates in Australia on their way through to Asia and probably Europe. I'd seen them play The Shetland two nights ago. The converted warehouse popping with old fans, faces glowing in the aftermath of their favourite singles, and hipster lesbians drawn magnetically to the gay Canadian duo and the prospect of a night away from Perth's clichéd and sleazy clubs.

Still, the idea of an in-store seemed pretty insane. Well, maybe not. But I was pretty sure that this was Carousel Shopping Centre. A sprawling mass of big names like Myer and Apple shoved between discount fashion outlets and oversize supermarkets on the eastern fringes of Perth.

What the hell were they doing at Carousel?

What the hell was I doing at Carousel?

Hold on. How did I know this was Carousel?

There was a Bags R Us store next to me. Shelves of cheap suitcases and tacky red-leather handbags. Next along was a salon. Part of a chain maybe. Then a chocolate store selling gift baskets, prepacked and wrapped in cellophane with snips of ribbon. One of these lay open between Taylor and Lizzy.

On the other side was Country Road. Larger than the other stores with classic-cut polos and pencil skirts stuck to beautiful mannequins in the windows. Next door to this was a gaudy looking Cotton On selling imitations at half the price. The place was weird without music. Normally I would be blasted with some crappy dance track standing this close to Cotton On. But not today.

I looked upward for some windows but there were none. This end of the centre was just one level. There was some light at the end of the corridor where the place seemed to open up into a kind of dome. Maybe that's why I thought it was Carousel. It had this ridiculous entrance where a bunch of doors led into a big round foyer with its roof cut off. In summer this left the sushi bar and café sweltering in forty-degree sunshine. In winter an awning was stretched across, leaving the floor slippery as hell when rain blew under and mixed with car-park dirt to form a greasy brown film on the tiles. Countless teenage dates were ruined by the embarrassment of a fall before the couple had even made it to the cinema.

The light down there seemed blue and artificial. From where I stood next to Bags R Us it was impossible to know if it were day or night.

Taylor and Lizzy were looking at me.

They had glanced my way a couple of times already. But now they were looking right at me and talking. Lizzy seemed to be suggesting something. Maybe Taylor wasn't so sure. Neither of them moved.

Nor did I.

It occurred to me how stupid I must look just standing there at the front of a discount luggage store. Why wasn't I walking somewhere or looking for something? I searched my pockets for my beat-up phone. But I couldn't pull it out now. The Finns were already looking at me. Instead I turned and stepped inside the store.

It was empty.

Not just of customers, which I might have expected, but seemingly of staff too. I browsed through some of the less tacky overnight suitcases and waited for a shop assistant to surface from the back of the store. Nobody did. I smiled a little at the idea that someone hated their job here so much that they didn't even bother coming out of the lunchroom for customers. I'd dreamed of this kind of behaviour at the stationery store where I worked but never had the guts to carry it out.

The only thing was I kind of wanted to buy something so I wouldn't have to leave empty-handed, looking like a fraud. I walked over to the counter and waited for a few moments. I took out my phone and put it down on the benchtop so that it made a decent noise. Still nobody surfaced to serve me.

This is stupid, I thought. Like Taylor and Lizzy Finn will care if I don't buy a suitcase. They probably weren't even looking at me.

I left the store and headed for the dome. The Finns were still there, focused back on their phones. But for some bizarro reason I didn't walk past. Instead I veered across in a weird curve and stopped awkwardly in front of them.

They looked up for a moment and gave me a couple of pretty friendly smiles. Lizzy returned to what looked like an X feed. Taylor waited for me to say something.

'Hi. I'm Nox,' I said.

'Hi, Nox,' Taylor replied.

I didn't say anything else straight away. Taylor shuffled over slightly on the couch. I lingered for a moment, then sat on the edge. Lizzy showed Taylor her phone.

'What?' said Taylor.

'Look at my network,' said Lizzy.

'You don't have one,' said Taylor.

'That's what I'm saying,' said Lizzy.

Taylor turned to me. 'Do you have a phone?'

'Yeah. But my network is shit in here.'

'All the time?' she asked.

'I don't know.'

Lizzy was listening too. She looked at me.

'This place is called Carousel, right?' said Lizzy.

'Yeah,' I replied.

'When is it normally open?' asked Taylor.

'I don't know. Most times I guess. There's a cinema and some bars down there.'

They turned in the direction of the dome. 'So it stays open pretty late,' I said.

Taylor and Lizzy glanced at each other.

'Are you guys doing an in-store?' I asked.

'We don't really do those anymore,' said Taylor.

'We did one last year,' said Lizzy.

'Not in Australia,' said Taylor.

'Or Perth.' I added.

They both looked at me.

'Not all bands do the west coast when they tour,' I said.

'We do,' said Taylor.

'I know,' I said. 'I've seen you guys play a few times.'

'Whereabouts?' asked Taylor.

'Saturday at The Shetland. But also Fremantle. And down south.'

'Where is down south?' asked Taylor.

'Just south of the city. People here drive down there on weekends.'

They nodded.

'What's your favourite song?' asked Lizzy.

'Lizzy. What the fuck?' said Taylor.

'What?' said Lizzy.

'There are probably some other things we could ask him,' said Taylor.

'Like what?' said Lizzy.

'Gee, I don't know,' said Taylor.

'I like "Josephine". But I don't really have a favourite,' I said.

They looked at me a little sceptically and nodded. Taylor dialled a number on her phone and waited for an answer.

'What are you doing?' asked Lizzy.

'Trying to call Patrick,' said Taylor.

'Why? I tried already.'

Taylor ignored this. Lizzy looked across at the Pure 'n' Natural kiosk ahead of us.

'What is Pure 'n' Natural? Like juices and stuff?' she asked.

'I think so,' I replied.

'Coffee?' she asked.

'I don't know. Maybe.'

'We need coffee,' said Taylor.

'There's a Coffee Club near the cinema, I think,' I replied.

'Is that like Starbucks?' asked Lizzy.

'Kind of.'

'So they'll have a machine yeah?' asked Lizzy.

'Yeah.'

Taylor laughed and gave up on her phone. I must have sounded sarcastic. Lizzy shook her head, stood up and stretched. Taylor watched her.

'Are you coming?' Lizzy asked Taylor.

Taylor looked across at me and didn't answer.

'Taylor?' she asked again.

'Hold on,' said Taylor. 'You don't work here or anything, right?' Taylor asked me.

I shook my head. Taylor nodded, then rose to head off in the direction of the dome. I stayed seated.

'Come on,' said Lizzy. 'We'll get a latte or something.'

I stood and shuffled forward to catch up to them. Ahead of us the centre lay completely empty.

2

Lizzy and I stood looking at the sky through the open dome while Taylor pushed on the doors at the front of the centre. None of them opened. The sky was crisp and blue. It was daytime and the centre was closed.

Lizzy left me and wandered over to the Coffee Club island. She opened a gate in the counter and walked inside. Taylor turned from the doors and watched as Lizzy took some milk from a fridge and studied the shiny espresso machine running along the counter. I trailed over and sat on a stool. A moment later Taylor joined me. Lizzy pressed some buttons on the machine. Steam shot out over the floor.

'Do you really want to do that?' asked Taylor.

'What?' asked Lizzy.

'Screw around with their stuff,' said Taylor.

Lizzy brushed this off. 'We're stuck in here, Taylor. What else are we going to do?'

'We're probably all over the security video by now,' said Taylor.

Lizzy ignored her. She had worked out how to grind the coffee beans and was filling up a handle.

'What are you having?' she asked me.

'Oh. A latte, I guess,' I said.

'Awesome,' she said.

Taylor rolled her eyes and toggled the airplane mode on her phone. Lizzy filled a jug with milk, turned on the steamer and spilled some foam across the counter. I smiled and Lizzy joined me. She poured the bubbly milk into three small glasses a quarter full with coffee. Mocking pride, she slid two over to me and Taylor.

'Thanks,' I said.

'Skim?' asked Taylor.

Lizzy shook her head. I watched the two of them look at each other. They seemed to do this a lot. It was hard to tell what was passing between them.

Lizzy looked around the open, circular foyer. 'So why are all of the shops open?' she asked.

Taylor and I followed her gaze. A giant Live clothing store dominated the space. Black and edgy and normally the loudest fucker of them all. But not today. The doors opened up to an abandoned counter tucked behind a silent array of leather, dark denim and leggings.

There were other stores, of course. Rebel Sport. JB Hi-Fi. Smiggle. An Apple Store. You could totally look at a Mac without talking to somebody in a blue shirt. I wondered whether the staff would suddenly appear if I walked in and applaud me as their only customer for the day.

Lizzy was right, though. The whole place was open for

business, bar the front doors. Seemingly all the doors. Yet we were inside.

I turned back to them. Lizzy was looking at some jars of giant cookies on the counter. She took one out and showed it to Taylor. It was pretty huge.

Taylor looked at me. 'How long have you been here for?' she asked.

'Not long. I stopped at Dymocks to look at some books, then came down the corridor and saw you guys,' I trailed off.

'Right,' said Taylor and sipped on her coffee.

'What about you?' I asked.

Taylor and Lizzy shared another look.

'Maybe twenty minutes before you. We were in the chocolate store looking at gift baskets. Picked one out but there was nobody at the counter. So we sat out on the couch and waited for them to come back,' said Taylor.

'Then we saw you looking for luggage,' said Lizzy.

I smiled a little and so did Lizzy. Taylor shook her head and looked around.

Something was bothering me.

'Why Carousel?' I asked.

'What do you mean?' asked Taylor.

'For the chocolates? Why did you come here?' I asked.

'We're still jetlagged. Woke up early looking for something to do. This weird cab driver dropped us here and said there would be good shopping,' answered Lizzy.

'You believed him?' I asked.

'He was oddly convincing,' said Lizzy.

She and Taylor glanced at each other as if to confirm this.

'Weird,' I said, to myself.

'What?' asked Taylor.

'I came by taxi too,' I said.

They kind of shrugged as if that were no big deal.

'I was heading into the city for the early shift at work but my car wouldn't start so I walked to the bus stop. While I was waiting this taxi pulled up and beeped at me. I figured *what the hell* and got in,' I said. 'The driver seemed kind of stressed. He was driving fast, taking a bunch of back streets. Next thing I know he pulls up at this big building that turns out to be the back of Carousel.'

The Finns sipped on their coffees and listened.

'Anyway, he didn't charge me anything. Just said he couldn't take me any further. Told me to go inside,' I added.

Lizzy nodded and thought this over.

'Surely some security guy must have seen us screwing around by now,' said Taylor.

'Do you want to check out the other exits?' I asked.

'Yeah,' said Taylor, and hopped down from her stool.

I led them through the complex, trying to remember how it was laid out. I'm not really good with shopping centres and at least twice I led us back through the same corridor. It's hard to tell if Taylor and Lizzy noticed. They seemed pretty curious about the shops we were passing. I heard them laughing a few times and turned back to smile like I was in on the joke. Or like I knew how hilarious this whole scenario was. Really, I just felt normal. Like this was something that was always going to happen. I've always felt underwhelmed in dramatic scenarios. People say I'm calm in a crisis, or hard to faze. Truth is I just go numb as hell.

Carousel had exits all over the place. Aside from the front, we found a series of side exits, and a large glass exit to a car park at the back. All of these were locked. The back entrance offered a pretty big view but mostly just of the car park, and a small patch of hills east of the city. Taylor and Lizzy stayed there for a little while, looking out at the view as you do in a new place, even when it's like stuff you've seen before.

The strangest thing we found was that all of the emergency fire doors were locked as well. Those doors with a small lever on the face that you just push to open. I didn't think they were ever locked from the inside. The significance of this didn't really dawn on Taylor and Lizzy. Actually, they both seemed a little tired.

I pushed on another fire door, without success, and turned to find them sitting on a corridor lounge, back on their phones. I went over there and took a seat. I looked at my own phone for a while, then just sat there looking at the light reflecting off the floor. Taylor was lying back with her knees drawn up. Lizzy was cross-legged, still glancing through her static X feed as if her flight was delayed, or her doctor was running late.

It felt comfortable. The three of us just sitting there, waiting for the inevitable opening. The snap of a door somewhere as a cleaner or security guard came on shift. Our voices echoing through the corridors to help them find us. Some paperwork to fill out. A few questions. Then the swish of a door as the morning breeze hit our faces. Taylor and Lizzy would want to go back to their hotel and get ready for their flight. Maybe we could share a taxi. I turned to ask them about this but Taylor's eyes were closed, and Lizzy's leg had fallen to rest, just slightly, against my own.

Instead I kept quiet and silently wished that the security guards wouldn't come. And that the cleaners didn't have to start a shift. That we wouldn't hear the snap of a door or feel the breeze on our faces.

3

I'd never heard the rain on the roof of a shopping complex. It had always been drowned out by people and music and a thousand other noises. But now, after seven months of emptiness, Carousel sounded cavernous. I could hear sheets of rain hammering against the long cinema roof upstairs. The lighter drumming and trickle of water against the glass of the back entrance. An occasional spatter of droplets on tiles as they reached down through the uncovered hole in the dome to the slippery floor below. The small rivers of water traversing the centre's complicated gutter system. And the dull hum on the roof above the homeware section of Myer where I slept.

I had chosen a single bed. Sometimes Lizzy would rib me about this, given there was a whole bunch of kings and queens in the centre. But I needed some sense of confinement. Sleeping in an empty shopping complex, with a whole level of Myer to myself, was room enough. I didn't need to roll over three times on a giant bed before I reached the edge.

It was actually a kids' bunk setup. One of those with a standard top bunk and a slightly larger bottom bed running at right angles beneath. I slept okay under there with my head up against the back of a display chest, and an assortment of colourful lamps running along a shelf down the side.

Taylor and Lizzy had tried a bunch of beds since the first night. Like they were still on the road, moving from hotel to hotel to play shows in different cities. I mentioned this once but it made them upset and a while ago the four of us had agreed not to do that. At the moment Taylor was back in Bed Bath and Home on a four-poster queen, and Lizzy had moved her favourite ensemble into a corner of Dymocks Books where the lighting was perfect for reading, but not too bright to keep her awake.

Lighting was a major drag for us. Most shops in the centre kept some lights on twenty-four-seven. Sometimes you could find the switches and screw around until you found which ones to turn off, but in the bigger stores they were often locked in electrical closets or offices. In Myer they were set to a timer that sent the upper levels into a three-quarter-dim at eight o'clock each night. This was still too bright for sleep.

A few nights in I tripped a fuse and cut out the whole kids section. But the place was too creepy in the dark and I quickly switched them back on. I think we all secretly felt this way. Behind our complaints on the first night there was unspoken relief that the lights hadn't shut down and left us alone and in darkness until morning.

This particular morning I had woken early with the rain. I lay there listening and looking around the level. The kitchen section was the closest to my bed. A constant shimmer of wine glasses and cutlery in selective downward lighting. I sometimes thought of taking a photo each week to see how long it would take for enough dust to collect to dim the reflections. One of the best carafes stood stained at a nearby table from earlier in the week. Taylor and I had taken our weekly pilgrimage down the east end of the centre to Liquor Central for a shiraz she had read about in a travel magazine.

Past kitchenware was the pastel warmth of the linen section. I had started to make a decent-size pile of dirty linen in a corner over there since Lizzy had introduced me to the novelty of fresh sheets.

'Come on. You can even have Spider-Man if you want,' she had said.

Before long I had a pile of vacuum-packed square sheet sets ready beside the bunks.

She was right about the sheets though. I didn't know what she and Taylor were on about when they ranted over thread counts or the cotton in Myer compared to Bed Bath and Home, but the crispy feel of sheets straight out of the packet, with their sweet, plasticy smell, was pretty addictive.

Linen eventually gave way to electrical and the walls of HD televisions that I had turned off long ago. Initially I was pretty excited about the electrical section. Watching DVDs and Blu-rays from JB Hi-Fi on huge 3D LCD LED ADD TVs. Gaming on the demo consoles chained to the cabinets beneath. But there was something kind of sullen about a TV with no reception. While Carousel had plenty of power, it was a total black spot for any kind of communication. No TV. No internet. Not even radio. Sure we could watch stuff on disc, and we did a lot of this, but every time I walked by the TVs I couldn't help but wish they were screening the latest *Modern Family* or *X Factor*. Shit, I'd even settle for *MasterChef*. Instead they sat dormant and lifeless. As disconnected from the world as we were.

Then there were the escalators. Static and exhausting. If there was a switch for these we hadn't found it. The increased fall of the stationary stairs meant that traversing was unusually difficult and made Taylor feel like she was 'going to die in this creepy mall'. I used a collection of long cardboard sheets to slide down to ground floor. After a few days practice it was relatively easy. The only downside was lugging all the sheets back up every so often.

Behind my bunk and out of view was a small giftware section. Several stands full of cards in sections like His Birthday, Her Birthday and Friendship. Every Sunday I would pick out the cheesiest card I could find from the With Regret section, sign my name, put it in an envelope and drop it off to Lizzy. She would respond the next day with the worst Happy Anniversary card she could find, trudging up my escalator while I was out microwaving soup or kicking around a soccer ball. One Sunday I started watching the *Lord of the Rings* box set and forgot to leave Lizzy her card. She brooded for two days. I realised then that the cards were important and I haven't missed one since.

It sounded like the rain had set in and I could come back and listen later if I wanted, so I got up and went to the bathroom. There were Men's, Ladies', Disabled and Staff toilets on my level. Fortunately the staff toilets had a shower.

At first it had been pretty uninviting. Basically a cubicle without the toilet. But, thanks to an abundant supply of toiletry items, it wasn't so bad anymore.

I stood under water, under rain, for a good half hour. Thankfully wherever the hot water supply was coming from, like the power, it seemed inexhaustible.

I towelled off and walked around to the Men's where I kept a basin. The Ladies' was closer, and I've never liked using a trough, but something still felt weird about going in there.

It had started getting cold in the mornings so I had laid out a series of bathmats in a collage surrounding the basin I used. Coupled with the piles of shave cream, toothbrushes and deodorants I had gathered, the room went from stark white to disco colour in a footstep. Being in there alone, with the long line of silent cubicles, could be pretty creepy.

A while ago I decided to prop the doors open with garden gnomes from Backyard Bonanza. I figured as long as the doors were open there couldn't be anyone hiding behind them. The others felt the same so we spent a day gnoming the whole centre. Now whenever you went to the toilet a gnome was stationed outside.

My radio crackled. I stopped brushing my teeth and listened. It was Taylor.

'We're moving to berry Pop-Tarts. Interested?' she asked.

'Yeah. Be down in a sec,' I replied.

'Awesome.'

We'd made a pact to keep the radios on after losing each other for a night during the first week. Taylor had stayed out late checking to see if any of the doors would open on the south side of the building. Lizzy was bunkered down in the alternative music section in JB's. I was supposed to stay by the dome to meet Taylor but got hungry and went to Coles. The corridor lights timed out and we chased each other's echoes around the place for hours before giving up and sleeping where we were. It felt like losing your mum when you were a kid. And the sounds had made it worse. Without people, parts of Carousel echoed like crazy. So when Lizzy started crying in Friendlies Chemist, Taylor and I could hear her. And when Taylor started too I couldn't really help it either. It was the first time any of us got upset. In the morning we found each other easily and all felt pretty stupid. So we charged some radios from Dick Smith and went shopping for belts to hook them on.

Now I didn't even notice it hanging by my side.

Right now breakfast was at the Pure 'n' Natural island. It had a microwave and toaster, but more importantly a freezer full of frozen fruit. Taylor and Lizzy were paranoid about getting scurvy after a former schoolmate of theirs contracted the ancient nautical condition. He was left to fend for himself while his parents were on holidays. They had a chest freezer full of frozen sausage rolls and party pies. So, thinking nothing of it, that's all he ate for a month. Until he collapsed at school with pasty white skin and sores all through his mouth.

Taylor and Lizzy Finn floated sleepily around the tropical-coloured island as I approached. Lizzy was putting together some weird fruit smoothie. She was slightly shorter than her twenty-six-year-old twin, but wispy in a way that made her seem taller than she actually was. She dressed herself in a lot of rock-star black but always with a flicker of feminine via a heart-shaped brooch or some smoky eye shadow.

Taylor was reading the box while she toasted some Pop-Tarts. She shared Lizzy's big, luminous eyes but hers had a kind of attitude that immediately distinguished her and somehow said both *What are you looking at* and *I'm really lost* at the same time. Taylor was all vintage denim jackets and high-cut boots. On their album covers Lizzy was usually photographed at the front, but in an ironic kind of way.

I gave them a little wave and stepped inside to clean a couple of plates at the sink.

'Is Rocky coming?' I asked, once Lizzy had stopped the blender.

'He's not answering his radio,' replied Taylor.

Lizzy shook her head and inspected the smoothie.

'We told him about that,' I said.

'I know,' shrugged Taylor.

The Pop-Tarts shot up and I plated them, leaving a spare in the machine for Rocky.

We chewed silently with a glass of purple smoothie to wash down the clumps of sugary dough.

'Do you need help moving equipment today?' I asked Lizzy.

'Sure,' she replied.

Taylor was quiet. She'd kept right out of Lizzy's plan to set up a recording studio from the equipment in the music store next to Target. I'd overheard them talking about it last week. Taylor telling Lizzy not to expect her to run in and play stuff once it was ready. Lizzy telling Taylor that she shouldn't assume she would be invited.

'I'm so into these blueberries,' said Taylor looking at her drink like it was mystical.

'I know, right,' said Lizzy.

'Are we on to berry Pop-Tarts because the others are out of code?' I asked.

Taylor nodded. Food wasn't our favourite topic now that items had started to reach use-by dates in all of the supermarkets.

'I was thinking that some of the stores in the food court might have storage freezers at the back with stuff inside,' I said.

They both nodded.

'Have you finished *A Dance with Dragons*?' Taylor asked Lizzy.

'Almost. You know there are like fifty copies in Dymocks, right?' Lizzy replied.

Taylor shrugged.

A whirring noise interrupted them as Rocky wheeled around the corner on one of his kid's-size mountain bikes. The three of us watched him coast toward us. He looked away, feigning interest in the stores flashing by.

'Hey, Rocky,' said Taylor.

'Hey,' he replied and leant the bike carefully against the island.

I swung off my chair and dipped his Pop-Tart down for a reheat.

'You forget your radio again?' asked Lizzy.

Rocky nodded and sheepishly sipped his smoothie. He looked young today. Acne blotching his lower face and neck. An oversized hoodie hanging loosely from his stooping shoulders. The three of us would often catch each other staring at him curiously like he was some study into puberty. Then remind ourselves to leave the poor guy alone.

'Do you want to come out to the south end with me today, Rock?' asked Taylor.

He nodded, as she knew he would.

'Awesome,' said Taylor.

There were all sorts of exits in the south end that Taylor had started testing after she finished with the back entrances. She would go out there with a bunch of different tools from Backyard Bonanza in the hope of wedging open one of the doors.

Taylor's desire to break out of the centre had remained pretty constant from the first night. For me it came in waves. I don't think this meant that Taylor necessarily wanted to be free more than I did, but maybe her need for a goal or routine was stronger. I found it easier to face the problem of our strange imprisonment when I was feeling okay with things than when I was down. But then I guess what got me down to begin with was probably being imprisoned.

I had drifted inevitably away from my parents and sister since moving out and starting uni. Driven back only by birthdays, holidays and the occasional family barbecue. As time went by the visits became even less frequent. I had graduated with average grades and an arts degree, and started work for a stationery store chain. Suddenly it was like there was no future to discuss. I was just twenty-two but it was as if I'd already arrived at my destination, and, although I don't think my parents held out any great ambition for either my sister Danni or me, my situation made things oddly uncomfortable. I don't know if I missed seeing them, but I definitely missed having the option.

Maybe it was kind of the same for Lizzy. But I hadn't asked. Something large and inexplicable was happening, maybe had happened, in the world, or at least in Australia, but Lizzy somehow found a way to rationalise. Or maybe not rationalise, but accept and move on. As much as that were possible in a giant, deserted mall. None of us knew what Rocky's thoughts were. He was just as happy, or maudlin (in Rocky's case the difference was small), helping Taylor bashing doors as he was playing *Turkey Shoot Arcade* in the foyer of the cinema. We knew he was fragile and the three of us kept a close eye on him. But in reality we had no idea what to look out for.

I liked Rocky, though. From the moment we found him in the PJ section of Target, still wearing his work uniform, lying on a roll-out camping mat. He'd been in there, quiet as a mouse, for over a week. Surviving on boxes of chocolate and bottles of Sprite. Crashing from sugar every two hours, before getting hungry and doing it over again.

Target was cold and severely fluorescent twenty-four hours a day. Rocky hadn't really slept since arriving early for his shift. Despite this, and the fact that he was dehydrated, malnourished and scared as hell, he didn't complain for a moment. Actually, Rocky never complained. I'd seen him come off his bike about a dozen times since he started coasting through the corridors and he never said a word. And there were other times when Taylor and I were fiddling around with a window somewhere and we would hear a jarring crash from another side of the centre as Rocky fanned out too wide on a corner and slammed into a shopfront. Only to pick himself up and pedal off moments later.

Rocky was the skinny kid in school that you decided you would stick up for, even if it meant you would get beaten up. Because watching him get beaten would be so much worse.

He and Taylor spent a lot of time together. Even when she wasn't looking for an exit. They would find different things to race around the centre on. Skateboards. Scooters. Shopping trolleys.

Some nights, the three of us would take Rocky down to Liquor Central with an phone and some beanbags and pass on our knowledge of vodkas and wines. Rocky would drink along obediently and listen to our stories of when we first drank something, or how crap we felt after drinking something else. Taylor and Lizzy's stories were a lot more interesting than mine. In the depths of Carousel it was easy to forget they were musical celebrities. Drunk Rocky was pretty similar to sober Rocky. There were just more bike crashes on the way back.

4

Lizzy and I were down the back of the music store. The place was part of a local chain that catered for kids learning guitar and retirees taking up piano where they left off fifty years before. Not a place to shop for half an indie-rock duo from Canada. But Lizzy was making the best of it.

'Wow. There's so much shit in here,' she said, stepping back and assessing our progress in collecting a pile of necessary equipment.

'Yeah. Even though the *prices are mental*,' I said, quoting a favourite sign of ours in the window.

We stood there for a moment, surrounded by trashy glinting guitars and big, blocky amps.

'I'll grab a couple of trolleys from next door,' I said and left her inside.

The centre was quiet now that the rain had stopped. I was wearing a pair of canvas slip-ons from Country Road that I liked because they were silent on the lino and they didn't echo through the whole fucking centre like some shoes did. Thankfully Taylor and Lizzy weren't into heels that much or none of us would get anything done.

I bypassed the trolleys at the front of Target and stepped through a checkout to look for some Vitamin Water that was still in code. We had pretty much cleared out the mini fridges at the head of each checkout. I walked past, just to make sure, but it was just old gossip mags and Extra gum. It was crazy how much chewing gum there was in a fully stocked shopping complex.

I turned down into the bulk food section where they kept some warm bottles alongside the still water and multi-pack soft drink. We had cleared out the good flavours, but there was plenty of orange-orange still in code. I grabbed two and turned back toward the entrance.

Something caught my eye and I stopped.

Rocky's abandoned campsite lay at the other end of the aisle. I had a clear view of the makeshift bed and empty drink containers.

I stood there, strangely engrossed by the window into our Carousel past. There was a pile of kids' pyjamas bundled up for a pillow and a small outdoor lantern alongside.

I suddenly realised that Rocky might have stayed there forever if we hadn't have been in here too.

It was one of the loneliest things I had seen.

I wanted to get the hell out of there but couldn't stop looking. I got a snap of dizziness and the centre spread out behind my eyes like a giant empty prison.

My radio crackled.

I jumped a little and took off back toward the checkouts.

'Just wondering if you would be finished trying on skivvies soon?' said Lizzy on the radio. I took mine out of my pocket to reply.

'Yeah, sorry. The checkouts are banked up like crazy today,' I said as I passed through the entrance with the Vitamin Waters. Outside I stopped and turned back, remembering the trolleys.

The radio crackled again. This time it was Taylor.

'Remember the blue one he found?'

'Yeah. It was so snug,' Lizzy replied.

I found a couple of trolleys that steered okay and put the drinks inside. The Finns' jokes continued.

'It was almost the exact same colour as his denim. Like a big grown-up onesie,' said Taylor.

Lizzy pressed her radio just to laugh. Taylor followed. I shook my head and glanced back at the eerie, fluorescent expanse of Target. I decided not to go back in there unless I had to.

I rounded the corner and found Lizzy sitting on an amp beside a small pile of equipment at the front of the store. She was still exchanging radio laughter with Taylor. I held my radio up.

'Hey, Rock. I'm going to be on channel four FYI.'

I switched channels. A moment later there was a solitary crackle to show he had done the same. Lizzy looked my way and mocked sympathy. I handed her the Vitamin

Water and started loading the gear to make her feel even worse. She just ruffled my hair and smiled.

Later in the day we were parked outside Rugs a Million. Lizzy had decided on this for her studio partly due to the sound-proofing options offered by the countless rugs and carpets, and also because it had an 'awesome middle-eastern vibe'.

We spent a couple of hours clearing out a corner at the back and carrying in some equipment. Lizzy was keen to keep working and get the place ready for recording. I wondered how much it had to do with Taylor. The topic of music was a polarising force between them. Taylor hadn't played, or discussed music, since we arrived in the centre, and whatever she was listening to on her headphones was hers alone. Like a mother preserving the bedroom of a teenager left for uni, she carefully sheltered the memory of their musical past.

Lizzy was the opposite. Funnelling time and energy into the studio with an unflinching resolve. She would blast the rest of us with impromptu DJ sets from Carousel's huge library, and power through music magazines and autobiographies.

And she would play. Cross-legged on a couch or bed. Pacing around an abandoned corridor. Her pale, perfect fingers skipping across a keyboard or guitar. One of my favourite things about being stuck in the centre was hearing

Lizzy's music drifting the empty halls. Rocky and I would stop cycling and coast in slow circles while we listened to the fractured and beautiful sounds. Once I had seen Taylor stop to listen also. Her back was to me but I could see that her head had dropped slightly and she might have been smiling. Or crying.

She and Lizzy lived in different cities on the outside and the confinement of the centre had complicated both their relationship and their music. But Carousel offered them time. It was its foremost gift.

We stopped for a break and some honey-flavoured trail bars. Lizzy had chosen a big circular rug for the floor of her studio. We lay on our backs, looking up at the cheap fibro ceiling, and slowly chewed down the bars.

'Okay, so after Michelle in high school there was Heather, then Chloe in college?' she asked.

'Uni,' I said.

'Uni, college, whatever,' she said.

'Yeah, I think so,' I said.

'What does *I think so* mean? You've forgotten because none of them were really serious?' she asked. 'Or is it some guy thing where you act casual about this stuff?'

'Yeah. That's probably it,' I replied.

Lizzy sighed and tore open another bar.

'Sorry. I should be more open about the details of my intimate relationships,' I added. It was pretty sarcastic and

Lizzy sighed again.

'We've been here for what, six months now?' asked Lizzy.

'Seven. Nearly eight,' I replied.

'You can't expect to be trapped in a mall with the last three people on earth and not get to know them eventually,' she said.

'There's just not that much to tell. Michelle and I were on and off from Year Nine till first year uni.'

'Freshman,' Lizzy cut in.

'Yeah okay, Freshman,' I said. 'I met Heather. Stuff got weird and confusing. She went overseas. I listened to The National a lot. I met Chloe in a film theory class. We both liked Tom Tykwer films. Went out until June last year.'

I had Lizzy's full attention but there was a smirk in her just waiting to surface.

'What?' I asked.

'Nothing. It's just like dot points or something,' she said.

I sighed.

'And *stuff got weird and confusing*. People call that love, I think,' she said.

'Right, okay. Thanks,' I replied. 'Do you want to tell me some more about Erica now? Maybe how her hair looks after a hot shower as opposed to a cold one. Or how she makes those tiny noises when she reads exciting books. Or how toast tastes different when she makes it.'

Lizzy smiled and punched me twice in the shoulder.

I glanced at her to make sure I hadn't overstepped. Carousel kept each of us on emotional tightropes that were increasingly shaky. Despite Lizzy's ribbing this was the main reason behind my general silence. I figured not bringing stuff up decreased its opportunity to affect me.

Pretty mental, I know.

Lizzy seemed a little reflective, but fine.

'Did you hear that truck noise outside a few nights ago?' I asked her.

'Yeah, maybe,' she shrugged.

'No big deal?' I asked.

'I don't know,' she replied, a little tiredly. 'We hear weird stuff out there all the time. It doesn't mean people are just carrying on with their lives and forgetting that there's a giant ugly mall sitting here. Plus we arrived here via the same cab,' she said.

I smiled. Lizzy had a theory that the taxi that dropped them here most likely dropped me also. And that this driver alone had the answers to Perth's countless mysteries. Unfortunately none of us could confirm this. Our memories of him were vague to begin with, and grew more so with every day that passed.

'Worst shopping advice in history,' I said.

'Or the best,' replied Lizzy.

We gazed back up at the ceiling and finished another trail bar. A dull banging rang out from some distant corner of the centre. Taylor and Rocky were trying to break through a door. We lay in silence and listened.

'Why do you think that none of the doors will break open?' I asked.

'They're not supposed to,' answered Lizzy after a moment.

'Why?'

'The same reason that the windows won't smash. And there's enough food to eat. And the power stays on.'

I nodded. It was the best explanation. We stared at the ceiling some more.

'Have you thought about what you're going to record in here once it's ready?' I asked.

'No.'

'Is that normal?'

'No. Yeah,' she replied. 'God, I don't even know,' she added.

I looked at her and nodded so that someone would understand. Even though I didn't at all.

After another hour or so of shifting equipment it was alone time. Lizzy and I were getting along fine but it was kind of unspoken that the four of us needed a certain amount of time away from each other each day to stay at least a little sane. It was strange to feel crowded in a massive abandoned shopping centre, but we often did. Taylor and Lizzy would usually declare it outright and head off alone to go shopping or read books. Rocky and I were less direct. He would just be cycling around us one moment, then slowly coast away out of sight the next. I usually had a plan worked out early in the day for somewhere I wanted to go later. It wasn't a secret, and I knew the others wouldn't follow me or anything, but I still didn't really like telling them about it. It had been the same outside of Carousel. I just hadn't realised it then.

After leaving Lizzy, I had gone to the Men's bathroom in the north wing of the centre. Having hundreds of toilets to choose from weirded me out a little so, having looked around a bit, I really only used the first cubicle in this room, and the last one upstairs on my level of Myer. If I ventured into another it was because we were 'out' somewhere unusual and I treated it like a public toilet. Mine I washed weekly and kept my favourite paper and fresheners inside. And some magazines.

I opened one of these and jerked-off quickly to the crouching bikini model inside. This was followed by the usual incapacitating rush of embarrassment and guilt. I couldn't believe that I had done that again in this place, with Taylor and Lizzy and Rocky probably just around the corner. Eventually rationality would swallow this down, but it always took some time, and I had to do something that made me feel better about myself in the hour or two that followed.

Reading through the literary section of the centre's three bookstores was my main focus at the moment. I had finished an arts degree but felt like I only just touched the surface of what it was to write or be an artist. Since then I'd been buying books online and convincing myself that every one was moving me closer to knowing what the hell I was on about. But really only getting security in the fact that there was slightly less that I didn't know.

Lizzy was probably in Dymocks so I headed to Collins where I had gotten through a shelf and a half of the Penguin classics and some of the film theory. Rocky and I had shifted a couple of sofas in there a while ago and I sat on one until I had read four chapters of *Scorsese on Scorsese* and felt like less of a loser.

By then I was hungry and always liked the process of walking through a section of the centre until I decided on something to eat. A lot of stuff was coming out of code so the selection wasn't quite as extensive as it had been, but with three supermarkets and almost a hundred food-selling outlets, it was still enough to make me a little excited. Nowhere near the first week or two mind you. That small window when the fresh food was still edible. The Finns and I had taken long breaks from our confusion and hysteria to gorge on gelato and mud cake and curry. Food really got us through those first weeks. Food and shopping.

For a while Carousel was like some giant grown-up playground. Rocky and I would pull the cash drawers out of shops and carry them up to the arcade games in the foyer of the cinema. There we would bunker down with bags full of Pringles, Mars bars and Red Bulls, feeding games with coin after coin until we were bored and moved onto another. Some games like *Hoop Fever* even stopped working because the coin slots were chocked full and we couldn't find keys to empty them.

Then there was the real gaming. Carousel had every console on the market and two stores full of games. Like a couple of teenage stoners, Rocky and I burnt weeks bedded down in futuristic cities fighting the undead with masses of state-of-the-art military ammo. For lightness we broke this up with epic *FIFA* tournaments.

I had always been solid at gaming but Carousel sharpened me to a level that would have destroyed any of my mates. Rocky was on another level entirely. Within a few days of playing a game he would be so good that he would get bored and start to experiment. How quickly could he kill a room full of zombies? How many times could he lap the field? How long could he survive with just a knife, when the other avatars held AKs and grenade launchers? Half of our time on *FIFA* was spent watching replays of the epic, ridiculous goals he scored on me.

For Taylor and Lizzy it was all about the shopping.

Tucked among the trashy discount stores selling torn-up daisy dukes and fluoro camis, there were enough big-name outlets to keep them busy. The two of them would drift off to one wing of the centre and return with trolleys full of jeans, tops and accessories. It was hard not to just grab anything that was remotely cool when price and time were taken out of the equation. This often left them sorting through their selections upon returning in a process that Lizzy called trolley shopping.

The rules of trolley shopping seemed pretty specific. Firstly it couldn't involve any shops. The base items had already been gathered and no further additions were allowed. Carousel was big and tiring, and this aimed to take that factor out of play. The only exception to this was sizing. If you liked an item but the size was wrong, it could be put aside and noted down for collection later, or Rocky could be asked to fetch a suitable size from the store in question. This sounds harsh but couriering clothes throughout Carousel on his pristine selection of mountain bikes was actually one of Rocky's favourite things.

Due to the ban on shops, trolley shopping had to take place in a corridor or corner somewhere. The Finns would drag over a couple of movie standees and some mirrors and set up a makeshift change area. Outside of this would be a couch or something comfortable to sit on, and a bank of clothes-filled trolleys. The two of them would walk along the trolleys, selecting items and trying them on in the cover of the standees. If an item made the cut it was placed in a smaller trolley that they each kept by the couch.

Trolley shopping was a gradual and relaxed process. There would be music and magazines, and pauses for smoothies and snacks. Only premium selections made it to the smaller trolleys. It would break my brain to see Taylor wheeling back a single pair of jeans and a scarf after a six-hour session. But often that's how it was.

Lizzy just shrugged and said that this was how Beyoncé would shop. No trudging around looking for needles in haystacks. Most of the choosing would be done already. Like you had a store just for you. You couldn't go wrong, just really right.

There were also the challenges we devised for each other, usually on trips to and from Liquor Central. Who could get their tongue to turn the bluest from drinking slushy. Who could stand amid the rotting fruit section of Coles for the longest without gagging. Who could get from the north end to the south on a bike without stacking once the corridor lights had timed out.

But gradually these things lost their shine. Like winners of some bizarre lottery, we had become jaded and were now only excited in rare moments by new discoveries.

I decided to cook myself a cheeseburger at McDonald's and make some extra to take back to the others. None of us had quite perfected the equipment in the fast-food outlets, but we could fumble our way through enough to make something recognisable. The packaging was the most exciting part. Whatever we managed to throw into a brown Macca's bag or a KFC bucket seemed at least slightly enticing.

I took enough ingredients out of the storage freezer for three burgers and fries. Rocky was a vegetarian aside from red beef curry. He also loved chicken nuggets so I grabbed a handful of these and shut the huge frosty door.

The freezer reminded me of my idea to check some of the other stores for frozen supplies also. I switched on a deep fryer and headed out to take a look while it heated.

McDonald's was part of a semicircle-shaped food hall at the south-east end of the centre. It had all of the regular fast-food chains you would expect, plus a clichéd selection of 'world food' such as Tasty Thai, Burrito Plus, Stars 'n' Stripes Carvery and Curry in a Hurry. I wandered over to the Indian place in the hope of finding a stack of delicious frozen curries out the back.

Each outlet had a counter, bain-marie and some drink fridges, as well as a small area used for storage and cooking at the back. I remembered venturing into a couple of these during the first week. But there was still plenty of food out the front at that time so we had never had a proper look.

Curry in a Hurry had a lock on the door to the storeroom. I knelt beneath the counter and looked around. There were a few dusty receipt books. Some spare till rolls. A half-full bottle of water. And, on a hook, a singular key. It matched the lock on the storeroom. I opened the door just a sliver and reached around for a light switch before going inside. Standard practice in Carousel.

With the light came the smell.

Dense and thick. It pushed me back like a pillow to the face.

Something was clearly rotting in there, but the smell was also spiked with a chemical sharpness I couldn't place. I stepped back and took a few breaths.

With my shirt pulled up over my nose I tried again. I got another snap of dizziness. Intense and warm like I'd stepped into heavy drunkenness. My legs wavered and, for a moment, it seemed like I would fall inside. Again the fractured visions of the Carousel floor plan swept past my temples.

I swayed back and brought the door shut with a bang.

I placed the key back under the counter and sat at a table in the food court for a few minutes while the sweat dried on my face. I felt nauseous and the place smelt overly bleachy for a centre that hadn't seen a cleaner in months. Curry in a Hurry stood dormant beside me. The trashy yellow sign with its chubby Indian cook full of kitsch and indifference. Something about the place unnerved me. I subconsciously added it to the list of places in Carousel that creeped me out.

It was growing.

Having put together my best impersonation of some Happy Meals, I picked up a bike from Sports Power to cycle them back to the others while they were still hot. Taylor informed me via radio that the three of them were watching *Breaking Bad* reruns in JB Hi-Fi.

'Awesome. What did you get?' she asked when I arrived with the Macca's bag. We still said 'get' like we were buying stuff rather than taking it or making it.

'Happy Meals. Nuggets,' I said and dished them out across the massive leather lounge we had positioned in front of a flatscreen.

'You're the best,' said Lizzy.

She resumed the show and we ate in silence while I tried to wipe the fetid smell from my mind.

Despite the massive library of films offered by the abandoned centre, we had drifted pretty quickly into watching television series. The extended narratives gave us all something to talk about, but also a sense of structure and rhythm. It was good to have something consistent in our weirdo lives, and if a TV series could offer this, albeit temporarily, we gravitated toward it, irrespective of the quality.

One of Taylor and Lizzy's favourite things was watching *Neighbours* episodes on DVD. Neither of them had seen one of Australia's most clichéd and long-running soaps before arriving in Carousel. They would talk pretty much the whole way through. The acting was bad and the plot lines seemed to repeat every season, but the massive bank of episodes held the security of continuation that most series couldn't.

Rocky and I had grown up with *Neighbours* and weren't keen to revisit something we didn't like the first time.

Instead we found our structure and security in *Futurama* and *Grand Designs*.

We also only really watched stuff on the one TV. There were countless others, a lot of them bigger and with surround sound or 3D. Sometimes during alone time or at night we would watch other sets around the centre. But most of the time we would sit happily on a couple of couches in front of our seventy-two inch. If Taylor and Lizzy were watching *Neighbours*, Rocky and I would kick a soccer ball around for a bit until they were finished.

I think this was like Taylor and the books. She would drive Lizzy crazy waiting on her to finish a book rather than get a new one off the shelf. Lizzy probably knew best why Taylor did it. Something about keeping a lid on the world. About making sure she still wanted things, because wanting was important. In some way, wanting was tied to survival. That's what I thought. But a lot of the time I didn't really know what was going on between them. Sometimes I felt like one day the doors would open and we would go our separate ways without any lasting impression. Like I was bouncing around outside of them this whole time and it meant nothing.

We finished with *Breaking Bad* and Rocky left for bed in Camping World. He kept a tent in there with a mattress on the floor. For a while it was a blow-up plastic one like he had in Target. When we realised, Taylor and I dragged in a pillow-top from Bed Bath and Home and got him the hell off the cold lumpy air. Rocky slept more than any of us, yet he always looked tired.

The three of us stayed on the couch in an early-evening daze while the DVD menu screen looped through.

'Did you look in those storerooms?' asked Taylor.

I nodded.

'No good?' asked Lizzy.

I shook my head, but couldn't get rid of their gazes.

'I didn't look in all of them. So there might still be something,' I added.

They nodded.

'How is Rocky?' I asked Taylor.

'Who knows,' she replied and was silent for a moment.

'We almost got a door open today,' she said, matter-of-factly.

Lizzy and I looked at her.

'Holy shit. Where?' said Lizzy.

'In the corridor beside Just Jeans,' replied Taylor.

'What happened?' I asked.

'It just moved. None of the other ones have. Rocky was using a crowbar and the door slipped a little. He didn't know what to do and I wasn't watching. By the time I raced over, the door had slipped back and we couldn't wedge it open again.'

'Wow,' I said.

'Yeah,' said Taylor.

'So that's it?' asked Lizzy.

Taylor looked at her for a moment. Something passed.

'We only had some small tools with us. With a bigger crowbar and mallet it might open,' she replied.

'Where do you think it goes?' I asked.

'What do you mean?' asked Taylor.

'Storeroom? Cleaners cupboard?'

'I think it goes outside,' she said.

The words resonated.

'Why?' asked Lizzy.

'Some of the doors have this feeling. Like a kind of pressure or weight. And others don't,' said Taylor.

'Does this one have that?' I asked.

'Yeah,' said Taylor.

The three of us sat there for a few moments, just staring at the looping faces of Walter White and Jesse Pinkman.

'What do we do if it opens?' asked Lizzy.

'Get the hell out of here,' said Taylor.

'Doesn't it depend on what's out there?' I asked.

'What do you think is out there, Nox? Zombies? A nuclear holocaust? You've heard the noises,' said Taylor.

'I've heard something that sounded like a harmonica. And some dogs barking. I haven't heard anyone come to do their shopping or catch a movie,' I replied.

'We have to go out there. All the food in this place will be out of code eventually. And I'm worried about Rocky,' said Taylor.

Lizzy put a hand on her shoulder. I stared hard at

the floor and wondered why the hell the idea of a door opening freaked me out so much.

'We need to take supplies,' I said.

The two of them looked at me.

'We can't just expect to go out there and catch a taxi to Pizza Hut,' I said.

'He's right,' said Lizzy. 'Wait. Are we all going?'

Taylor and I looked at each other. She nodded. So did I.

5

I left JB's and cycled through the half-lit centre to put some supplies together and think over Taylor's news. We had agreed to head to the door after breakfast tomorrow and I had volunteered to gather supplies for whatever we might face outside. I didn't often cycle around alone at night. The mixture of shadow and light, as some shops shut off and others stayed on, tipped Carousel over its creepy threshold. Plus with so many areas on different timers you never really knew when the place you were in would black out and send you into momentary panic.

Tonight I felt numb and I told myself I didn't care. The news of the door had my head racing more than it had done since all of this started. The idea that the four of us could be outside this time tomorrow was too bizarre to comprehend. The logic of our existence in the centre – me, teenage shop assistant Rocky, indie rock duo Taylor & Lizzy – seemed stronger than everything else now. The outside world was not just foreign; it contained too much possibility to be real. Somehow it felt fictional and I hated it.

I looked around for backpacks for a while, even trying

Bags R Us. Shopping for Taylor and Lizzy was pretty impossible these days. Eventually I settled on four small hiking packs from Mountain Designs and set about filling them with whatever items our hypothetical adventures might require.

I started with the obvious stuff. Two large bottles of Mount Franklin in each. The most expensive first aid kit I could find at Friendlies Chemist. Multivitamins. Chocolate and vanilla energy bars. Some water purification sachets. Four of those extra-warm sleeping bags that somehow bundled up into tiny balls. I actually unrolled one to check it out and couldn't get it back into the bag. So I left it on the floor and took another.

With the four bags swinging from my handlebars I coasted over to Army Depot. Thankfully all the lights were on and I wouldn't have to fish around in the dark while the gas masks followed me with their big black eyes.

I ran through survival movies in my head for packing ideas. This relaxed me a little and I started to kind of enjoy the process. I packed a premium slimline Maglite torch in each bag, along with some backup batteries. The Swiss Army knives were in a glass display case on the counter. I stepped around and took out four small models before carefully closing it again.

What else?

There was no point packing clothes because Taylor and Lizzy would only wear what they wanted, and Rocky had his own bizarro outfits. I did find some plastic pullovers that would keep us dry and folded down to the size of a golf ball. Pretty cool.

A compass seemed pointless because Perth was pretty easy to navigate. West was the Indian Ocean, north and east were hills, then desert, and if you headed south you could follow the freeway all the way down to reach the forests.

That left the masks.

They covered a wall behind the counter like a shrine to Cold War sci-fi and post-9/11 paranoia. The thought of pulling one on terrified me, but of all the things I had thought to pack it probably made the most sense. There was a reason that nobody had come to Carousel for the countless days we had been trapped inside. That reason could be innocent. But it most likely wasn't. And if that were the case then something widespread must have happened. In most of the movies I could think of, widespread meant airborne. So I picked out the least creepy mask and packed one in each bag.

I hooked a trolley onto the back of the bike (something that Rocky and I had eventually perfected), loaded up the bags and cycled over to Coles to choose some food items. Cans were heavy but the only viable option given their distant expiry and the lack of preparation required. I selected a decent range that would feed us for around a week, then took everything over to the lounge out front to finish the packing.

Out of the dead Carousel air Lizzy started to sing.

The echo was small so she wasn't far away. Maybe just on her bed in Dymocks.

I stopped and sat down amid the cans and bags. She was playing with a song I hadn't heard before. It was gentle but had a poppy kick in the chorus that I liked straight away. She drifted off a few times before just thumbing through some chords. The lights in Coles timed out behind me. The corridors were close to dark now, but I stayed to listen.

Abruptly Lizzy switched into 'Over Early' from *Sophomore*. I'd never heard her play a full song in the centre before. For a moment I wondered if Taylor and Rocky could hear, but realised that of course they could. Bouncing around the night-filled centre it was sad and beautiful and loud as hell.

Lizzy had started singing to herself, but ended up singing to all of us. We were together then. Like we were that first day on the lounge. Or in Target when we found Rocky. Like we would be tomorrow at the door.

Suddenly I wondered if Lizzy was offering Carousel an early goodbye.

In the morning we met at Pure 'n' Natural for breakfast as per normal. Taylor had a trolley full of tools from Backyard Bonanza. I had my own trolley carrying the four backpacks I had filled the night before. We were all a little pensive about the door. Lizzy tried to lighten the mood with a joke about my choice of backpack. We all smiled, but it was fleeting and we remained focused on our food.

Just Jeans was in a part of the centre that had been refurbished since construction in the seventies. The floor was parquetry with a matt finish and the walls a light shade of mauve. Taylor and Lizzy would shop down there sometimes. Browsing through the small clothing outlets with a concentration that belied our situation. Only occasionally finding something they would wear in front of the other. Sometimes talking through their shopping predicaments, often assessing each other silently, noting what worked and what didn't with an objectiveness that kind of intrigued me.

Taylor led us to the store, even though we all knew the way. Rocky cycled along beside us. He had mastered the art of riding slowly without toppling sideways. I glanced at him. He seemed calm and free of anticipation. I don't know why I expected anything else.

Taylor was clearly edgy.

She had been there when the door slipped partially open. A glimmer of hope after countless rejections. She felt that it could be forced to happen again, and that the door would lead not to another room but outside to freedom. She had been waiting for this opportunity since our first week in Carousel. And now it was here.

Lizzy confused me. She seemed more relaxed than Taylor and me. Strolling casually and sipping on some leftover smoothie. She was making jokes, too. Actually, maybe not jokes, that wasn't her thing, but kind of witty observations that you wouldn't laugh at straight away, but maybe smile about two days later when something reminded you. Watching her I wondered if she was actually more nervous than anyone.

My own anxiety had drifted into numbness. Whatever waited outside the door, I was sure it wouldn't be my job at the stationery store. Or my housemates at our crappy apartment. Or the lonely spread of suburban Perth on a Tuesday. Our situation would continue. This had drifted me to sleep when Taylor and Lizzy had chatted through the night on the radio, talking with expectation about Canada, apartments and girlfriends.

The corridor beside Just Jeans was fairly short, with just four doors. Two headed to bathrooms, one was labelled *Cleaner Only* and the fourth stood blank. We pushed the trolleys against the wall. Taylor grabbed a large crowbar and a mallet and carried them over to the fourth door. We followed.

The paint was scratched slightly from the day before.

'So I'm going to try and wedge this inside like Rocky did yesterday,' said Taylor holding up the crowbar.

'When I get it in you need to hit the door,' she told me and passed me the mallet.

'Okay,' I replied.

Lizzy watched us both. Then turned to look at Rocky a little way behind us.

'Hey Rock, come over here, yeah,' she said. He followed obediently.

'If it opens and we go outside we need to prop it so we don't get locked out there,' I said.

Taylor and Lizzy looked at me curiously, as if they couldn't see how this would be a problem.

'Use the mallet,' said Taylor.

I nodded.

Taylor edged in close to the door and positioned the crowbar on top of the previous scratches. She glanced at me. I shuffled forward with the mallet to stand ready by her shoulder. She angled the bar back a little, wedged it in close to the frame, and pulled.

Nothing happened.

Taylor pulled again. Still nothing moved.

She leant closer and levered her weight against the bar. The door held quietly firm.

'More angle,' said Rocky softly.

Taylor stopped to look at him. She held the bar out for him to replace her. He hesitated for a moment, then padded slowly across. He took the crowbar and pointed it awkwardly at the door as if it were alive. We watched as he drew it back almost at a right angle and struck the edge of the door before quickly levering sideways.

The door shifted an inch or so inward.

'Shit,' said Lizzy.

'That's it, Rocky. Go again,' said Taylor.

I shuffled closer with the mallet and Rocky held up the bar for another blow.

He struck down again. There was a noise. Air.

The door slipped back and the steel of the crowbar wedged in between the wood and the frame. I swung the mallet automatically, just missing Rocky and landing a dull thud on the door.

It swung open.

I expected light but it was darkness that greeted us. Darkness and the smell of rubber and concrete. Neither Rocky nor I moved. Taylor shifted in behind us. She put a hand on Rocky's shoulder and he stepped aside. She paused, then took a careful, deliberate step down and out of Carousel.

'Wait,' I whispered harshly.

Taylor froze.

'The bags,' I whispered again, unsure of why I had lowered my volume.

Lizzy took them out of the trolley and passed them around. Taylor pulled hers on and continued down the steps. I motioned for Rocky to follow, then Lizzy. I left both the mallet and crowbar wedged in the frame so the door wouldn't close behind us.

I took a final glance at the familiar fluorescence of the corridor and turned to follow them down.

We were inside a car park. Not one of the large customer parking areas at the back of the centre, but a smaller version, for staff maybe. There were three steps leading down from the door, then a cold concrete floor with vehicle bays. Taylor had stopped a few metres from the door and seemed to be sniffing the air.

Immediately I thought of the masks. It had been stupid to head out there without putting them on. I inhaled cautiously. The smell was a new one. Not fresh, but with a kind of life we didn't have in the centre. Maybe it was the lack of air conditioning. A sudden chill ran across my shoulders. The air was cool.

A car park had to have an exit, but in the darkness there was no sign of one.

'Did you pack torches, Nox?' whispered Lizzy.

'Yeah, in the pocket inside,' I replied and reached around to find mine. The others followed. Our rustling resonated through the space.

We scanned the area in front of us. Concrete floors ran into brick walls broken only by the labels of stores in the centre. Coffee Club. Curry in a Hurry. Dinkum Donuts. Dymocks Books. Lizzy shone her torch across this sign.

'My park is free,' she said.

I smiled but nobody could see.

Rocky's torch was fixed on something near the left wall. Taylor and I noticed and turned to look. It looked like a ramp down to a lower level.

'Turn your lights off,' whispered Taylor.

'No fucking way,' replied Lizzy.

'Just for a second,' said Taylor.

She switched off her torch and the rest of us followed. For a moment it was close to pitch black. When our eyes adjusted we noticed a dim glow of light emanating from the ramp.

'It's light down there,' I whispered.

'Holy shit,' said Lizzy.

'We should take a look,' said Taylor.

We switched our torches back on and moved carefully over to the ramp. I turned and looked back at the door into the centre. It was open as we'd left it.

At the incline of the ramp the light ahead was still dull, but somewhat wider. We headed downward, swinging our Maglites around to catch anything out of the ordinary. The concrete levelled beneath us. There were no further ramps.

We were on the ground floor.

It was easy to see where the light was coming from. There was a large roller door on the far wall. The sides of the door didn't seem to fit squarely against the concrete wall. Daylight seeped in from outside creating a dull hue around the door.

The four of us drifted to it like lemmings.

The door was big but not huge, just enough room for two cars, side by side. Taylor gripped a metal crossbar and tried to lift it.

Nothing moved.

We shone our torches along the base. Something was fastening the door to the concrete floor, but it wasn't visible.

Lizzy and I moved to the side, close to the dull blue light. To our disappointment the slit of daylight was minuscule. We wedged our heads in against the wall and tried to gaze out. The view was grey and, in all likelihood, just of another wall outside.

'Fail,' whispered Lizzy next to me.

'Yep,' I replied.

Taylor was doing the same on the other side of the door. I shone a torch at her face. She looked deflated. She shone hers back at Lizzy and me. We shrugged.

Suddenly I remembered Rocky.

I swiped my torch sideways to find him. Taylor and Lizzy followed, seemingly with the same thought. We found him a few metres behind us. He was standing still with his torch fixed on something. We followed his light across the car park. Lizzy inhaled beside me.

There was a car parked in the corner.

The three of us stared at it. Rocky fidgeted and looked back at us.

'It's a Ford Fiesta,' he said, his voice booming through the space.

'Shhh, Rock,' said Taylor, moving past him.

Lizzy, Rocky and I followed. We kept our torches fixed on the car and approached.

Rocky was right. It was a newish Ford Fiesta parked roughly across a couple of unmarked bays behind the ramp. The tinted windows reflected our torchlight so that we had to get right up close to see inside. The cab was clean and empty. No rubbish or shopping. Just a folded-up sun reflector on the back seat, and a pine tree freshener hanging from the rear-view mirror. Lizzy took hold of the passenger door handle and looked at us.

Taylor nodded slightly. Lizzy pulled back on the handle. The door was locked.

I slowly circled the car, looking for dust or dirt or something that would tell us if it had been parked there for a while. The body was clean but not shiny and gave nothing away. I noticed Rocky had a hand on the bonnet. I placed mine beside his. The steel was cool to touch.

'Not today,' he said softly.

I nodded and gave him a smile. Taylor and Lizzy were together by the passenger's side. Both looked a little freaked out. I moved over to them.

'Do you want to try the crow-bar on that roller door?' I asked Taylor.

She turned and looked at the door as if she had forgotten it was there.

'I don't know. What do you guys think?' she asked.

Before we could answer there was a sharp snap from the upper level. We jumped and looked at the ramp. The light drifting down from the door had gone. Like it was closed.

'Fuck. Fuck,' I said.

'Did you prop it?' asked Taylor.

I looked around for Rocky but couldn't find him.

'Nox?' she asked again.

'Rocky?' I said.

Suddenly he was beside me.

'Nox!?' asked Taylor a third time.

'Yeah I propped it. Come on,' I said and pulled her and Lizzy toward the ramp.

We forgot the car and bolted back upstairs under the weight of our bags. As the ramp levelled off we turned to find only a sliver of light spilling from the centre door.

'Shit,' I whispered.

The aircon in the centre had timed out and the drop in pressure had sucked it shut.

We raced over, fearing we had trapped ourselves out. The crowbar had fallen flat with the force of the door. My heart sank at the sight of the mallet head beside it.

Taylor crouched and followed the handle with her torch. The very end was still wedged in the door. She slipped her fingers in the small gap of light that remained. I followed. We pulled backward but it didn't move. For a horrible moment it seemed like the airlock would be too strong for us. We pulled again. It broke and the door swung open freely.

A moment later we were back in Carousel.

6

We didn't speak about our venture outside the centre for some days. Taylor's and Lizzy's nerves were shot. Mine too, probably. Rocky seemed normal, which was slightly concerning in itself. We had closed the door and trudged back to JB's, backpacks full of supplies, where we watched *Parks and Recreation*, ate junk food and were gentle with one another.

When it was really late and we could no longer pretend we weren't scared to be alone, each of us left JB's. I walked back to my bed in Myer, too tired to cycle with just a Maglite to guide me. The normally welcoming glow of the fragrance section felt dull and lifeless. I passed giant glowing advertisements with Natalie Portman and Beyoncé like they were old trees in a neglected garden and trudged up the escalator, not bothering to carry any cardboard for the next trip down.

The lights had already timed out to three-quarter dark but I switched off the torch, knowing my way without them. I stopped at the pile of sheet sets bundled outside my bunks. I had only replaced my sheets a few days ago but felt like

I could do with some fresh ones again tonight. I grabbed a random bundle and stepped through into my cove.

I made the bed in the murky light and ran over the events of the morning once again. Our failure to break out of the centre was no big deal. Well, perhaps it was, but I don't think any of us, even Taylor, were really expecting success. I had packed the backpacks as comprehensively as I could, but never felt that my decisions would prove significant.

Even the discovery of the car park was a little underwhelming. We were always finding new places within this sleeping giant of a centre. Some nice toilets next to the Wendys outlet. A new row of video games at a bend in the corridor at Hoyts. The small garden with real plants lining some windows at the back entrance. I guess we could just add the staff car park onto this list and forget about it.

But there had been the Fiesta.

Nowhere else in our limited view of the exterior of the centre had we seen a car. Perhaps if they had been present from the first day, left outside or undercover at the back entrance, another part of our bizarre new world, then the solitary Fiesta might not have creeped us out.

I couldn't think of a reason why there shouldn't be a Fiesta in the staff car park. But Carousel had a kind of weird logic that its presence there disrupted. There were four of us. The power remained on. The food supply was abundant. This was the logic we understood. Or if not understood, at least accepted.

The Fiesta left us swinging limply in the realm of fate. It reminded us that, however much we adapted to the centre, our existence remained fluid. We could attempt to break out and set our own agenda. But the reality was that our circumstances were being defined for us, and the Fiesta was part of that.

It also meant that there could be someone else in the centre with us. The thought sent a spike of adrenaline through my arms and I tucked the sheets in hard. Discovering Rocky in Target had been a great thing for us, and him. But there was something sinister about the owner of the small hatchback parked below. All of us had felt it. The way they had parked the car across two bays. As if well aware that the centre was, or would remain, empty. If this person had been here since the first day then they were actively hiding from us, or dead. If they had arrived recently through the fastened door then they were somehow in on the Carousel phenomenon. Either way the Fiesta appeared to spell trouble.

I finished with the sheets and turned all the lamps out bar one. I slid into bed and pulled a quilt up around my face. The level felt too quiet for me to sleep, so I played some XX on a new phone and stared at the display chest opposite. I was almost asleep when I realised it was Sunday and I hadn't given Lizzy a With Regret card.

I lay still and considered whether the day's events rendered this acceptable. I sighed, knowing that if anything they probably made the card routine even more important.

I dragged myself out of the beautiful warmth and pulled on my favourite grey hoodie and some jeans. Not wanting to clunk around the centre and wake up the others, I went for some quiet loafers. Then I took the Maglite over to the giftware section to find a card.

I had given Lizzy some truly terrible cards over the weeks. *Life gets in the way – I'll make it next time.* Or *The dog ate my homework … you know the deal.* Bordering on delirium, I wasn't too fussy this time. I went for a card with an illustrated bird flying through a grey urban landscape on the front, with the destination of a solitary birdbath on the back. Inside it said, *Good luck in your new oasis, my apologies that I couldn't make a splash.* It didn't make a lot of sense but I wrote inside, sealed it up and set off to Dymocks.

Lizzy was in her bed reading *Burning for Revenge* from the John Marsden teen series. She dipped the cover at the soft shuffle of my approach and looked at her watch.

'Cutting it fine, Nox,' she said.

'Yeah,' I replied and passed her the card.

She opened it and smirked briefly at the contents. I sat on a sofa beside the bed and wrapped myself in a blanket.

'You okay?' she asked.

'Yeah. Bit creeped out,' I replied. 'You?'

'Not really,' she said.

'Serious?'

'I bet the normal demographic for Fiesta owners in

Perth is like, female, nineteen to twenty-six,' she replied.

I smiled a little.

'You think there's been a car-full of ladies shopping in Miss Shop all this time?' I asked.

'Most likely,' she said.

'Wow, they must be shy,' I said.

'Shy is fine,' said Lizzy.

Usually we could go on talking crap like this for a while. Tonight it felt a little forced.

'How is Taylor?' I asked, more seriously.

'No idea,' she replied.

'Do you really think there's somebody else in here with us?' I asked.

'God, I don't know,' she answered.

We sat in silence for a while.

'I was thinking about last time we played here in Perth. At that old arts centre,' she said.

'In Fremantle. I was there,' I said. 'You guys totally ignored me.'

'We're famous. Of course we did,' said Lizzy.

'Anyway, we were so pumped about hanging out in the place before the show. It's like this tiny castle, yeah. They pretty much gave us an entire wing to ourselves. I remember sitting in this big room after sound check, drinking a beer and looking up at the awesome ceilings. And Taylor was just wandering through the halls, looking at people's art projects. Nobody around.'

I nodded.

'Then we googled and found out the place was built as an insane asylum where they locked people up and dished out shock therapy and shit like that. Both of us got creeped out and spent the rest of the pre-show in a van out the front.'

Lizzy looked at me.

'Nothing changed in the place except what we knew about it,' she said. 'I don't want that to happen here. I'm not going to let a fucking Ford Fiesta creep me out of the only good stuff about being alive and living in a mall.'

Her eyes were fierce and they were posing me a question. Maybe not a question, but a challenge. The idea of not meeting it scared the hell out of me.

7

Life in Carousel felt pretty normal in the weeks that followed. There wasn't much we could do about the mysterious Fiesta. If it meant that somebody else was in the centre then it seemed inevitable we would eventually meet them. But we weren't going to go out looking. They would have to come to us.

Plus we weren't exactly hiding away or keeping quiet. If anything there was more of a party atmosphere than ever. Lizzy had pulled together some DJ decks and a projector and had taken to turning the dome into a weirdo abandoned club with music mashed to old sci-fi movies. Rocky would coast around on a series of bikes and scooters in a kind of Zen state that belied his entrapment, while Taylor and I would hang out on a couple of deckchairs from Backyard Bonanza, drinking a new region of wine and looking up at the dim twinkle of stars through the distant hole in the dome.

We'd often talk of how we might scale the long, curving walls to reach freedom. The top of the dome was three storeys up and made predominantly of glass. Without cleaning, the glass had developed a greenish film that looked slippery as hell. If a rope could be somehow thrown up to catch on the top, and the weight of the climber was not enough to pull the whole structure down, scaling the slippery exterior would probably result in you breaking your neck in the sweet fresh air of freedom.

Drinking away to Lizzy's maniacal performances led to more bizarre ideas involving catapults and skate ramps.

I was getting through a lot of reading, more than I ever have before, and started thinking about working on a few short stories to see if that was something I might want to do. I kept quiet about the focus of my reading, leaving Taylor and Lizzy with something to gossip about in their now banal lives. I think that gossip was one of the things they missed the most. Their lives pre-Carousel seemed pretty full and there were always things to discuss regarding other bands, touring venues, girlfriends, shopping, haircuts. The list was long and constantly updated.

One night Lizzy actually started writing a list of the things she missed on the floor. Taylor and I frowned upon this initially as it seemed to go against our pact of keeping a clean and tidy centre. But then Rocky drifted over and tagged HIGH SCHOOL GIRLS in massive cursive letters outside Smiggle. It gave him one of the biggest smiles we had seen and somehow made the whole thing okay.

I kind of liked it now. Maybe not the writing so much, but discovering what the others had done. Walking down to Pure 'n' Natural for breakfast and noticing a huge B outside

Myer, then following it along until it spelt out BEACH.

One day I stopped outside JB's and noticed a tiny, beautiful word scribed in the corner. I couldn't stop staring at it. It said *Mum*.

Taylor continued working her way around the centre checking the doors. The events surrounding the car park didn't seem to put her off. She was happy with the routine and hopeful that one of the thousands of doors would swing open to reveal some sunshine and a logical reason for us being here.

Generally I thought it was best for all of us to assume this would never happen and get on with living as best we could. I don't think it was resignation or giving up. You just couldn't think of Carousel with normal logic or it would do your head in.

I started to notice that Rocky was looking paler than normal and slightly flabby, despite his thin frame. He was always on a bike but with the smooth floors and new tyres, riding around the centre didn't really require any effort. So I goaded him into doing some daily exercise to keep him, and me, in some kind of health.

We tried a bunch of things before settling on a hybrid form of indoor soccer played in a rectangular arm of the central corridor that was kept vacant for exhibitions, charity car raffles and school performances. It was pretty normal for a shiny new car to be parked in centres like Carousel with a desk in front selling tickets for a chance to win. But, for whatever reason, there was no car there when we arrived. I often wondered what we might do if there was. Whether one of the windows could be smashed through instead of rebounding whatever we threw at it. Or just how quickly we could get around the place. I'm sure Rocky had thought about this too. He seemed to like cars. Or maybe just anything with wheels. The idea of him racing around the narrow corridors in a new Commodore was pretty frightening.

We had taken a rubberised beach net from Sports Power and set it up at the back of the rectangle, which was walled in to give any stage that was erected a single frontage. The walls kept the ball from straying off into David Jones too often and we had a few pretty intense half-court games of one on one.

At around lunchtime on a Friday I found myself open with the ball rebounding nicely off the side wall for a shot on goal.

I hit it flush, but offline. The ball smashed through the glass of the Sussan store adjacent. A crunching noise rang through the centre.

Rocky and I stood still and stared at the glass. Both fighting down the heavy dose of guilt that would come with this type of thing outside of Carousel. A few seconds later our radios chimed.

'Are you guys okay? asked Taylor.

'Yeah, sorry,' I radioed back.

'Is Rocky with you?' asked Lizzy.

I looked at Rocky and nodded to his radio.

'Nox smashed the window at Sussan,' he said, ratting me out.

'Nice one, Nox,' said Lizzy.

'Sorry. I know it's your favourite,' I replied.

'Are you cleaning up the glass?' asked Taylor.

'We're talking to you,' replied Rocky, deadpan.

I smiled.

'Thanks, Rocky,' said Taylor. 'Maybe you can once we've finished, yeah.'

'We'll do it now,' I said.

'Hey, when you've quit screwing around come down to Kitchen Warehouse. We're making soup,' said Lizzy.

'Okay, cool,' I replied.

The ball had made a jagged hole halfway up the front window. I didn't know if this was unusual, but it looked pretty fragile. We gathered the glass on the floor into a messy pile and I left to find some gaffer tape to run in a cross over the window like I'd seen on TV. The Two-Dollar Shop only had cheap looking masking tape so I trudged down the hall and around the corner to Dick Smith.

When I arrived back Rocky was standing still, looking at his hand. A steady flow of blood was streaming from his palm onto the floor.

'Shit, Rocky. You cut yourself?' I asked, putting the tape on the floor.

He nodded and kept focused on the blood. I took his

wrist and gently turned it over to look at the wound. A coin size chunk of glass was sticking out of the fleshy part of his hand.

'Fuck,' I said.

I looked at his face. It seemed calm, as per usual. I kept a hold of his wrist and reached over to grab a thin scarf from a rack nearby.

'I'm going to take it out, okay? When I do, can you put this scarf in your hand and clench it into a fist?'

Rocky glanced at the scarf for a moment.

'Can I have a blue one?' he asked.

I looked at him, then at the beige scarf in my hand.

'Mum has that one,' he said.

'Yeah, of course,' I replied and reached back for a blue version.

I put the scarf in Rocky's good hand and took a firm grip on the glass. I hesitated for a second, then pulled upward. Rocky gave a small shudder as the glass slid slowly out of his flesh.

It was a fucking iceberg. The glass inside him more than double the size of that outside. I stared at it, slightly astounded, until I realised that Rocky hadn't clenched the scarf in his hand. Instead he was watching the increased flow of blood run down his pale fingers.

'Rocky! The scarf,' I said.

He came to and limply clenched the scarf. It quickly turned red.

I used the gaffer tape to circle his hand and stop the bleeding until we could get to Friendlies Chemist. When it was secure and the pool of blood on the floor had stopped expanding, I radioed Taylor and Lizzy and prepared for a blasting.

The three of us spent an hour or so in the kitchenette at Friendlies dealing with the wound. We realised quickly that it probably needed stitches but none of us were physically or mentally capable of performing this. So for a half-hour we just cleaned and disinfected and thought through our options.

Eventually the bleeding had almost stopped so it was plausible that keeping the wound dressed and clean would eventually see it scab over and heal. The trouble was that the gash was right in the middle of Rocky's hand, so any movement would open it up and restart the bleeding. We settled on a large swab of cotton padding, wrapped tight to his palm by gauze, which we taped over with medical adhesive. It was large and a little clumsy and we could see it coming off within hours unless Rocky stayed still.

Scanning the long fluorescent aisles, Lizzy found a kind of hessian glove used to exfoliate dead skin. When she arrived back in the kitchenette wearing the glove and a manic smile, Taylor and I thought she had lost her shit. But, to Lizzy's credit, the glove made for a perfect outer barrier to Rocky's makeshift bandage. It kept all the dressing in place but still allowed his skin to breathe underneath. Taylor popped open a couple of Panadol Rapids and gave them to Rocky for the pain. She put the remainder of the packet in his shorts along with dosage instructions. Rocky listened, but had shown no real sign of discomfort throughout the process. Before long he had drifted back to JB's.

I met Taylor and Lizzy at Kitchen Warehouse a little while later. They were hovering over a pot of soup simmering on a small portable gas burner at the back of the store. I sat sheepishly on the bench adjacent. Neither of them could look at me.

'I think he did it on purpose,' I said, after a moment.

They fixed their deep brown eyes on me.

'What do you mean?' asked Taylor.

'The glass was in really deep. Like it had been pushed there,' I said.

'Holy shit,' said Lizzy.

'Are you sure?' asked Taylor.

'No,' I said.

We were silent. Somehow all knowing that it was true.

'Well, you can't screw around with him like that anymore,' said Taylor, bitingly.

I nodded. Lizzy glared at her. We all watched the soup for a while.

'This is ridiculous,' said Lizzy.

'What?' asked Taylor. 'Being trapped in a mall?'

'Yeah,' said Lizzy.

'Quite an observation,' said Taylor.

They glared at each other.

'Rocky won't last in here, like this, forever,' said Lizzy, staring at the soup.

'None of us will,' Taylor said.

Taylor was a tight ball of stress. I'd seen it building in her shoulders for a while, but now it seemed constant and dangerous. She needed music more than ever, but was moving further away from it with every day.

'He's a teenager,' I said, eventually.

The two of them looked at me.

'Remember how that was?' I said. 'We just need to give him space. Let him brood stuff over,' I said.

'Have you guys ever spoken about his family?' Taylor asked me.

'Not really. I know he has a stepdad and a baby sister,' I replied. 'I kind of figured he was talking to you while you guys worked on the doors.'

'You don't think he should be taking antidepressants or something?' asked Taylor carefully. She and Lizzy both looked at me. It seemed like something they had discussed already.

'Shit, I don't know, maybe. Probably. It's hard to tell in this place,' I said.

We were pensive for a few moments.

'There's also his arrival here,' said Lizzy.

Taylor looked at her. Maybe they had discussed this too.

'What do you mean?' I asked.

'Well, he came to work. What makes somebody turn up to shift during the apocalypse?' asked Lizzy.

'God. What does that even mean, Lizzy?' asked Taylor.

'Nobody else did,' she replied.

'I asked him already. He said he got to work early that morning,' said Taylor. 'Probably missed the whole thing.'

'Rocky got to work early?' replied Lizzy.

Taylor shrugged. I had a stupid thought and let out a small laugh. The Finns stared at me.

'What?' asked Taylor.

'Nothing. Sorry,' I replied.

They glared at me until I spilled.

'I was just thinking. Do you think working the apocalypse pays double time?'

Lizzy flashed one of her huge *oh my god that's funny but I'm not going to laugh* smiles. Taylor smiled ruefully and sighed.

'You're a maniac, Nox,' she said.

Lizzy picked out some bowls for the soup and wiped the dust off them. We sat together and spooned in the comforting mixture of country chicken and vegetable and frozen corn. I don't think any of us thought Rocky's problems were just about being a teenager. But it gave us a little security. Barely a decade older and full of our own insecurities, we knew we weren't cut out for the support and guidance he seemed to require. Carousel also had a way of highlighting things that could normally be ignored. We didn't know exactly what these things were for Rocky, but they seemed serious.

8

During the following week Carousel was battered by the first in a series of severe storms. Brewed in deep masses of low pressure in the Southern Ocean, they were buffeted north and east to smash against the state's coastline. I had been wondering when the winter cold fronts would come. The third level of David Jones offered a sweeping view of the sky to the south via a series of windows throwing light on the linen section below. I liked to wander up there when the wind seemed to pick up outside and watch the walls of rainclouds roll towards us. Taylor and Lizzy would look at me curiously when I arrived back saying it would rain in half an hour.

The first storm made for a pleasant break from routine. We huddled on couches at the back entrance, watching the lightning with cups of powdered milk and Oreos that were magically in code for another six years.

Lizzy and Rocky both loved lightning. They would already be seated, gazing out at the distant and infrequent flashes, when Taylor and I wandered down to join them. Often they would stand right at the windows as a storm passed over. Rocky stationary, his exfoliating glove glowing softly in the dark. Lizzy hopping about with excitement, pointing out each flash retrospectively. Taylor and I weren't quite as pumped. But we both liked seeing Lizzy and Rocky together. They were often the odd couple in our weird little group. Rocky and Taylor still spent a lot of time together on the doors. Even more since Rocky cut his hand. I was still helping Lizzy with her studio in Rugs a Million. Although, from what I could gather, it was almost ready and she often played in there without recording. Usually loud and late at night, as if to remind the world that we were still alive. My relationship with Taylor was a bit fractured. We often skirted around each other as if to avoid something that neither of us quite grasped. But then we would hang out and drink wine, or work out things to cook, and get along fine. Seeing Lizzy and Rocky stand together at the window, watching the lightning, was kind of like having our girlfriends get along, or watching distant cousins find some common ground to dispel the awkwardness of their forced relationship.

I think we were all quietly thankful for the storms.

It wasn't until the third front, and the largest, that we were presented with an opportunity to escape.

It had come during the night. Gusts of moist southern wind whistling across the ageing patchwork of steel that made up the cinema roof. Wind was our best reminder that a world still existed outside. Carousel had cracked and groaned with the hot easterly in the summer, and now it buckled tightly under winter's gusty bursts from the south.

The sky had been clear when I ventured up to David Jones at sunset so I was surprised to be woken by such force during the night. Of course the view only offered a short-range forecast. If I had the internet I might have seen a huge brooding low spitting out cold fronts that stretched all the way from Geraldton to Esperance.

As usual, the first one was the angriest.

I sat up in my bunk for a while, listening to the wind and wondering when the rain might start. There seemed to be an unusually long build-up. Tucked back into the north-east corner of the centre, Myer was relatively sheltered. I could hear the dull hum of wind, with the occasional echo of some loose roofing or gutter smacking against steel somewhere on the sprawling roof. But, for a long time, no rain. I had drifted back to sleep by the time the first spatterings began.

By morning the noise was immense.

I walked downstairs to join the others at breakfast. Lizzy and Rocky were already eating, keen to get out to the back entrance and watch the storm roll through. There was half a bottle of Shake 'n' Pour ready for me on the bench so I dripped out a couple of pancakes and watched them cook. Taylor arrived looking tired with a big fluffy robe pulled over her jeans and t-shirt. I held up the mix. She nodded so I poured out two more. The noise of the rain drowned out all sounds so there was no point talking. Before long, Lizzy and Rocky were cycling off to the back entrance.

Taylor and I sat through a pretty lazy breakfast. After the pancakes we swallowed a selection of daily vitamins put together by Lizzy. A multi. Some fish oil. C with echinacea. These were altered due to what was still in code and what new condition she considered posed us the most risk. On top of these we piled coffee. In contrast to the first day, time and practice had developed our coffee skills to a barista level. Even now that we were well out of fresh and frozen milk we could still churn out pretty perfect lattes using powder. Taylor sipped hers and read a *Gourmet Traveller* magazine. I worked my way through some Sylvia Plath.

When we were done Taylor packed together her tools to head out and check some doors. I decided to tag along given her usual assistant was busy watching the storm.

As we walked westward through the centre we noticed several patches of wetness on the floor where rain had blown in under gutters or gathered too heavily at fissures and seeped inside. The noise changed as we approached the front entrance and the dome. The echo disappeared, replaced by the sound of direct rain. We hadn't erected the winter awning over the dome when the season started to turn. There was a control panel by the sushi place, and a good chance Rocky could figure out how it worked, but the idea of adding to our confinement and losing our only real patch of sky didn't appeal to any of us, regardless of the weather. With today's rain the floor was wet and slippery all the way back to the Apple Store.

Taylor led us upstairs past the cinema. Halfway across I reached out and tapped her on the shoulder. She looked back and I nodded down at the entrance.

The scene beneath the dome was pretty surreal.

A miniature tornado swirled down through the opening to the tiles below. The falling water was condensed and circular at the top, but fanned as it lowered and the wind swirled in every direction. Leaves and dirt littered the floor, carried outward by tiny rivulets of water. The whole thing was backlit by the daylight seeping through the large windows at the entrance. Our centre had its own waterfall.

Taylor and I shared a smile. It was beautiful and awful at the same time. Like a lot of stuff in Carousel.

We continued on to an amenities area adjacent to the cinemas. There were a couple of corridors with various doors similar to the one we had broken through near Just Jeans. Taylor stopped out the front of these and unpacked her tools. I stood by her side and looked up at the ceiling to listen to the rain. It really was intense.

Taylor handed me a mallet and we started on one of the corridors. She had established a pretty comprehensive system by this stage. First she would check the locks and handles to see if they could be jimmied with a series of small screwdrivers. Failing this, she located the position of the hinges to see whether the door could be knocked free. Then there was the crowbar approach which had magically worked for Rocky. When none of these freed the door, there were other, more forceful options.

It had been ages since I'd seen Taylor really flip out on a door. Occasionally you would come across one that she had taken to during our first week, with axe marks near the hinges and large mallet indentations surrounding the handle. But most of them seemed to be tested thoroughly then left alone. I don't think any of us, including Taylor, really thought we could bust a hole in a door or smash a window to break out of the centre anymore. Somehow it was more complicated than that.

We tried the first door, and the second, with no luck. At the third a giant crashing noise stopped us dead.

Taylor and I stood looking at the cinema. Something had fallen somewhere inside. The sound had reached us above the rain.

It must have been big.

We glanced at each other. There were a lot of weird noises in an abandoned shopping centre, but this one had been different. Something had changed. Neither of us needed to say anything. We put down our tools and headed to the cinema.

Just because we weren't talking about our discovery of the Fiesta didn't mean we weren't thinking about it. That day had caused a slight but permanent shift in our lives. We looked at things differently. Kept together at night. Talked more on the radio. Walking into the foyer, the dull blue hatchback was forefront in my mind.

We had pretty much left the cinema alone aside from a half-baked attempt to run a movie on one of the complicated projectors. It was a maze of darkened, sound-proof rooms. Not the type of place you want to frequent in our situation.

But the noise we heard had definitely come from somewhere inside. We paused at the candy bar and considered our options. We were reluctant to search each cinema, one by one. There were nearly twenty of them and tons of corridors, toilets and projection booths in between.

Taylor sighed and headed off in the direction of the first cinema. I grabbed her arm. She turned and looked at me, confused. I tapped my ear, signalling for her to listen. Amid the chorus of falling water there was something else. A kind of swirling noise. Dense, like an indoor pool. It was coming from behind the candy bar.

We slid over the counter and walked around the corner to a door labelled *Office*. Taylor tried the handle. It turned. She held the door open and I reached inside for a light switch. There was a bunch of them by the door.

A long room was illuminated under a series of fluoros. There were some desks. A large stack of movie standees and posters. A kitchenette with a sink, fridge and water dispenser. And a series of doors leading up to projection booths.

The noise was definitely louder in there.

We moved through the room, listening cautiously. It was above us, in one of the projection booths. We scanned the doors, trying to decide which one to investigate first. A small pool of water had gathered at the base of the door to Projection Booth Four. We looked at it carefully as if to confirm it was real. The noise was a constant hum from behind the door. Taylor glanced at me and took the handle of the door.

'Stand on this side,' I said loudly, above the rain.

Taylor stared at me blankly. She couldn't hear. Rather than try again I took her arm and pulled her over to the other side of the door. She looked at me like I was weird, then turned the handle.

The door flung open and a wall of water exploded into the office.

Straight away I realised we should have left the entrance open. The room was large, but if it filled with water we would be screwed.

I left Taylor gaping at the river we had created and dashed across the office to the candy bar entrance. I think she must have thought I was getting the hell out of there because I half heard her yell, 'What the hell, Nox!'

The water had reached the door before me, which made it hard to pull it back against the flow. When I did I had to find something big and heavy to keep it propped. There wasn't really anything close by so I pushed it back fully against the wall so that the water pressure would hold it open rather than closed. Then I dragged across a desk and propped it there just to be sure.

Trudging back I noticed the pressure decreasing already.

Taylor looked at me and nodded with a half smile.

We waited by the door until the flow of water had subsided a little more, then moved carefully up the stairs inside.

The walls and ceiling were wet all around us. Water had completely filled the staircase. It was pretty narrow and although another rush of water seemed unlikely, neither of us felt totally comfortable in the space. There was also a light source somewhere ahead. I'd noticed it as soon as the door had opened, and I'm sure Taylor had too. This didn't necessarily mean anything. But it created an automatic anticipation.

Taylor double-stepped the final section of stairs and disappeared around the corner. I shrugged off visions of her being thrown back by a wall of water or falling down some huge Carousel chasm, and followed.

Inside was carnage.

Reams of film were plastered all around the long, hall-like projection booth. Two of the big, clumsy looking projectors had been tipped over by rushes of water. All of the small square windows to the cinemas were burst through and dripping with water.

A section of the roof had collapsed under the pressure of the torrential rainfall. Maybe something had blocked up the guttering during the summer. On a flat roof like Carousel's this would create some serious pooling. The section had fallen away from us so that the opening faced the opposite end of the booth. From where we stood there was just a downward sloping ceiling that met the floor in a messy and jagged pile of soaking rubble. However, through pockets of this, and to one side, there filtered the unmistakable grey of daylight.

Taylor looked at me with big, excited eyes.

We stepped carefully forward to the edge of the collapsed roof. I was a little nervous. Water was still running freely beneath our feet and there was a shitload of electrical items in the room. Many of these were switched off, but probably not everything, and I could never remember how conductivity worked. We both had rubber-soled shoes. Did this mean we were safe?

'The gaps aren't big enough,' said Taylor, crouching.

I followed her gaze and saw what she meant. There were only small pockets of space where the water and light were reaching us. It looked like there might have been something bigger when the roof first came down. But since then a growing pile of debris had banked up against it from the outside. None of the holes that remained were anywhere near large enough to climb through.

It seemed like the hole in the roof was out of reach.

'Maybe from the other side,' I said.

Taylor nodded and moved back past me toward the exit. We ventured swiftly into the two adjacent projection booths to see if they had also been breached or somehow offered access to the hole.

Both were intact.

More deflating was the discovery that all booths seemed to share the exact same layout. Basically a long hallway-type room with a solitary entry via a staircase. This meant that the roof had collapsed right at the end of Projection Booth Four, and there was unlikely to be any other access to the small area beneath the hole.

Taylor wanted to check all of the booths, just to be sure. I followed for a while, suspecting it was futile. With two remaining, I gave up and trudged back through the office, leaving her to finish alone.

We had made a real mess of the candy bar and foyer by opening the doors. Dirty brown water had spilt out onto the plush red carpet in a widening semicircle. Several of the temporary queuing barriers had fallen over in a tangled mess. A giant standee for the latest Adam Sandler film lay flat and dejected.

I sat up on a bench beside the pick'n'mix candy dispensers and chewed on some stale jellybeans. Taylor surfaced a few minutes later. The sparkle had left her eyes. She sat beside me and grabbed a handful of beans for herself. The rain seemed to have eased.

'Maybe the other side will fall in, too,' I said, without conviction.

Taylor nodded but didn't look at me.

She was crying.

I reached over to put a hand on her shoulder. We were sitting a little too far apart for it to be comfortable. After a moment I withdrew. Taylor sniffed and chewed on some beans.

'Sorry,' I said, mainly for being crap at comforting her, which I was, but I was also sorry about the roof, and everything else in the stupid centre.

'You don't care,' she said.

I swallowed and looked at her.

'About what?' I asked, already knowing what she meant.

'Getting out of here,' she said.

I stared hard at the damp and dirty carpet.

'I just feel numb,' I said. It was true, but didn't really explain anything.

Taylor wiped her nose and put the stale jellybeans aside.

She looked at me. I didn't meet the gaze. I wasn't up to the intensity that Taylor seemed to whip up out of nowhere. I felt bad for her, stuck here with the rest of us, the only one really trying to get out. She kept up her gaze. She and Lizzy would do this sometimes. As if they thought they could draw emotion from me via sheer force of will. The sweet stale sugar burned in the back of my throat. I swallowed and wiped a couple of tears away.

'I'm not some mental fan who wants to be stuck in here with you guys forever,' I said.

Taylor waited for me to continue. I tried to come up with something more to say.

'I have a family and friends out there,' I said.

It was the easy answer but Taylor seemed to let up.

'You're worried we'll get out of here and your life won't have changed,' she said after a few moments.

'Yeah, maybe,' I replied. This was exactly how I felt.

'I doubt that's the case, Nox,' said Taylor, sounding tired.

I felt like such an idiot. Petrified that we hadn't seen the apocalypse. That the world was okay and going about its business as normal. Having Taylor Finn, and most likely Lizzy, know this was how I felt.

We sat in silence for a few minutes and listened to the distant grumble of thunder.

'We should watch *Happy Gilmore* later,' said Taylor, looking at the Adam Sandler cut-out on the floor.

'I like *Big Daddy*,' I said.

'Are you serious? *Big Daddy* is the worst,' she said. 'That court case at the end where the dad gives that bullshit testimonial.'

'It's funny,' I replied, shrugging her off. 'And *Happy Gilmore* is about golf. Do you like *Tin Cup* too?'

'Oh fuck off, do I like *Tin Cup*,' she said. '*Happy Gilmore* is awesome. Everyone likes it. Unless you're a weirdo and prefer *Little Nicky* or something.'

'*Little Nicky* rules. So does *The Waterboy*,' I replied, deadly serious.

'Yeah? And *Zohan*?' asked Taylor.

'And *Zohan*,' I replied.

We were both smiling now. It felt good to be talking crap again.

I hopped down and sloshed onto the wet carpet. Taylor followed.

We walked over to the corridor and picked up her tools. Neither of us wanted to continue with the doors today. Instead we retraced our steps back past the dome to JB's where we warmed up watching old episodes of *Friends* and waited for Lizzy and Rocky to get bored with the storm.

9

We had been back to assess the hole in the projection roof
a few times since the weather had cleared. In sunshine the
tiny holes threw brilliant sparkles of light through the long,
messy room. They were pretty and alluring, but offered
no indication of how we might escape through the gap
above. The room definitely only had one entrance, which
sounded crazy when Rocky revealed to us how flammable
film stock could be. Death via the shitty new *Transformers*
film would be a sad way to go.

With this off the cards, and the Ford Fiesta fading from
our minds, we shivered through our first grey and mindless
winter in Carousel. There was no shortage of heaters in
the centre, but with such large areas to keep warm, we still
found ourselves hanging out in coats and jackets. Taylor
and Lizzy refused to wear any kind of ugg boot. They were
'so trashy' and the wool inside was like 'walking on top of
some poor animal'. I tended to agree that they were pretty
trashy, but we were living in Carousel so in a way it kind
of made sense. Rocky had taken to wearing a black pair
that came halfway up his shins. Combined with his skinny

jeans and oversized hoodies it gave him a mythical look akin to a character out of *Harry Potter* or *The Lord of the Rings*. The Finns and I often avoided making eye contact when Rocky surfaced in the morning for fear of flat-out laughter.

Not that the rest of us were looking our best either. Taylor's and Lizzy's hair was a constant source of angst. They would begrudgingly trust one another to perform trims and treatments in one of the boutiques. More often than not they would be unhappy with the results and sulk around the centre beneath a hood for weeks. Cutting Rocky's and my hair was a much simpler exercise. I was currently getting around with one side of my head shaved close, along with the back, while the rest was left longer to produce a pretty deliberate edgy look that seemed way out of place in Carousel.

I tried to look at the style as part of a new artistic persona. I was writing regularly. Churning out poetry full of thinly veiled explorations of entrapment and confinement. I had also started, and abandoned, several novellas based on my angsty teenage years, my first year at university, or anything else that I could pull from something I was reading and adapt to fit my own history. I had no real sense of their success, but they all felt pretty fake after the first few pages and I wasn't able to commit to one over the other.

I also started experimenting with the clothes I was wearing on long ventures throughout the centre. During one of these I found a brown leather jacket in Live. It was the type of thing that I would never normally consider wearing because it was so obvious. You didn't just happen to throw on a leather jacket, you chose to wear one. Even if it looked good, this decision was somehow significant, and the kind of thing I usually avoided. But I liked this jacket. It felt natural and fitted my slightly longer arms and thinnish torso perfectly. After a few trips back to the store I decided to take it.

Taylor and Lizzy noticed me wearing it immediately. I did my best to act natural and play it down, but figured there'd be some comment flung my way. But there wasn't. Until almost a week later when Taylor stopped and looked at me seriously.

'You look fucking awesome in that jacket, Nox. With the hair and shit,' she said, and turned away without adding anything further. I nodded and nearly broke my face holding in a smile. The compliment left me feeling more fragile than any criticism ever could.

Now that Lizzy's studio was just about ready for action I decided to learn how to work the recording gear so I could help her out some more. It was mostly done on a computer program but we had also set up a small mixing desk to control the sound coming in. A lot of the time I just stood around listening to loops on headphones, playing with dials and quietly revelling in how cool it was to be hanging around a rock star in their studio. Lizzy had a whole bunch of stuff she had been tinkering with. But oddly nothing that was ready to lay down.

Taylor and Rocky had added gardening to their daily tasks. The four of us had watched a couple of movies recently that depicted post-apocalyptic stories of survival. They seemed a long way removed from our lives in Carousel, but still made us realise what a shit job we were all doing of staying alive.

The obvious way of remedying this seemed to be growing some food.

So, as winter set in, we all ventured to Backyard Bonanza and piled every pot we could find into trolleys, along with dozens of packets of seeds for lettuce, carrot, sweet corn and whatever else we had been craving. Unfortunately they didn't have soil so we had to cart this from Coles, who kept small generic bags of potting mix in the pest control and electrical aisle.

We filled the pots and set them in a neat circle beneath the dome where they would at least get some sunlight.

Many of the pots had remained barren. Trying to grow stuff like tomatoes and sweet corn inside a shopping centre in the middle of winter had proved overly ambitious. But other stuff like rocket and mushrooms had gone crazy. It was probably one of the most exciting things we had done in Carousel. Eating a rocket salad, or some mushrooms in a pot with powdered butter, or even just walking past the small pocket of green below the dome made us feel like we weren't just sitting around, eating our way through a shopping centre. With the garden, and the doors, and the music and the writing, we were doing something more than just existing.

Something that was probably keeping us alive as much as anything.

Our makeshift lounge room in JB Hi-Fi seemed to expand by the week. We now had a variety of couches forming a large u-shape facing our favourite flatscreen. There were two glowing space heaters beaming up at us from in front of the screen, and a big square coffee table from Freedom, floating like a messy, urban island in the middle. It was strewn with a constant supply of DVDs, magazines, books, snack foods and dinner plates.

As the days grew colder we found our desire to venture to other places within the centre diminishing. We now cooked and ate in JB's most of the time. We wheeled in a little gas cooker and a microwave and cleared off a table full of discount CDs for a prep area. Dishes were problematic as they required plumbing and the closest available was at the Coffee Club island. So Rocky and I constructed a kind of giant dish rack similar to those at Ikea restaurants and the four of us would take it in turns to wheel it over to the Coffee Club dishwasher once it was full or started to smell festy.

I glanced away from the TV and looked over at Rocky working through the dishes inside the island. He opened the dishwasher, releasing a wave of steam into the air. He coughed, holding his gloved hand up to his face. Rocky had developed a raking dry cough early in winter that he had been unable to shift.

'Do you think that steam is bad for his cough?' I asked the Finns, who sat on a couch adjacent.

They followed my gaze to Rocky.

'It's warm. Shouldn't it be doing him good?' said Taylor.

'He needs echinacea. But I can't find any more that's in code,' said Lizzy.

'Have you seen his hand lately?' I asked them both.

They nodded. Despite regular bathing and a chemist full of supplies, Rocky's hand still hadn't healed. He now walked and rode with it cupped in front of him like he was holding a tennis ball or asking for change. None of us knew what else we could do.

'There is a bunch of antibiotics at Friendlies. I found a book that says most of the penicillin stuff works the same,' said Lizzy.

'You want to just flip him some pills and see how it goes?' asked Taylor.

Lizzy glared at her.

'We might have to. If we miss a dressing, or he gets some dirt in there, he could get blood poisoning or something,' I said.

We were silent. None of us wanted to go down this path, but the alternatives were too frightening to get our heads around.

Rocky wheeled the big floating dish rack back over to us.

'Alright, fine,' said Taylor. 'Rocky, have you ever had penicillin before?'

Lizzy sighed. Rocky left the dishes inside the door and carried his hand back to his spot on the couch.

'Amoxicillin. For my throat,' he replied.

Taylor and I looked at Lizzy. She shrugged.

'We're going to give you some antibiotics for your hand,' said Taylor.

'Are you allergic to anything, Rock?' asked Lizzy.

'Don't think so,' he replied.

'You'll have to stay off the booze for a bit, yeah,' said Taylor. 'No more Tia Maria.'

Rocky smiled. I couldn't help but laugh. Somehow Taylor was both the funniest and most serious person in Carousel.

'This episode is shit,' said Rocky, looking at the TV which was aglow with our latest fad, nineties cult series *The X-Files*.

'*Call of Duty*?' I asked, referring to our gaming setup at the other side of the store.

Rocky nodded and we left Taylor and Lizzy alone on the couches. They watched us go.

We played for a few hours before Rocky was tired. I left him to sleep on the couch, covered in blankets and away from moisture. We took any chance we could to get him out of his damp and dingy tent at Camping World. I gave Taylor and Lizzy a wave and strolled out into the frigid, lonely centre.

It was Sunday and I'd already chosen a card for Lizzy earlier in the day. I picked up a bike I'd left at Pure 'n' Natural and cycled it over to Dymocks. Lizzy's bed lay tucked cosily into an aisle between *Travel* and *Self Help*. It looked warm and inviting. Lizzy was one of those people that always had a comfy looking bed, or found the best spot to sit on a train, or the best table in a restaurant.

I left the envelope beside her pillow. It contained a new short story I had written about a kid who took the wrong bus after school and rode it all the way across the city.

I started putting snippets of my writing in with the letters about a month ago. I was pretty sure Lizzy was reading them, but so far she hadn't said anything. I don't know what I wanted to happen. I guess for her to tell me they were good. But I wasn't sure if this even mattered. Right now just putting them inside and having her say nothing felt fine.

As I left I noticed a shelf lined with cards from previous Sundays. It was chocked full. It struck me how many weeks we had seen in Carousel already. Once winter was over it would be almost a year. I wondered seriously whether there would be enough With Regret cards to last us the distance.

Walking back to Myer I fantasised about the owner of the Fiesta. Lately it felt like the only thing I thought about. She was in her twenties. A little older than me. The soft, rounded face of a girl I'd been to high school with. She was always warm. Tucked up in track pants and a red pullover. Sitting on my bunk listening to Bon Iver. Sipping on a smoothie at Pure 'n' Natural. On the couch beside me watching old Hitchcock films.

I would fight her out of my mind, then quickly bring her back again. There was comfort and distraction in the fantasies. My imagination had always been strong enough to make something feel tangible, at least temporarily. I convinced myself that these moments were worth the comedown of reality that followed. Plus they turned the Fiesta into something I wasn't afraid of. The girl was stronger than any of my nightmares, pushing them away somewhere deep and controllable. I began to bank on her for this.

I stood motionless under a hot shower for a half-hour to warm myself after a day of shivering. The air was frigid in Myer and the bathrooms were the coldest part. I cycled through towels and dried and dressed in the tiny steam-filled cubicle to delay the cold. Then I hopped about at the mirror, brushing my teeth and assessing how my hair was growing out. Until I noticed the cubicle.

The second one from the end. Its door was closed. The guarding gnome stood solemnly outside.

Our bathroom pact had been breached.

I walked straight over to it. The fear still in my feet but threatening to rise up and overwhelm at any moment. The latch was open. I pushed and the door swung inwards.

The cubicle was empty.

I stood there with the toothbrush in my mouth. Minty foam gathering at the edges of my lips. The toilet stared back quietly like a witness claiming ignorance. I held the door open and slid the heavy little gnome back to where he should be. Where he was until somebody moved him.

Back at the bunk my legs jittered with nervous energy. The warmth of the shower had vanished in an instant. Somebody had used my bathroom. If it was one of us they had broken our biggest rule of keeping cubicles gnomed unless in use. This was subconscious now. Not something any of us would forget.

I fought down a violent urge to bolt out of Myer. Any security I felt about the place had vanished. I needed to tell the others. To radio them and talk it through. Not because they would have a solution. But so they would freak out too, and I would try to rationalise things and calm them down, and in the process calm myself.

But something held me back.

I don't know what it was. Maybe it was the thought of leaving. The cubicle seemed like confirmation that our world would inevitably be smashed open, leaving us hanging outside of fate. Forced to create our identities again like kids out of school.

But my fear of this happening didn't completely eclipse my feelings for the others. These were strong and the de-gnoming left each of them vulnerable.

I picked up my radio.

Before I could talk the speaker crackled and Lizzy screamed.

I arrived down at Dymocks just after Rocky and Taylor.

Lizzy was pacing about anxiously.

'Rocky, you fuck! What were you doing in there anyway?' said Lizzy.

Rocky shuffled uncomfortably, his hand twitching in front of him. The three of them glanced at me as I walked through the door.

'What happened?' I asked Taylor.

'Rocky forgot to gnome a cubicle in Lizzy's bathroom,' said Taylor.

The words left me stunned.

I stole a look at Rocky. He seemed a little confused, but otherwise normal.

'The gnome was lying on its back outside,' added Lizzy.

She was pumped full of adrenaline.

'It's hard with my hand,' said Rocky.

The three of us looked at him. It was difficult not to feel for the guy.

Lizzy sat back on the edge of her bed.

'You just need to tell us, Rocky,' said Taylor. 'If you can't prop the door just tell us so we know it will be closed.'

He nodded. I sat next to Lizzy and gave her shoulder a squeeze. She didn't respond, instead focusing on the floor and trying to slow her breathing. Taylor watched us.

'Did you open the door?' she asked.

'No. I ran the fuck out of there,' Lizzy replied.

'Okay. I'm going to go open it,' said Taylor and turned to head out of the store.

'Wait!' I said and jumped up to follow.

'Jesus, Nox,' said Lizzy, bewildered.

'I'll come,' I said to Taylor.

She stopped and waited for me. Lizzy and Rocky were left alone by the bed. Lizzy and Taylor shared a look.

'Rocky, come with us, yeah,' Taylor said.

Rocky padded over to join us.

We rounded the corner and walked down the corridor to where the words *Named Lizzy* had been scrawled underneath the label *Ladies*, on the toilet door. My pulse thumped through the back of my knees. It took all my control to follow Taylor casually into the room.

Rocky didn't follow.

'Shit. Rocky!' called Taylor, as the door closed behind us.

She edged back past me to find out where he had gone. I followed and we found him stopped a few metres away by a different door.

'Come on, Rocky,' she said softly.

Rocky looked confused but followed obediently into the room. Taylor moved bravely over the cubicle and pushed open the door.

I started feeling weird again. A familiar dizziness swept down from somewhere above my head and flooded into my eyes. The layout of the centre swept out before me. A kind of three-dimensional floor plan with colour and texture. I felt myself towering above it on a savage tilt that would soon see me crash inside. I tried to get my bearings and find somewhere soft to land but swayed backward with a rush of nausea.

'Nox,' said Rocky softly.

I came to. He and Taylor were looking at me oddly. The cubicle was open and Taylor was retrieving the gnome from the floor.

'Sorry. I'm still half asleep,' I said.

Taylor nodded and put the gnome back in place.

'Are we all sorted?' I asked.

'Yeah,' said Taylor, walking past me. 'Weirdo.'

Rocky followed. I glanced at the cubicle, then trailed behind.

Lizzy was back reading in her bed. Taylor moved over to the free side and climbed in under the covers. Lizzy watched her silently, looking neither pleased nor annoyed.

I really didn't feel like hanging out with Rocky, but it seemed like the Finns had decided this for me.

'Come on, Rock. You hungry?' I asked and waited for him to follow me out of the room. Taylor and Lizzy glanced at me as we left. A hint of thanks in their gaze.

Rocky and I stayed up playing *Mario Kart* and eating stale Doritos until morning. As I wove my tiny machine around the colourful tracks my mind churned with a heady cycle of Fiestas, gnomes and cubicles. Every so often I would remember Rocky beside me. His body still. Gloved hand clumsily holding the controller. Avatar nailing turn after turn. Eyes dull in the flicker of the screen. Our adopted teenage brother. Chocked full of mystery, now more than ever.

10

I didn't get a chance to think through the events of that night until a few days later. At Lizzy's suggestion we conducted a kind of Carousel busy bee. Cleaning up the floor beneath the dome where our fledgling garden had been built. Mopping the corridors that we used the most. Tidying up JB's after a winter of eating in and watching TV. Checking that all the toilets were gnomed. I was pretty sure that the season hadn't yet broken outside of the centre but it felt as close to a spring-clean as anything.

Thankfully, due to the size of the centre, we were still able to hide away from our increasingly epic stockpiles of rubbish. Early in our stay we had collected the centre's supply of rubbish bins and liners and created a giant grid inside Big W. In the aisles between bins we had laid an assortment of pest control – roach baits, ant rid, mouse traps – to keep the place from becoming infested.

The bins had filled much quicker than we expected and we had soon started using anything that was airtight. The environment in Big W was still hygienic; in fact, none of us had seen a single cockroach, something we were pleased about but which didn't necessarily bode well for the situation outside, but we knew it wasn't feasible forever. Like a bunch of cliché politicians, our rubbish management accommodated the present, with a clear disregard for the future.

Luckily we had remained pretty strict with our recycling. Life on earth may be over, but our bottles, papers and plastics were beautifully separate from our food waste and ready for the factory. This meant that Lizzy and I could experiment with our genius idea of using the decomposed slush at the bottom of our first bins to grow vegetables.

Taylor and Rocky watched our stupid grins as we wheeled bins into position beneath the dome and edged the lids open to heavy wafts of weird gases. We decided that the best way to control the smell, and potentially grow something edible, was to top up the bins with soil and wet everything together. With the mini bags of potting mix from Coles already running low this raised the stakes on our plan and left both Lizzy and me deliberating carefully over the number of seedlings and the position of bins, hoping something would grow in one of them so Taylor wouldn't have us shovelling the soil back out a few weeks later.

The clean-up was a good idea. The collective tasks smoothed over our fractured relationships and gave us all something to concentrate on. Rocky had been particularly active and we were all pleased to see the second brand of antibiotics finally chasing the infection from his hand. The cough remained but that seemed a part of him now.

We spent nights relaxing with beer and stretching out muscles that were sore for the first time in a while.

After a long day on the mop I left Rocky watching TV with the Finns and drifted back to Myer to finish my beer and revisit the cubicle saga.

I coasted through the corridors on a BMX, nursing my drink and passing the stores like houses in a tired and familiar neighbourhood. I tried to stay relaxed as I headed into Myer and trudged upstairs. Discovering the de-gnomed cubicle had changed the dynamic of the place. The familiarity I had worked hard to develop had gone, leaving me anxious and eager to switch bedrooms to somewhere else in the centre. But with my discovery still a secret, and no really plausible reason to offer the Finns, I felt stuck there until something changed.

And I had no idea if it would. Lizzy's discovery and Rocky's admission had confused the hell out of me. It was hard to imagine Rocky using the toilet and leaving the door closed by accident. Even given the state of his hand this would mean he stepped over a gnome and left the room in a way he'd been drilled not to from day one. We'd all seen him do some pretty bizarro things, so maybe forgetting to gnome a door was pretty possible, even inevitable. But what was he doing in Lizzy's bathroom?

I think this was the thing that concerned us the most. Dymocks was at the opposite end of the centre to where Rocky slept. It wasn't close to JB's or Hoyts or anywhere else he hung out regularly. Plus there were at least four other bathrooms within maybe a hundred metres of Lizzy's. If Rocky really needed to go, there were other options.

Of course none of these questions even touched the issue of my own cubicle discovery. Whatever the hell this meant, and how, if at all, it was connected to Rocky, I had no idea. The simple assumption would be that Rocky was also responsible for de-gnoming my bathroom. He had a wild night where he roamed, full-bladdered, through all corners of Carousel using select toilets to break the centre's only rule, and scare the crap out of his housemates.

As I lay on the bunk looking up at the ceiling the absurdity of this was enough to make me laugh. But what if it was somebody we didn't know. Someone who had chosen to hide from us. Someone who knew things about Carousel that we didn't. Someone who had now decided to silently, definitively, announce their arrival.

As long as the owner of the solitary Fiesta in the staff car park remained faceless, our imaginations ran in overdrive. This, combined with my cubicle discovery, pushed me dangerously close to the edge of something. My dreams changed. No longer tangible or relevant, they swept out over massive vistas of time and space, dwarfing me physically and emotionally, and leaving me fragile and jittery in the mornings. I was also in constant worry over the safety of Rocky and the Finns. I would mask my relief at their arrival at breakfast, and make up excuses to radio them late at night.

None of this was sustainable. I had to tell the others, but felt I couldn't until I found out more. I told myself this was to protect them from unnecessary stress. And maybe it was. But again I was crippled by the thought that the news would somehow see us thrust out of the centre. I understood that we had to break out. For Rocky, Taylor, all of us. But every instinct screamed at me to delay.

I stayed up late, bargaining with myself. If I wasn't going to tell the others about the de-gnoming of my bathroom, I had to at least investigate and find out who was responsible. I would kill off my imagination with facts, then decide how to act on them.

I started spending my alone time looking through the centre for signs of another occupant. Lizzy didn't really need me in Rugs a Million anymore, and Taylor and Rocky were occupied with doors and gardening in the dome, so I generally had the rest of Carousel to myself.

It might have been a Wednesday when I headed east toward the back entrance. This was the opposite side of the centre to where the Fiesta was parked, but I didn't think that was relevant. The car was parked randomly and away from any of the labelled bays. This didn't give me a lot to go by, but did suggest that maybe the driver wasn't a storeowner in Carousel, or at least didn't want to look like one. For some reason this pointed me eastward to the cheaper, less permanent stores.

The back of the centre was an area we generally left alone. It didn't have any real food outlets except for a Wendys where the superdogs and thickshakes were long expired. It was also draughty and cold, only receiving a sliver of afternoon sun. I remembered there being some novelty stores and a Two-Dollar Shop where we found some buckets for waste storage, and also some offices that seemed like a management area. But otherwise it all felt fairly new and unexplored.

I had no method, wandering slowly through corridors, looking for something out of the ordinary in a centre with nothing but. The build-up of dust was really noticeable in the east end. Counters and benchtops held a thick film of grey.

Human skin.

I remembered this from a movie we'd seen recently. They had said that dust was predominantly human skin. Yet here it was in a centre without people. Maybe it was already in the air when we arrived here, and the static centre had since let it drop. The skin of a thousand dead shoppers.

It was easy to creep yourself out in Carousel.

I considered the dust a good thing though. Its heavy

build up meant that any disturbances should be pretty noticeable. I started looking at it closely. Noticing how it sat fatly on horizontal surfaces, but also held in thinner clusters on the vertical. Testing different items, I noticed that dust could be disturbed in several ways. Touching it directly, sweeping past the vertical, creating a soft flow of wind with an arm or leg. I also noticed how it gathered in clusters at the edges of ventilation ducts, on surfaces that were smooth but not slippery. How it would sit, almost invisible, in the cotton of a shirt. CSI Carousel. I ran over snappy lines of dialogue in my head and considered adding forensic drama to my list of sketchy novella concepts.

But, from what I could see, the dust in the east end was stable and undisturbed. The costume stores and locksmiths sat dormant and steadfast. These were stores that were used to being quiet. They didn't seem to miss people like Live or the Apple Store did. My presence in them was neither welcomed nor despised. Another window shopper, showing fleeting interest, but holding a separate agenda.

Centre Management was a series of nondescript shopfronts in a cul-de-sac leading away from the back entrance. The glass was tinted and there was a list of stickers identifying who could be found inside. I pushed open the heavy glass door and stepped into the coldest room in the whole freezing complex. I shook out a shiver and looked around the reception area. It was all pretty bland. A desk with a computer and a secret stash of gossip magazines.

A couple of chairs for people waiting. A fish tank bubbling away with a solitary guppy anxiously circling the corpses of his tankmates. Doors leading to several offices and a kitchenette.

I sniffed at the stale, dank air and stepped around the desk to drop a bunch of fish food into the tank. The guppy gulped at it eagerly. I watched him and considered a rescue. There was a dreaded bulge at the back of his stomach that seemed more buoyant than the rest of him. It had him tipping dangerously upside down whenever his swimming slowed. I didn't like his chances and spread some extra food across the surface. At least he wouldn't go hungry.

The offices looked the same bar one, which was bigger and had its own couch and sitting area. I decided that this must be the manager's office and worthy of some poking around. Inside I loaded up the computer and fished through some drawers. I found applications for liquor licences. Several giant-size Snickers bars. Unopened letters from a local politician. A packet of menthol cigarettes. A calculator. No master key or secret escape button.

On the computer I snooped through the private folders of the potentially deceased manager. Again, nothing unexpected. Without the internet I couldn't refresh the email account, but the existing inbox was still pretty interesting. There was a lengthy exchange between Cathy, in whose seat I was sitting, and a potential shop owner named Mike from Ra's Emporium. Mike sold Egyptian ornaments out of Victoria Park but wanted to relocate into the centre. Cathy reiterated that they had received his application but no spaces were currently available. Mike wasn't able to accept this and asked Cathy to remove the lowest-paying existing tenant and offer him the space at a slightly higher price. Cathy had explained several times, in a polite yet businesslike tone, why this wasn't possible and suggested he tried the Southlands complex or wait for a vacancy. Mike wasn't happy. In his final email he confusingly called Cathy a capitalist anti-Semite and threatened to curse the centre. Ironically Mike signed off every email with *Kindest regards to you and your family*. Maybe Cathy should have listened.

There was also a brief email from Centre Security. It contained an update on the installation of some new security cameras in the car parks. We had often thought that the security department might give us some answers on our situation, but had been unable to find their offices in the centre. For a fleeting moment I thought they might have been in with the management but this wasn't the case. I searched through Cathy's folders for further correspondence with Security but found nothing of note. Frustratingly their email signature didn't reveal their position in the centre either.

Back in reception, I found a rack of keys behind the desk. I shook these into my pocket without much hope and left the icy room behind. We had a massive stockpile of unlabelled keys already and none of them had proven very useful. The most exciting discovery was when Taylor found one that opened the Giant Claw vending machine and we freed the stockpile of cheap stuffed toys.

I slipped some coins into a vending machine next to Best & Less and drank a Solo. We were actually running low on coins at the moment so vending machines were a bit taboo. There were notes all over the centre, but no use for them. Coins on the other hand got us gameplay on the video games in Hoyts. Wash cycles in the laundromat beside Coles. And the chance to validate a hypothetical parking token and get the hell out of this place.

I drained the can and lay down on a couch beside Wendys to listen to The National. The centre was different with a soundtrack. The emptiness filled and it felt possible to think about people that I used to know. It gave my imprisonment a momentary context. I felt alive in these moments. Like I had as a teenager in a pot-filled garage with Rage Against the Machine. Or in bed with Heather while Soko played on Triple J. But Carousel really amplified the comedown at the end of the song. It was deathly quiet and still. A great big emotional vacuum. This kept my music listening limited and selective.

'Hello? Nox?'

It was Lizzy. She sounded bored and a little annoyed. I lifted my radio to reply.

'Yeah. Hi,' I said.

'What were you doing?' she asked.

'Sorry. Listening to music,' I replied.

'Who?'

'The National.'

'*Trouble Will Find Me*?'

'*High Violet*.'

'Nice.'

She was silent for a moment. Then we both tried to radio at the same time.

Static.

'Sorry,' I said, getting through a moment later. 'Are you still in Rugs?'

'No. The Apple Store. I need a new iPad,' she replied. 'Where are you?'

'Just riding around,' I said, having prepared for this question earlier.

'What are we going to eat later?' she wondered out loud.

'I can't eat any more refried beans for a while,' I said.

'Oh. You too?' she asked.

'What? No. I'm just over them.'

There was a little silence.

'You love that Apple Store,' I said.

'Yeah. It's rad. I'm pretty stupid though. I keep checking to see if the iPhones have been updated.'

I laughed but forgot to radio this through.

'What else you doing? Surfing the net?' I asked.

'Yeah, I wish,' she replied.

The internet had been down since our arrival. This bummed out Rocky and me but we were used to it now. For Taylor and Lizzy I think it was still like a phantom limb.

'Maybe we could have a pizza,' said Lizzy.

Lizzy often suggested this but we had long since used up the frozen bases and none of us had bothered to learn how to make a dough.

'Yeah,' I said, noncommittal.

There was some more silence. Radios weren't really designed for Taylor and Lizzy's kind of rapid-fire, mindless chatter. There was a delay that provided an opportunity to shape questions and answers. Plus the act of pressing a button to speak placed an inherent importance on the message.

'Or hash browns,' said Lizzy.

I looked up at the ceiling as Lizzy continued to radio through whatever food slipped into her mind. It reminded me of primary school. Cheap looking square panels boarded by a thin steel frame. We used to jump up from chairs to push them upward into the roof cavity.

'Are you back on your phone?' asked Lizzy.

'Yeah. Sorry. Should I have been listening?' I joked.

'Asshole,' said Lizzy.

'Where are you, Nox? Rocky and I want to race your ass.' Taylor had joined in on our conversation.

I hesitated.

'I'm heading back to JB's. Lizzy made me hungry,' I said and rose from the couch.

'Chicken,' said Taylor.

Or maybe it was Lizzy.

'Sounds good,' I replied.

I set off swiftly westward, not wanting to run into them in the east end and get a bunch of other questions I hadn't prepared for.

Lizzy and I snacked and watched some TV in JB's for a while before she drifted off to play some CDs at the other end of the store. Rocky and Taylor returned from their racing and caught their breath on the couch beside me. Lizzy's deejaying was a little higher than conversation level and drifted in over the television. I waited for Taylor to snap, but she surprised me and wandered over to join Lizzy at the stereos.

The pair of them flicked through albums and talked in a way I hadn't seen them do in a long time. They were separate from the world. In a bubble, not just born out of their sisterhood, but out of talent and status, and whatever else separated famous musicians from the rest of us. I watched and was almost relieved to feel a pang of envy. Carousel hadn't changed them yet. It was trying, and maybe it would eventually succeed, but for the moment Taylor and Lizzy Finn were still awesome.

The world retained an iota of sense.

11

At breakfast Taylor announced her plan to venture back into the staff car park and try to open the garage door. None of us were overly surprised. She was pretty determined to test every door in the centre, and the garage door was one of them. But the car park and the Fiesta were topics we'd steered away from, so there was automatic anxiety.

'You don't have to worry about the backpacks or anything,' Taylor told me. 'I'm just going to jiggle it around a little and see if it moves. If anything happens we can figure out a plan afterward.'

Lizzy and I chewed down our porridge quietly. Rocky hadn't surfaced yet.

'I'm coming,' I said, my cubicle secret weighing heavier by the minute.

Taylor and I looked at Lizzy.

'I'm not staying up here alone while you two take off into the city,' she said.

Taylor sighed.

'You should stay in the corridor so that fucking door doesn't close on us,' I said.

'A doorstop, Nox?' said Lizzy.

I nodded, mocking seriousness.

'And Rocky?' asked Taylor.

Taylor and I were silent. It seemed like Lizzy should decide on this.

'He has to come,' she said after a moment.

We nodded and continued with our breakfast. On cue, Rocky cycled around the corner.

I left breakfast and hastily put together a backpack in Army Depot. Taylor had told me not to bother but there were basic things we would need and there was no way I was heading into that car park unprepared. I stashed a couple of stronger Maglites in a bag, as well as a freestanding light that could be placed beside the door while we worked on it. I also stuffed in one of the gas masks. It seemed stupid to take just one, rather than four, but I didn't have a lot of room.

Before I left I packed one final item. A large, vicious looking hunting knife from behind the counter. I felt ridiculous tucking it inside. Any danger that we were about to face would surely not be quelled by a hunting knife. But I had to take something. None of the others knew what I knew. Even if that wasn't much.

Taylor exited her bathroom and glanced at me with the backpack. She didn't say anything, but to ease the tension I put a couple of her tools inside. Rocky seemed to have been briefed on the plan and stood waiting in the corridor, flicking a skateboard around. Lizzy poured out the contents of a smoothie into a couple of takeaway cups, handed one to Taylor, and we set off.

This time Rocky and I had the door open without any problems. The three of us stepped outside while Lizzy took up position on the step.

I handed her a torch.

'Your radio on?' I asked.

'Roger,' she replied.

We turned on our torches and set off toward the ramp.

'I'm eating the last Tim Tams if you guys take too long,' said Lizzy.

The extra power of the torches lit up a lot more of the space. Not that there was anything to see. Just a big empty car park slowly filling with dust.

At the base of the ramp the three of us immediately turned around to locate the Fiesta. It was there, just as before. With this confirmed, we headed for the dull columns of light escaping down the sides of the roller door. Taylor stopped beside the door and put down her tools. I took off the backpack, pulled out the portable light I had packed and switched it on. It threw a steady pocket of illumination across the door.

Taylor nodded, impressed.

'Stick around, Rocky. Okay?' she said.

Rocky nodded, looking slightly bored.

Taylor proceeded to wedge various crowbars under

the steel while I searched around for a switch or lever that would open the door and make us all feel stupid. Sometimes I wondered if our escape from Carousel was as simple as pushing a door instead of pulling it and this whole experience had been completely avoidable.

There were a couple of control panels on the wall but nothing that seemed to relate to the door. Taylor had been able to wedge a crowbar underneath the door, but not move it upward even a fraction. She gave up and moved over to one side to see if it might shift that way. I turned to join her but Rocky stopped me.

I looked at him curiously. He nodded in front of me and held up his torch. I followed the light to find a spider web strung between pillars with a tiny spider suspended in the middle. I patted Rocky gratefully and bypassed the web. His arm lingered on mine, as if there might have been something else. I glanced at him, but he kept quiet.

Taylor could increase the gap at the side of the door a fraction using all her strength on the crowbar. I watched as the column of light widened slightly on one side, and almost disappeared on the other. It was kind of exciting, but I couldn't really see how it would get the door open. Taylor stopped, seemingly thinking the same.

'Alright. At least I can sleep now,' she said as we both stood staring at the door.

'Yep,' I said and gathered a few of her tools.

Our radios crackled.

'So I'm thinking *Gossip Girl* season three, Coke Zeros and those pizza shape biscuit things,' said Lizzy from upstairs as if sensing our failure with the door.

Taylor and I smiled.

'We'll be back up in a sec,' Taylor replied.

I turned off the light and passed it to Taylor who had the backpack. She placed it inside but it wouldn't zip up. She took it out and shuffled the other contents. Her hand stopped on something.

I swore silently. It had to be the hunting knife. Taylor edged it aside, packed in the light and handed me the bag without saying anything.

'All set, Rocky?' she asked.

He nodded tiredly and followed us back up the ramp. I took a final glance at the Fiesta. It glinted dully and then was lost from view.

Lizzy seemed uninterested in our attempts on the door. She simply stood up and led us back into the centre.

I think we were all a little relieved. Taylor and Lizzy sat through a bunch of *Gossip Girl*, with Rocky looking on, feigning boredom even though he was clearly into it. I made us some packet mash potato with gravy, and heated some frozen garlic bread. A huge carbo load but one of our favourite meals.

Late in the afternoon Taylor returned from her bathroom, sat down and rubbed her temples.

'What?' asked Lizzy.

Taylor was still for a moment, then took her hands away. She was pale and looked like she was trying to remember something. All three of us watched her.

'Taylor?' asked Lizzy.

'A cubicle in my bathroom was de-gnomed. While we were in the car park.'

I went cold.

'Are you sure it was gnomed when we left?' I asked. Taylor looked at me. She was.

'Shit. Shit. Shit,' whispered Lizzy in a kind of anxious daze.

'What do we do about this? I mean, somebody is in here with us, right?' said Taylor.

I kept quiet.

'Why wouldn't they come and talk to us?' asked Lizzy.

'They're obviously not the making-friends-in-empty-malls type,' said Taylor.

'It's just one door. The other one was an accident. Do we really want to turn this into something dramatic?' replied Lizzy.

The lump of guilt in my stomach rose into my throat.

'I think they did my bathroom, too,' I said, looking down.

Taylor and Lizzy stared at me.

'You think?' asked Taylor.

'It could have been me. I'm pretty out of it in the morning.' I copped out.

'When was this?' asked Lizzy.

'A few weeks ago. Sorry.' I said.

I looked up at them and was scared as hell that they would hate me forever.

'I thought it would just freak everyone out so I didn't say anything. But now it makes sense.'

'The knife,' said Taylor softly.

I looked at her but she turned away from me. Lizzy seemed confused but gave me a tiny, sympathetic smile.

I looked across the couch and realised that Rocky was with us. These weren't the type of conversations we normally had when he was around.

'They de-gnomed my bathroom, and Nox's,' said Taylor, thinking it over.

'And Lizzy's,' said Rocky, abruptly.

We looked at him.

'That was you, Rocky. Remember?' said Taylor soothingly.

Rocky shook his head. We all watched him.

'I used the toilet next door. Forgot to gnome the door in there,' he said.

'Oh my god,' said Lizzy.

I suddenly remembered him lingering weirdly outside the adjacent bathroom as we went back into Lizzy's bathroom.

'You didn't say anything,' said Taylor.

Rocky dropped his head.

'Did you get confused, Rock?' I asked.

He nodded.

'How come we didn't see this when we were cleaning?' asked Lizzy to nobody in particular.

'I gnomed it again in the night,' said Rocky.

'Holy shit, Rocky. You gotta stop creeping around the place in those giant boots,' said Lizzy.

It was funny as hell but none of us dared to laugh. Rocky kept his head down. We were silent while Leighton Meester chirped away on the TV.

'We need to find the security office,' said Rocky.

None of us followed.

'Watch the screens to see who is moving around,' he continued.

'Rocky. That's awesome,' said Taylor genuinely.

And it was. Shoplifting was rife in Carousel. There were cameras everywhere.

'Didn't we look for that already?' asked Lizzy.

'Yeah, but it's got to be here somewhere,' I said. 'Have you guys seen anything while you're working on the doors?' I asked Taylor.

It felt good to ask her something. Like I was out of the woods.

'There are some rooms we could check out. But it's pretty vague,' she replied.

'Somewhere on the perimeter,' said Rocky. 'So they can come late at night and check on the car parks,' he finished.

We nodded. This made total sense and narrowed the search significantly.

'It's got to be in the south, right?' said Lizzy. 'All the perimeter stores in the north are boutiques. The east is bordered by that car park. And the west is the dome.'

Taylor and I nodded. None of us seemed to have anything else to say. In the morning we would search the south end for the security office. If we could find it then Carousel's mystery fifth inhabitant might be revealed. I looked over at Rocky to give him a nod or something that said good job and sorry we all accused you of being a demented freak. He was back watching *Gossip Girl*.

We made an unspoken decision to remain in JB's until morning. Shit was going down in Carousel and nobody seemed keen for any more right away. Taylor curled up on the couch with a blanket. Rocky didn't move. I shuffled over to the gaming couch with a sleeping bag and some chocolate bullets. Lizzy picked up a guitar.

She thumbed softly through some songs from *Holy Noise* and *The Quell* on a beanbag amid the DVDs. It was gentle and only for herself. I turned over and listened the best I could from my couch. After twenty minutes or so I noticed the TV noises had stopped. Taylor had turned it off. JB's was silent but for Lizzy.

She finished her song, paused for a moment, then put down the guitar.

12

I was beginning to hate that our breakfasts were becoming a prelude to some big venture. I just wanted to sit around with Lizzy, chewing on pancakes and making perfect lattes. Not spoon down serious porridge covered in dirt-coloured supplements and stress about what we were about to find. But that was pretty much the deal the following morning as we prepared to search for the security office and whatever horror it decided to reveal.

The four of us moved steadily southward through the centre. We stopped briefly at the dome to water our strange, sprawling garden. Lizzy and I quietly noted the lack of any growth from the seeds in the rubbish bins. The place was going to need a decent clean-up once the winter rains had stopped. At the moment any heavy rainfall was flushing through the pots and spreading dirt in an increasing fan across the tiles. We left, carrying this on our shoes past the cinema and further south.

It was hard to get a handle on what type of stores were in the south end. The east was similarly mishmash but held together by the theme of thrift. You could buy a pair of sneakers, and a giant bottle of shampoo. And both would be at a bargain price. This wasn't really the case in the south. There was a Freedom furniture outlet selling sleek rectangular lounges and glass coffee tables, as well as a bubble-tea house covered in kitschy yellow pandas. If anything, the smaller stores seemed like filler for the corridors leading to big outlets like Woolworths, Coles and Big W. For us this meant the south was our major source of food in the centre. Twice a week we would trolley back to JB's with a pile of whatever was still in code and prepare what we could to eat.

Beyond the big stores were a series of smaller corridors leading out to car parks. There were stores lining these routes but it was pretty average real estate. Shoppers were either on their way in for groceries and nothing else, or on their way out after marathon ventures throughout the centre, too exhausted to look at another mobile phone plan or wall calendar.

As we suspected, several of these stores had exterior facings that provided independent access to the centre after hours. Rocky deemed this vital to a potential security office. His stepdad worked night shift for Guardhouse Security in the city so none of us were in a position to doubt him.

We paced along looking for anything that wasn't retail. There were a couple of offices that had us momentarily excited until we noticed the *To Lease* listing on the counter.

Otherwise all we found was a series of random shopfronts where you could picture the shop assistant shamelessly tapping their smartphones as you browsed inside.

Right at the end of one of the corridors, beside an exit leading onto a ramp and most likely a car park, Rocky noticed a hallway. We wandered over and found a couple of cleaning closets and a large cupboard housing firefighting equipment. The end of the hall was pretty dim and we nearly dismissed it, but for some open space on the right. Moving closer we found a small staircase leading up to a singular door.

It had to be the security office.

For some reason it made perfect sense that the office would be upstairs, above the surrounding stores. I doubted whether you could see any more from up there but it somehow fitted with the security office's omniscient feel. Rocky stopped at the base and looked back at us like a well-trained puppy. We nodded and followed him up the stairs.

The door was locked and looked like it swung outward, which would make knocking it in problematic. Taylor produced one of her crowbars and wedged it in between door and frame. We stepped back and she braced herself for a great heave.

The lock gave meekly and the door swung open towards us.

'Some security office,' said Taylor and headed inside.

We followed and were relieved to find a simple room with a wall full of closed-circuit TVs. Each one offered split screens with multiple live angles of the centre. The checkouts at Target. The box office at the cinema. The dome. Our little hideaway in JB Hi-Fi. Every exit in the centre. It was all there.

The four of us stood and stared at the screens. It felt strange looking at our centre from up there. Kind of like we had somehow gained objectivity. We were able to see our situation, our entrapment, for the absurdity that it was. We had been wandering across these screens for months and months. Tiny black figures lingering in places we shouldn't.

'This is weird,' said Lizzy.

'So weird,' said Taylor.

The coverage was impressive. Every corner of the centre that we recognised seemed to be on-screen, and then there was a bunch of places that didn't look familiar at all.

'We have a Domino's?' I asked.

'You didn't know that?' asked Lizzy.

I shook my head.

'No bases though. It's tragic,' she continued.

'Holy crap, you can see outside!' said Taylor.

She pushed a chair aside and leant in close to a couple of screens trained on the surrounding car parks. The four of us huddled around, eager for a glimpse of the outside.

Taylor sighed. We were foiled by angle. All the cameras seemed to be positioned up high, pointing down at the car parks and exterior doors. This made perfect sense for surveillance, but gave us no hint of horizon or even the immediate suburb. The city could be burning with a thousand corpses but these cameras would still offer an indifferent empty car park.

A little deflated, we wandered around the room looking for anything interesting. I think Rocky was disappointed that the place didn't have its own exterior door as he'd said it would. I wanted to tell him that he had still helped us greatly in suggesting we look for the place. It felt like we had a real shot of finding our fifth housemate now and that was because of Rocky. But the truth of the matter was that we had all blamed Rocky for the de-gnomings. Each of us citing his absentmindedness or something worse. Rocky knew this and things were even more awkward now than they had ever been. Every supportive gesture felt like a guilty admission. Every grumble felt insensitive and crass. Including him was all we could do now.

'So I guess we just watch,' I said.

The others nodded. Rocky sat and coughed a little. Taylor followed. Lizzy slid down the wall and sat cross-legged on the floor. I leant on a bench. None of us seemed too pumped. We were used to comfort and entertainment and the security office had neither. I don't think anyone wanted to say it for fear of sounding precious. This was one of the rare times that Carousel had asked us to focus. There seemed to be a collective resolve not to screw it up.

Four hours later Lizzy and I left the office to get some supplies.

Finding the security office had been a little easier than we expected and we weren't really prepared for the long hours of surveillance that would follow. We had no idea what kind of schedule the resident weirdo kept in the centre. Normally you might assume they would stalk around at night but the de-gnomings were seemingly carried out during daylight. Taylor's room was done yesterday but this also didn't necessarily mean there would be more activity right away. This person could have been in the centre all along. Hiding out, devouring food and making some rationalisation as to why talking to the chatty twins, or the skinny teenager, or the wannabe writer was a bad idea. Basically we had to sit and watch the screens until they decided to surface – whether this was days, weeks or months. We couldn't ignore this like the Fiesta.

With this in mind Lizzy and I pulled the most comfortable set of cushions from a large couch in Freedom and lugged them upstairs with a pile of blankets and pillows. Heading back down we raided the shelves of Woolworths for food and were happily surprised to find a decent selection still in code. Coles was a lot closer to us at JB's so Woolworths had remained decently stocked. The fruit and veg section smelt terrible, as you'd expect. Rows and rows of oozing, mould-covered blackness that used to be apples and bananas. There wasn't much we could do about this kind of thing in a big centre like Woolworths. We'd closed the doors to smaller stores like Nick's Fruit 'n' Veg early on in our stay and watched with fascination as the room filled with gas and mould then slowly, eventually, returned to looking like a regular store with empty, albeit stained, shelves.

'There are Tim Tams on the shelf behind you,' radioed Taylor at one point.

'Oh my god. You can see us,' replied Lizzy looking upward for a camera.

'That's the idea,' said Taylor.

'So creepy,' said Lizzy.

I checked the Tim Tams. They were soft to touch and out of code.

When we rejoined Taylor and Rocky they were quickly becoming tired of the static vision.

'I can't believe they haven't even moved yet,' said Taylor. 'Rocky says they could have redirected a camera.'

'Or maybe they just sit around most of the time, like us,' I said.

The others nodded.

'Should we run shifts?' said Lizzy.

'Good idea,' said Taylor and pulled away from the desk. 'Come on, Rock. You and I are on break.'

Rocky padded over to join her on the sprawling bed we had assembled on the floor.

Lizzy and I dragged ourselves up to sit at the screens. There was no reason why we couldn't return to JB's or our own beds when we were off shift, but it didn't seem like the right thing to do. At the same time I hated leaving our stuff unattended. Not that we really owned any of it. But it felt like we'd gone out and left the house wide open. My eyes gravitated immediately to the cameras on JB's and Myer, scanning for any hint of movement.

Lizzy and I took up watch as night closed in on the centre. We chatted to Taylor and Rocky for a while before they drifted into sleep and their soft breathing asked for silence. Eventually Lizzy broke this.

'The boy that takes the wrong bus, why doesn't he get off at the first stop when he realises?' she whispered.

The question caught me out. It was the first time Lizzy had mentioned the stories I had been slipping in with her cards on Sundays. I glanced over my shoulder at our sleeping roommates.

'I think he's too embarrassed to do anything. So he just sits there and acts like he's on the right one,' I replied softly.

Lizzy nodded and pondered for a moment.

'But he has a pretty awesome adventure. Seeing all that stuff for the first time,' she said.

She was looking at me seriously. I felt under pressure to have an answer.

'Does it seem like he did it on purpose?' I asked.

'Maybe not, initially. But the bus stops for a while at that first station. While that homeless dude is screwing around. I mean, he knew what was happening by that stage, and he could have gotten off, yeah,' she replied.

'I guess so,' I replied.

'So he decides to stay on and have an adventure?' she asked.

I had no idea and started to sweat, despite the cold. I silently pleaded for some demented lunatic to run onto the screens and save me from answering.

They remained static and empty.

'Yeah,' I said.

Lizzy nodded but I could see that she wasn't satisfied. I wished I'd never written the story, let alone given it to her to read. What was I thinking? She was Lizzy Finn. Just because we happened to be trapped in a shopping centre together didn't change that.

'How is the studio going?' I asked.

'Fine,' she replied.

The room was deadly silent but for the breath of our sleeping housemates. I focused on the screens. Lizzy flicked through a magazine. Nothing happened.

It wasn't until the end of our second shift that Rocky saw the woman.

13

For some reason we were all exhausted after a solitary night of watching the screens. When Lizzy and I clocked on for our second stint, the idea of remaining awake for another four hours seemed impossible. But somehow we ground our way through, chewing Hubba Bubba and sipping Ribena juices. We watched as lights timed on across the centre and it prepared for an opening that never arrived. Conversely the car park lights flickered out as daylight crept across the centre. For a while a tiny bird hopped about on the pavement giving us a window into something we hadn't seen for a long time.

Taylor and Rocky woke a little while before we were due to finish and volunteered to make coffees at the Muffin Break down the hall. They returned with four jumbo cups and a packet of Pop-Tarts.

'Oh, wow. Thank you so much,' said Lizzy as they passed us the coffees.

'Cold?' I asked of the Pop-Tarts.

Taylor nodded to Rocky who was unpacking a toaster, fresh off the shelf.

We sipped and chewed and gradually swapped shifts. My back felt balled up and tense from my conversation with Lizzy so I tried to remember some yoga on the floor. Taylor and Lizzy joined me and the three of us put on a pretty amateur display. Rocky sat attentively at the screens, sipping his giant mocha through a straw.

'There's a lady,' he said abruptly.

The three of us looked up.

'There's a lady,' he said again, pointing at a monitor.

We scrambled up and plastered our heads to the screens.

'Where?' asked Taylor.

Rocky pointed again. It was one of the exterior cameras. A figure, most likely female, was holding a cup of coffee and fumbling through her pockets. We watched in stunned silence as she found a swipe card and disappeared from view.

'Shit. Shit. She's coming inside!' said Lizzy.

'Shhhh,' said Taylor harshly.

'Where is she?' I said.

We scanned the other screens, frantically trying to locate the lady's position.

'Coles,' said Rocky, pointing to one of the screens to our left.

'Oh my god,' said Taylor.

There she was. Without the high angle we could see her clearly. A middle-aged lady in jeans and a polo shirt. Light hair pulled back from a suntanned face. A thermal coffee cup in one hand, a handbag in the other. We stared in awe at the perfectly normal looking human walking through Carousel.

'She knows where she's going,' said Taylor softly.

We watched her closely as she traversed the corridor adjacent to Coles. It was true. She didn't have the walk of a shopper or a visitor to the centre. She knew where she was going, and seemed eager to get there.

'What do we do?' asked Lizzy.

'Watch,' I replied.

We followed her as she moved away from Coles and took a turn down a narrow corridor beside Kitchen Witch.

'Where did she go?' said Taylor as she disappeared from one screen and didn't surface on another. We scanned the monitors.

'Stick to one corner,' I suggested, concentrating on the screens to the top right.

Again Rocky's video game prowess came to the fore.

'There. She has a bucket,' he said.

We scuttled over to find her on-screen. She had emerged from a storeroom and was pushing a trolley, holding a mop bucket and some spray bottles, across the floor toward some bathrooms.

'Holy shit. She's a fucking cleaning lady,' said Lizzy. 'Isn't she?'

None of us answered. But it was true. The lady wheeled her bucket over to the Men's, propped the first door open and disappeared inside. Around ten minutes later she surfaced and moved along to the Ladies'. The four of us watched in silence.

After she finished the Ladies' she left the bucket and walked back out into the main corridor to take a seat on a couch. She took out what looked like a muesli bar and sipped on the remains of her coffee.

'Oh my god. She's taking a break,' said Lizzy.

The rest of us nodded, transfixed. She finished the muesli bar and looked at a smartphone for a while.

'You think she has a network?' asked Taylor.

As if to answer the lady held her phone upward and moved it around, searching for reception.

'Doesn't look like it,' I said.

She checked the time on her watch and hauled herself back over to the bucket. We followed her as she wheeled it back into the storeroom and resurfaced with some additional products. She wheeled away from us, toward the dome.

'Where's she going now?' asked Lizzy.

'Toilets near the Apple Store?' suggested Rocky.

He was right. The lady trudged down the corridor and pulled up outside the next set of toilets. She was in there for quite a while. From memory they were pretty big. The four of us watched the process silently. At one point the lady strolled out into the corridor and over to the Coffee Club island. She looked around, then reached over the counter and grabbed a bottle of water from the fridge.

The fact that only a scattering of bottles remained didn't appear to bother her.

She seemed to take less time on the toilets as she went, only spending a few minutes in the Men's at the end of the corridor. Then she wheeled the bucket out and trudged back towards us. She glanced at her watch and wiped her forehead. She had gotten through a lot of cleaning in just over an hour.

We watched her closely as she returned to the storeroom and disappeared inside. Where would she go next? If she ventured much further down the corridor past the dome she would close in on JB's and our sprawled out living areas. Luckily there weren't any toilets right by JB's. Still, I think it was on all of our minds. But we weren't just apprehensive. The room buzzed with a weird sense of excitement too.

A few minutes later she shuffled back out of the storeroom.

'No bucket,' said Rocky.

'She's carrying something,' said Taylor, her face up to the screen.

'Looks like her coffee cup,' I said.

We watched her moving away from the storeroom and back towards Coles.

'Oh shit, she's going home,' said Taylor.

For some reason none of us had considered this possibility.

'Can she get out?' asked Lizzy.

'She can't be,' I said.

'Why not?' said Taylor.

'Shit. What do we do?' said Lizzy.

We stood up. Suddenly things were urgent.

'We need to speak to her,' said Taylor.

'Too far,' said Rocky.

He was right. The lady was already turning down the corridor towards the door she entered earlier. By the time we reached it, she would be outside.

'Fuck. We're so stupid!' said Taylor.

The four of us stood in silent, dejected limbo as she disappeared from our screens, then reappeared outside. She put her coffee cup down on the ground, pulled the door shut, and disappeared off the screens completely.

There was a heavy silence.

None of us wanted to look at each other.

'I'm going to check that door,' said Taylor.

She picked up a few tools and took off down the stairs. The rest of us followed.

Carousel felt different. It had been breached by reality, or some weird version of it. The corridors felt like part of an empty shopping complex again. Foreign and unwelcoming. Not somewhere we had been living for months on end.

We passed the corridor with the storeroom and glanced cautiously sideways. It was as empty and boring as always. I looked up to find the cameras we had been viewing it through. Once I started looking I noticed them everywhere. Small glass domes that didn't give away the direction. Larger rectangular versions that were designed to stand out and shout that you're being watched. We had been under twenty-four-seven surveillance since the morning we arrived.

Taylor disappeared around a corner into a small cul-de-sac. We followed her to a regular looking door at the end that must have been the lady's entry point. There was the usual small tagging mechanism with a red light on the wall. Taylor pulled on the door. Without a card it was fixed shut like any other.

We gathered around as Taylor put her tools down on the floor. To our surprise she calmly took a hold of the heaviest mallet and began viciously pounding the door. Large round dents appeared all over the timber. The door didn't shift but Taylor continued. Lizzy sighed and said something that I didn't hear. I turned to look at her but she was already walking back out into the foyer. Taylor took a breather, then continued. Rocky stood behind her, watching sheepishly. The door held firm like the hundreds before it.

I surfaced from the cul-de-sac to find Lizzy on a couch near Coffee Club. She was cross-legged and as serious as she was when I'd first seen her. I sat beside her and we listened to the dull thumping on the door continue from behind us.

'Hello! It's not going to open!' yelled Lizzy over her shoulder. 'Idiot,' she said to herself.

I glanced across at the toilets the lady had cleaned. I rose and walked toward them.

'What are you doing?' asked Lizzy.

'Checking something,' I replied.

I opened the door to the Ladies' and gazed inside. Lizzy appeared at my shoulder. The place smelt like bleach and had definitely been cleaned. All of the cubicles remained open and gnomed.

'So weird,' whispered Lizzy.

We checked the Disabled. It was similarly clean and open. In the Men's, one of the cubicles was closed. Lizzy and I shared a glance and ventured over to the door. It was the final cubicle at the far end of the room. I pushed it open and we found the gnome standing inside. He was close to where we would have expected. By the right-hand side of the toilet, back enough to let the door open. I edged him forward an inch until he propped the door once again.

'You think she just knocked him back a little as she left?' asked Lizzy.

'Probably. She's left everything else gnomed. For some fucking reason,' I replied.

'So weird,' Lizzy repeated.

We surfaced from the bathrooms to find the thumping noise stopped and Taylor seated on a couch down the corridor. She was curled up with her head hidden in her knees. Rocky stood awkwardly beside her, tracing imaginary words on the floor with his sneakers. Lizzy looked at her sister and sighed. I put a hand on her shoulder.

'Can you take Rocky back to play some video games?' Lizzy asked.

I nodded and watched her move over to sit beside Taylor. She said some things that I couldn't hear. Taylor lifted her head slightly to reply. She was crying pretty bad.

Rocky padded over to me with his head down. I gave him a brief one-armed hug that didn't feel too awkward and we left Taylor and Lizzy Finn alone in the giant, messed-up centre we made our home.

Rocky and I played *Call of Duty* for a while before I headed back to Myer for a night in my own bed. Taylor had done the same earlier. We were all pretty tired and it felt like the edge had been taken off our fears. The corridors were dim and lifeless. Natalie Portman was where she always was, as was Beyoncé. My steps were heavy and slow on the escalator and I fell into my bunk on arrival upstairs.

I rolled over onto my back and noticed an envelope beside me. It was Lizzy's Happy Anniversary card from Monday. With all the surveillance business going on I hadn't been back to open it. Inside was a horrible pink card with some kind of lace stuck in a border around a generic married couple. Inside Lizzy had written *Another anniversary Noxville? You total slut!*

I placed it on a pile beneath the bed.

There was no way I could process the fact that there had just been a cleaning lady in the centre so I put on some Bright Eyes and drank the remainder of a hundred-dollar shiraz that had been airing in a carafe. When it was finished I curled up under the quilt and tried to think about my fantasy Fiesta owner. Picture her lightly tanned skin or something she would say. Normally I was good at imagining this stuff. But our reality had grown too complex. She would only surface in fleeting, superficial waves that I couldn't cling onto.

Home, however, had started to flood into my subconscious with vivid and unexpected clarity. Lying there on the bunk I could see my dim, grungy share house in full colour. My roommates and I drinking on the couch with plans to go out that would never eventuate. The stale quiet of the morning when I got ready for work while the others slept through their ten-thirty lectures. The four months with Chloe when she would stay over and I would cook something in our dirty kitchen and we'd eat outside in the overgrown garden before having quiet, friendly sex in my bedroom. Afterward when Heather came back from Berlin and we decided wordlessly to hook up and eke out some security in our collective limbo. Trips to my parents' place in the hills for birthdays, long weekends and sometimes without a reason, just to sit in their routine and feel okay about a regular life.

Carousel had drifted me welcomingly away from these things, and only recently had they returned. Our existence in the centre was in flux and I think my subconscious was trying to figure out what this meant. The possibility of a return to my previous life was an assumption but surely not a reality. My visions weren't tinted with sadness or anxiety, but they probably should have been.

These thoughts took me to sleep and kept me there until late in the morning. I woke feeling dopey and hungover. The spiking cold of the bathroom woke my skin, but nothing far beneath. I wandered downstairs and found the Finns making smoothies at Pure 'n' Natural, having only just arrived themselves after a long night wrapped in their own emotional blankets.

I sat on a stool and continued to wake up. Rocky wasn't around. I took out my radio and was about to call through to him when Taylor stopped me.

'He's in the security room,' she said.

'Oh. Okay,' I replied. 'Did he go there on his own?'

She nodded.

'I guess there's a chance she'll come back,' I said.

'Why?' asked Taylor.

'It's her job,' said Lizzy with a chunk of sarcasm.

'You think she's been coming here every week since we arrived?' said Taylor.

'Maybe,' said Lizzy.

'She doesn't think it's weird that the bathrooms stay

clean and there are gnomes all over the floor?' said Taylor.

Lizzy shrugged.

Taylor shook her head. 'I'm pretty sure we would have run into her by now,' she said.

'This place is massive, Taylor. Aside from you and your door fetish we hang out in like ten percent,' replied Lizzy.

Taylor gave her daggers.

'Can we not do this,' I said, surprising myself with the sharpness of my tone.

'What?' said Lizzy.

'Try to make sense of all the bullshit,' I said.

'You're going to have to eventually, Nox. You can't just float around in here for the rest of your life saying "oh well",' said Taylor.

'Who says I have a choice,' I replied.

'The cleaning lady does. And the Fiesta,' she replied.

'A hatchback says I have a choice?' I replied.

Lizzy smirked. Taylor glared at me.

'Seriously?' she asked.

We held onto a silent stand-off for a little bit before Lizzy broke in.

'Let's just wait and see if she comes back, and if she does we'll be quicker and we'll follow her out that door. Yeah?'

'Yeah,' said Taylor.

I nodded.

'I'll go sit with Rocky for a while,' I said and rose from the stool.

Taylor stopped me and handed over her smoothie.

'Thanks,' I said.

I climbed awkwardly onto one of Rocky's bikes.

'Are you hungover?' asked Lizzy.

'Probably,' I replied.

I stabilised myself and wobbled off with the drink in one hand. As usual I would have given anything to hear what they were saying once I left.

Rocky didn't turn from the screens when I arrived. He just sort of sniffed a greeting and kept up his vigil in the black and white flicker. I sat beside him and watched for a while. It wasn't that Rocky looked overly serious about the surveillance. He held the same distant expression I'd seen on him as he watched TV or ate potato chips. But there seemed to be something attracting him to the screens. I wondered if it was connected to his stepdad.

'How long has your stepdad been at Guardhouse?' I asked him, casually.

'Ages,' he replied.

'He alright?' I asked.

'Yeah,' he replied.

Rocky sniffed, then coughed a little. It wasn't the sort of question that would get much out of him.

'Man, I wonder if she'll come back,' I said.

'Might be someone else,' said Rocky.

I hadn't thought of that. I don't think the Finns had either.

'Yeah, maybe. Whoever is on shift,' I said.

Rocky nodded.

'Geri works here as a cleaner,' he said.

Geri was the sister of one of Rocky's schoolmates. I'd only heard him talk about her once, on the way back from a drinking session at Liquor Central. But I think he liked her.

'Ha. It would be pretty awesome if she came in,' I said, joking.

Rocky nodded seriously. I glanced at him. He seemed to think this was a possibility.

I guess it was. Shit, pretty much anything was.

But normally we didn't hope for stuff like that. I felt a rush of concern for Rocky that was hard to shake. I needed some air.

'You want a mocha?' I asked.

Rocky nodded absently.

'Cool. I'll be back in a sec,' I said.

I put music on my phone and walked down to Woolworths for some powdered milk and coffee beans. There was plenty left so I grabbed a bunch of packets and carried them to the Muffin Break island so that we would have coffee supplies for a few weeks of surveillance. I made Rocky a jumbo mocha, heating the chocolate powder with the milk so that it cooked a little and tasted better. It looked pretty delicious so I made myself the same, knowing that all that powdered milk would probably churn up my guts all afternoon.

My radio crackled through the music. I paused the song.

'Hello, Nox?' said Lizzy.

'Yeah hello,' I replied.

'Who were you listening to?' she asked.

'The Panics,' I replied. 'They're local.'

'Okay. When do you and Rocky want to be replaced?' she asked.

'I'm okay,' chimed in Rocky.

'Oh, okay,' said Lizzy. 'And you, Nox?'

'How about two thirty?' I said.

'Awesome. See you then,' she replied.

I put the giant mochas in a carry case and shuffled back to the surveillance.

14

Rocky didn't break his surveillance vigil for a week. It might have gone on even longer had the cleaning lady not reappeared. Same time, same camera. Coffee cup in hand, ready for another shift.

His reluctance to leave the security room had divided the Finns, while I hung in the middle like a kid in the back seat. Lizzy thought it was fine, as arbitrary as any other activity we used to kill time in Carousel. Taylor thought it was out of character and obsessive, a sign of Rocky's mental instability that needed to be addressed. I tended to agree that it was unusual, particularly given his comment about Geri. But on the other hand it wasn't like he was neglecting anything to take up the surveillance. As Lizzy said, his existence in Carousel was as arbitrary as any of us, and it was normal to cling onto something that offered a hint of purpose.

One thing we were all concerned about was his cough. It had been around forever now, but had only recently gained a rattle that rose from somewhere deep within his spindly frame. When it was obvious he wasn't keen on leaving the room I moved a couple of heaters up there and Lizzy increased his daily doses of vitamin C and E. Other than this all we could do was keep an ear out for it. Taylor and I read a couple of articles in a book that outlined the differences between Rocky's symptoms and something like pneumonia. It all seemed pretty grey.

Taylor was up there with him when the lady arrived for another shift. She radioed Lizzy and me immediately. We weren't going to sit back and watch this time. She had a key and Taylor wanted it badly. We bounded out of the studio in Rugs a Million and cycled for Coles where the lady had just entered.

We arrived before Taylor and Rocky and found the lady with her head in a storage cupboard. We lingered behind her for a second before it seemed like one of us should say something.

'Hi there,' said Lizzy.

For some reason we were both on the edge of hysterics.

The lady backed out of the room and turned around. She was middle-aged, maybe just into her forties but thin and still held a good figure so it was difficult to tell. The skin on her face was a little too tanned to be healthy. She looked at us vacantly for a second or two before replying.

'Yeah?'

Talk about an anticlimax. The first person we'd met in who knows how long, and it was as if she'd seen us a million times before.

'We're um … stuck in here at the moment. Would you mind letting us out through that door?' I said, nodding in the direction of her entry.

She looked at me, then Lizzy. Weighing up if she gave a shit.

'I gotta finish my cleaning first. Then I'll let you out,' she replied and turned back into the cupboard. 'If you help me, it'll be quicker,' she added.

Lizzy and I looked at each other. It sounded like a fair trade.

She wheeled a bucket out past us into the main corridor. Taylor and Rocky arrived simultaneously. They pulled up from a full sprint and sucked in some air. Rocky coughed, dangerously. The lady glanced at them and continued across toward the bathrooms. Taylor dragged her eyes away from the new human in Carousel and looked at Lizzy and me. We gave her a stupid thumbs-up.

'What does that mean?' whispered Taylor, stepping closer.

'She's going to let us out once she's finished cleaning,' I said.

Taylor shook her head, not satisfied.

'Excuse me,' she called after the lady. 'Sorry. We really need to get out of here now.'

The lady turned and looked at Taylor tiredly.

'It's a long story but we can give you some cash,' she said.

The lady lightened a fraction. Cash was a good idea.

Lizzy and I hadn't thought of that.

Taylor pulled out a hefty wad of fifty-dollar notes and passed them to the lady. She pocketed them and looked at Taylor, then Lizzy. I was pretty sure she had no idea who they were. But maybe I was wrong. She sighed and left her bucket in the corridor. The four of us followed her back toward the cul-de-sac where she entered.

It all felt so mundane and underwhelming. This woman was about to rescue us from a lifetime of shopping centre imprisonment.

I looked at Lizzy, then Rocky, then Taylor. None of them would meet my gaze. Everyone's eyes were stuck on the cleaning lady as she reached the door and rummaged through her pocket for the security card. My pulse began to thunder. She stopped and lifted a white card to the scanner.

The light stayed red.

She tried again. Still red.

Taylor's head dropped.

'Fuck's sake,' said the lady.

She pushed on the door and waved the card about. Still nothing happened.

She was stuck here, too.

'Oh well. Fucked if I'm cleaning anything until this is sorted,' said the lady.

None of us could bear the thought of explaining our situation. But eventually we would have to. It wouldn't be

Taylor though. She was inconsolable, even to Lizzy.

'Are all the doors fucked?' the lady asked.

None of us answered, all hoping someone else would do the job.

'Yeah,' I said eventually. 'I'm Nox. This is Rocky, Taylor and Lizzy,' I added.

'Rachel,' she said.

Lizzy offered a tiny smile. Rocky coughed.

'Security here are useless,' said Rachel.

None of us responded. I think we were all trying to process what had just happened.

'You been helping yourself to some food? I would have,' said Rachel.

I nodded and wondered what she would say when she saw the shelves at Coles.

'Was everything okay on your drive to work, Rachel?' asked Lizzy.

'Who says I wasn't on the bus?' asked Rachel, suddenly defensive.

'Oh, sorry. I just assumed,' replied Lizzy.

'What number?' asked Rocky.

Lizzy and I looked at Rocky curiously. Rachel seemed to notice him for the first time.

'I take the five-oh-nine,' she replied. 'But since it's not running I drive. Nothing I can do about that.'

Rocky was silent.

'How was the drive?' asked Lizzy.

'Fast, sweetheart,' she replied, deadpan.

'What about when you got up? Or last night?' I asked.

Rachel looked at me, then the others, as if she was trying to figure something out.

'Same old,' she replied, and lit up a cigarette.

Eventually we led the increasingly agitated Rachel back to JB's for some TV and a reality that we worried might break her tiny suburban brain. Along the way we waited as she tried her card on dozens of doors. Even trudging up to the east end to the door she apparently used to use. None of them opened.

I think she began to fully process what had happened to us when she saw what we'd done to the store. We didn't even notice anymore, but I guess to a fresh pair of eyes it must have looked pretty crazy. Our living area took up a huge section in the middle of the shop. All the stereos and DVDs that had once been there were piled up against a wall in a shiny electronic mass. A series of huge flatscreens bordered our enclosure and cut off the draughts that drifted around the centre like wraiths.

'Shit. You guys have made yourself at home,' said Rachel.

Lizzy, Rocky and I sat on the couches and waited for her to register. Taylor distracted herself in the kitchen area.

'You've been here for a while, haven't you?' said Rachel, like it was a big fucking secret.

I nodded.

'And none of youse can get out?' she asked.

We shook our heads. Lizzy glanced at Taylor across the room.

'How long have you been cleaning here, Rachel?' I asked.

'Fifteen months. Nine to go,' she replied.

'Until what?' I asked.

'Bullshit parole deal is over,' she replied.

I nodded and stole a look at Lizzy.

'How come we haven't seen you before?' asked Lizzy.

Rachel shrugged. 'I work the east end. Switched down here a few weeks back. Sick of freezing my arse off in that mouldy shithole.'

My stomach tightened. I'd smelt her bleach down in the food court not three or four months ago.

Rachel took a seat on our couch.

'Mind you, you guys could be cleaner,' she added.

'You knew we were here?' asked Lizzy.

Rachel looked at her dully.

'Hello. It's fucking gnomesville in here,' she replied.

'Why didn't you come and talk to us?' I asked.

'None of my business,' she replied.

She flicked through a gossip mag, tossed it aside and flicked through another. We watched her in a kind of stunned silence until she finished that one too and sat back and looked around.

'Well, it's nicer than my place. And there's no kids around.'

'You have kids at home?' I asked.

Rachel shook her head. 'They're with my ex,' she replied. 'If he hasn't left them somewhere.'

I held my head and tried to work out what her being stuck in Carousel meant for the kids. Lizzy seemed to be doing the same. Rocky seemed anxious and had barely moved a muscle, instead just swallowing down his cough with a noise that sounded like a small dog.

We weren't adjusting to our new roommate very well.

'Rachel. We were going to crack open some liquor this afternoon. Are you interested?' asked Taylor, stepping over from the kitchen looking suddenly casual and composed.

It was a good call from Taylor. Getting on the booze couldn't hurt. Judging by Rachel's positive reaction, it may even help. It had been a long time since we drank properly and with all this stuff going down we desperately needed to get outside our heads. No thoughts of tomorrow. No plan for how we would deal with Rachel. No talk about what her arrival meant for our existence in the world.

We just trudged across to Liquor Central with a phone and some beanbags and reassured Rachel that taking some drinks wouldn't get her in trouble with the law. She seemed pretty paranoid about this. Probably for good reason.

'Why do I feel like I'm on fucking *Big Brother* all of a sudden,' Lizzy whispered to me as we cracked open our first bottle of vodka and mixed it in with some Deep Spring Lemon Lime.

It was true. Carousel didn't feel real with Rachel around. It felt like an experiment to see how we would handle this new arrival, coupled with all the other shit facing the four of us.

'Yeah totally,' I replied.

It would pass, of course. Rachel would eventually see what was going on. She would settle into the strange rhythms of the centre. Bring things to our group that we didn't like, and surprise us with other things that we did. We would eventually regain the faux equilibrium we once had, and live out our weirdo lives the best we could.

But not tonight.

Tonight we would drink and convince ourselves that we could be anywhere.

Lizzy played DJ on her phone as it grew dark and we worked our way confidently through the first bottle, and onto another. She played a bunch of great artists: The Smiths, Gang of Youths, PJ Harvey – later in the night even a bit of Taylor & Lizzy. Taylor pretended to ignore it, while Lizzy and I watched Rachel to see if anything about the catchy songs and the identical Canadian twins drinking with her would register.

It didn't.

Rocky kept up with us easily, often holding out his empty cup to signify he was ready for more. I gave up on worrying about him for the night. I got the feeling the Finns had also. Rachel's arrival reminded us that we had precious little control over the universe right now, and Rocky's fate was unlikely to be decided by any of us.

Alarmingly, Rachel seemed to get pretty sloppy after just a couple of drinks. But, to her credit, she seemed to maintain this level for most of the night. She was chatty and told us a bunch of things we probably shouldn't know about her welfare dodging and sexual partners. Rachel was the type of unfiltered, excessively honest semi-bogan that thrived in reality TV land. She was addictive in the way of a painful back massage. We screwed up our faces listening to her, but didn't want it to stop.

Taylor drank harder than anyone. She concentrated on each cup like it was a door she was trying to open. Making sure it all went down, before refilling and starting over. Several times I noticed Lizzy watching her. I think she was trying to gauge how low her sister had fallen. How much the latest disappointment was weighing on her. For anyone else the jovial booziness would have made this impossible to assess. But I got the feeling that somehow Lizzy knew.

We spread out from the smallish store into the adjacent corridor and watched Rachel bust out dance moves with bottles of pre-mix in both hands. I couldn't work out whether she was an amazing dancer or an awful one. Her style was interpretive and random and none of us could drag our eyes away. It was kind of beautiful watching somebody so uninhibited fill a room like that. It made me think of kindergarten where I remembered kids proudly announcing their names like kings and queens at the top of tiny playground forts, oblivious or embracing of their scrappy clothing and unemployed parents. Seriously drunk, Rocky joined her and found himself smiling happily as the middle-aged mother ground herself against his skinny frame.

He remained on the dance floor when Rachel had tired and gave us an amazing hacky sack performance. We had all seen Rocky messing around with the small red sack before, but had no idea of his talents. He kept it in the air forever with a series of kicks and shoulders that had him dancing all over the floor and us in hysterics watching.

At one stage I saw one of the Finns comforting the other as she cried into her hands on a beanbag. I assumed it would be Taylor who was upset, as she had been earlier, but was surprised to see it was Lizzy being comforted. My heart sunk a little.

I think she might have been worried about the seriousness of her sister's drinking. I saw Taylor put her vodka aside and drink some water. This seemed to calm Lizzy and within a few minutes she was back out in the corridor kicking around a soccer ball. Somehow Lizzy had ended up as the middle child in our Carousel family and I suddenly realised how much that must suck.

Before she passed out on a beanbag, Taylor grabbed me by the jacket for a drunken D & M.

'Nox,' she said, eyes all glazed and hair falling everywhere.

'Yo,' I replied.

She pushed me over to a very specific spot on the floor. We sat and drank a little more.

'You're awesome, Nox. But you haven't worked it out,' she said accusingly.

'Sorry,' I said.

She hugged me and spilled her cup out onto the floor.

'I love you guys,' I said.

Taylor brushed this off and pushed me on the shoulder like I was the drunk one.

'I'm getting us out of here. And you need to stop. You need to start …' she trailed off.

I looked at her and nodded, trying desperately hard to be sober and serious. Lizzy was watching us with some amusement from across the store.

'Nox,' said Taylor.

I waited. She had something else to say but she wavered unsteadily and couldn't get anything out. Arms wrapped around me from behind. It was Lizzy with a bear hug.

'Why so serious?!' she said in a deep voice, pulling a line from *The Dark Knight*.

Taylor looked up through her hair and a flicker of something passed between them. She stumbled to her feet and kissed us both on the head. Lizzy let me go and we watched Taylor fall onto a beanbag and into sleep.

Her final sentence hung, unfinished and forgotten.

Rocky crashed out next. He had been sitting upright on

a beanbag for a while, his head dipping with sleep every few minutes before bobbing back up to look around and smile. After a while Lizzy slid over and shuffled the beans so that he could lie back more comfortably. A minute later he was asleep.

I had been pulling myself back from total drunkenness for a few hours, knowing that another quick drink or two would end my night and bring forward a morning that none of us wanted to think about. I walked out of the store and over to the adjacent Men's toilets. Rachel stood at the basin as if she was about to wash her hands, but her drunken mind had wandered. A de-gnomed door stood behind her.

'Hey!' she said, as if I'd walked into the Ladies'.

I smiled and trudged into one of the cubicles. I started pissing, oblivious to the churning noise I was sending throughout the room. Rachel was still at the basin when I finished.

'You okay?' I asked.

She swung her head up and smiled. 'Drunk,' she said, defiantly.

I smiled and leant back against the cool of the tiled bench. Rachel ran some water over her hands. The music coming from the liquor store had stopped and the bathroom felt oddly peaceful.

'Everybody's dead, aren't they?' I asked her softly.

'Bullshit,' said Rachel. 'The TVs are just fucked.'

'What happened?' I asked.

'The fuck should I know?'

'Why do you keep cleaning this place?' I asked.

'I do my job. They can't send me back there,' she replied, with a flicker of drunken defiance.

'Back where? Prison?' I asked.

Rachel grunted.

'Are there other cleaners?' I asked.

'Geri?' she replied. 'Never heard of her.'

Rocky must have already asked.

'Have you seen your ex or your kids?' I tried.

'Left his place wide open. Nothing there now,' she replied, laughing.

'Are you worried about them?' I asked.

Rachel ignored this and turned from the sink to look me up and down.

'You guys are artists, hey?' she asked.

'Taylor and Lizzy are. They're in a band called Taylor & Lizzy,' I replied, pretty confused.

Rachel swayed forward and pushed her face up to mine. Her hands slipped down past my chest to my pants and she rubbed the front of them. I watched it happening, but felt disconnected. Suddenly her hair was in my face and she was kissing me. She smelt like Pantene and her tongue moved in a practised rhythm that belied her inebriation. She fell back against the basin and laughed, waiting for me to follow and continue with things. I was hard and felt like

I had to, but something stopped me. I swerved back out into the milky light of the corridor.

Lizzy was curled up on the last beanbag in the store. I stood above her, and the others, and tried to think of where I should sleep. Rachel wandered across to a softly lit corner housing whiskey and liqueurs. She circled the carpet like a cat, then curled up and fell asleep without a blanket, pillow or anything.

I left Liquor Central and found myself walking back to JB's. At one point I realised this was wrong, not knowing why, but certain that I had to go back and sleep with the others. I was shivering in the icy dark of the corridors so I ripped a picnic blanket out of a basket in Kitchen Witch and pulled it over my shoulders. Shortly after I found myself on a couch out the front of Liquor Central. I wrapped myself up and squinted to make out the lumpy outlines of my housemates on their beanbags inside.

Sleep swallowed me with a darkness that felt immense.

15

Rachel left Carousel early the next morning.

Somehow I knew she had gone. The place felt normal again. Not crazy and hyper and part of some weird experiment.

Plus I think I had seen her go.

I had woken suddenly from a deep, drunken sleep on the thin leather couch. The morning brightness of the eastern end was overwhelming. Immediately I retreated, rolling over and tucking my head beneath the blanket the best that I could. It was too short though. Out of a gap in the top I saw a figure moving down the corridor. Tight, faded jeans and a wash of bottle-blonde hair. Quickly I willed the sleep to take me back.

The next time I woke, Taylor was tapping me on the arm and telling me we had to go and find Rachel. The four of us searched and yelled through enough of the centre to confirm that Rachel had either left, or was hiding from us and didn't want to be found. This seemed unlikely so we ventured back to the cleaning cupboard and found it packed away and locked as it was before she arrived.

Lizzy also noticed that one of the display MacBooks in the Apple Store had been ripped from its cable.

Taylor and I checked Rachel's door. It was locked and cold and gave nothing away. None of us said a word. I felt like I had maybe an hour before my morning-after drunkenness morphed into a severe hangover.

'I'm going home to sleep,' I said.

I set off down the corridor toward Myer without waiting for a reply.

A few steps later I felt Rocky and the Finns behind me, each carrying their own fragile bodies back to bed. I stopped at Friendlies and took some Panadol Rapids from the shelf, along with two one-point-five litre waters and a handful of energy bars. I wanted to crawl into bed and stay there for weeks. Carousel had been willing me to do so since we arrived. Finally I was ready to submit.

Winter eased during our hibernation in the weeks that followed. It wasn't sudden. Few things were in Carousel. The mornings were still cold, the light still filtered grey. But the days felt longer and we seemed to lounge about for hours before the lights timed out and darkness crept its way through the centre. Forgotten seeds sprouted in pots and bins beneath the dome as proper sunlight swept across for a time at midday. We watched them curiously as they grew from identical green spikes to form something recognisable. Most powered upward to a height of a few inches before wilting and growing pale due to a lack of nutrients in the generic potting mix. Hardier plants like lettuce, basil and shallots managed to survive, offering us strange salads and a break from the diminishing supermarket items.

I spent long mornings in the bookstores reading with a purpose I hadn't experienced before. I read Hemingway, Coetzee and Murakami. Starting with one title and churning right through the shelf until it was done and I caught my breath with some magazines. I also read a lot of history. Filling gaping holes in my knowledge of World War II, the Space Race and early Australian explorers.

At the end of these sessions I would change into Skins and cross trainers and jog the circumference of the centre, stopping at the dome where the air felt fresh like a forest or a beach. The jogging had stripped me of a few kilos but I was gradually gaining them back with weight training in Sports Power. I was lean now, but moulded, my body a project that I could focus on to burn through the hours. I carefully searched the centre for supplements that would provide amino acids and protein to my overworked muscles, leaving them tight but defined as the spring took hold.

Long ago, Taylor and Lizzy might have ribbed me for these sudden obsessions. But now we each had commitments that were perhaps irrational but also crucial to our survival in the centre. Lizzy continued to tinker with the studio that had seemed ready for use months ago. She would add another instrument, drape another rug, decorate the already spectacular space to the point where it seemed perfect, before taking something down and starting over. With every week that passed, the idea of her recording in there seemed more and more remote. It had become something else now. A shrine perhaps. She would play anywhere but Rugs a Million. Plugging a keyboard into a socket in the dome while we were gardening, or thumbing her favourite guitar on a stool at Coffee Club.

For Taylor the obsession with the doors still held firm. It had grown into something more than escape. A kind of responsibility or obligation. A groundsman checking the lawns and gardens. An architect building a huge mental map. Lately she would head out alone with her phone and a backpack, checking the radio every hour with a double tap before resuming with her work and mystery playlists.

Rocky had stopped joining Taylor on these ventures but for the odd occasion. He was sick and we encouraged rest without great confidence, but with nothing much else to offer. While our hangovers from that bizarro night with Rachel had lingered for a day and a night before drifting into tiredness and rabid hunger, Rocky's had stayed, morphing with his cough to form a weird virus that took the remaining colour from his face and left him placid and couch-bound. During the days we would be reassured by his appetite and eagerness to see us as we dropped in and out of JB's for cups of tea and to pick up things we had conveniently left behind. But at night, in the stale, cool air of the centre his cough would take a hold and each of us would listen carefully as it seemed to lower into his chest and rumble with an echo that made us shudder.

Rocky had something that his body couldn't shake. It gave Carousel a clock that in the past had never existed.

We hadn't seen Rachel since our night in Liquor Central. Our time with her seemed faded and distant almost as soon as it had passed. My mind couldn't place it as a good memory or bad. The drinking and debauchery had been long overdue, and in a way vital to our existence. Taylor and I had spoken honestly and, although the words had been clouded with booze and time, our connection had been reaffirmed and remained strong ever since. But Rocky had grown sicker that night, and the only human we had seen since arriving had chosen to abandon us after less than twenty-four hours in the centre.

Rachel's existence built on a mystery of which we had long since lost comprehension. I had spent hours at the foot of Lizzy's bed talking through the parameters of Carousel without ever managing to map the world. Rachel's arrival confirmed that life existed outside of the centre, although she offered little concrete information about this, or none that we could remember. Our memories of the night with her were clouded and we cursed ourselves for the level of our drinking. We remembered that she was on parole for something, and that her job as a cleaner here was somehow a part of that agreement. The fact that she had honoured this parole duty and kept turning up to clean an abandoned shopping centre, despite whatever it was that had happened in the world, suggested that Rachel was a little mental, but also pretty keen to stay onside with the law. Until she found out we were trapped here and seemingly decided to never return.

It was difficult to know what all of this meant for the four of us in Carousel. Taylor and I fought pretty hard to keep our situation somehow rationalised. We both knew that there was obviously some crazy stuff going on. Maybe even something fantastical. I was trapped in a shopping centre in suburban Perth with Taylor and Lizzy Finn, after all. But we still weren't keen to accept the notion that we would never be free of the centre, and that freedom wouldn't hold a world similar to the one we remembered, with some answers as to what the hell we were doing in here.

Lizzy had been more accepting of our situation from the beginning. She never believed Taylor could force a door open, or that somebody had locked us in here maliciously. Lizzy saw the mystery of Carousel for what it was and didn't waste her time labelling it as anything else. There was defeat in her perspective, but in a strange way it also held the most hope.

The fact that Rachel could exit the centre alone, but

not in our presence, was particularly unnerving. Maybe this was a coincidence. Or maybe she just swapped cards on us. But it also seemed possible that someone, somewhere, may have stopped Rachel from letting us out. This wasn't exactly a reassuring thought, but it kind of aligned with Lizzy's idea that our entrapment in the centre wasn't arbitrary, and could even be seen as some bizarro protection against the apocalypse – if there actually was one.

But then why was Rachel so eager to get back out there? Her kids were the obvious answer. She'd told me that they had disappeared somewhere with her ex, and probably the rest of the city. But maybe they were still out there somewhere. Even the remote chance of reuniting with them meant she couldn't risk staying in Carousel. I got that.

But maybe Carousel wasn't the type of place you wanted to stay in anyway.

This wasn't something the Finns and I chose to discuss. However, our diminishing food supplies and Rocky's mystery illness made a decent case for it. Rachel seemed a little strange, maybe even outside of the context of whatever was happening in the world, but her desire to get the hell out of Carousel and not come back was seriously unnerving. Rachel was a survivor. Somebody that had probably been knocked down continuously throughout life, but had kept pulling herself up and struggling onward. She had an instinct that a lot of people didn't. And this instinct had told her to leave.

16

In the angsty aftermath of Rachel's visit, and the ongoing concern over Rocky's sickness, the Finns and I made an effort to keep some lightness in Carousel. I had pulled a barbecue into the dome and started constructing a tiki-style 'outdoor' area ahead of the warmer weather. There were bamboo torches in Backyard Bonanza, and a trashy party goods outlet in the east end had fake lanterns and plastic decorations. With these in position against a wall near the sushi bar I began shifting in some outdoor furniture.

Rocky and I discovered a kind of hand-operated forklift a while ago, out the back of Bonanza. With a large platform on wheels and a handle that could be pushed or pulled, it quickly became a favourite around Carousel. I loaded up a couple of deckchairs and set out westward to the dome.

Lizzy crossed through an intersection on her mountain bike ahead of me. I didn't think she saw me but a few seconds later she re-emerged around the corner and coasted my way. She was wearing her favourite pea coat from David Jones and some cherry-red boots. I continued to haul the chairs behind me.

'Whoa. Nice one, Nox,' said Lizzy, circling behind me.

'The best they had,' I replied. 'What you up to?'

Lizzy shrugged and slowed down to roll alongside me.

'It's your birthday soon,' she said.

I nodded. Birthdays were touchy in Carousel. They confirmed the passage of time. Plus we'd pretty much taken anything of interest from the shelves, making gifting problematic.

'Still no writing?' she asked.

'Not really,' I said.

In truth I had been writing at night quite a lot but hadn't included anything in with Lizzy's cards since our discussion of the kid on the bus story.

'You gotta get onto that, man. We'll be out of here one of these days and you could have a bunch of stuff ready to publish,' she said.

Both ideas seemed pretty ridiculous.

'Is it true that we're out of vitamins?' I asked.

Lizzy nodded solemnly.

'There's some zinc left. And some D's,' she said. 'Just random stuff.'

'We have to grow more vegies,' I said.

Lizzy nodded. The gardening wasn't working out as well as we'd hoped.

'Remember last summer at the dome? All those bugs dropping down on us?' I changed the topic.

Lizzy shuddered. 'Yeah, but the stars were awesome.

And your tiki stuff is going to rule,' said Lizzy.

I nodded and we rounded the corner toward the dome.

The following afternoon the four of us sat on deckchairs amid shredded sunlight and sipped on limey cocktails mixed by Taylor. The temperatures still seemed pretty low outside and the massive concrete slab that was our home would need a few good months to thaw out from the winter. So our deckchairs were adorned with rugs rather than beach towels and none of us were keen to reveal our pasty-white shopping centre skin. Rocky lay tucked deep within a hood, sipping his mocktail through a long straw and looking up at the sky. Lizzy read a book, while Taylor and I hid comfortably behind our sunglasses.

I hadn't thought about what we actually had to cook on the barbecue when I wheeled it across from Bonanza. Other than the occasional can of beef and vegetable soup or frozen chicken nuggets we were effectively rendered vegetarian these days. In the end all we could think of were some puny mushrooms from our garden and a packet of frozen wieners Lizzy found in Wendys. It was rough losing food as a topic of conversation. In the beginning Taylor and I had chewed through a heap of time reading copies of *Gourmet Traveller* from the waiting area of the surgery and thinking up meals we could make with our abundant food stocks. Now food was just something we needed to find enough of to survive.

When the sky turned from blue to pink I sizzled our tiny meal on the giant hotplate and Taylor made up one of our weirdo salads. We were still picking away at the food when the sky deepened to navy and a triple-seven jet flew over.

It was easy to forget that Carousel was just a couple of suburbs away from the Perth airport. With the runways flowing north–south, it was also beneath the flight path for what was once a shitload of air traffic heading in and out of the state. Either by accident or some hair-brained plan the hole in the dome offered a regular and unobstructed view of the belly of these planes, accompanied by the shattering roar of their engines. Or at least it had until we arrived.

During our first few days each of us had thought we'd heard the sound of distant planes. I had imagined a fleet of domestic arrivals converging on a city in chaos, runways without controllers, terminals without staff, too far into their fuel to divert to anywhere else in the giant, sprawling state.

But those had been nothing like this. The deep growling stopped us dead.

'What the fuck is that?' asked Taylor.

She didn't wait for an answer, instead dropping her plate and walking out of the tiki enclosure towards the garden. Lizzy and I followed. We gazed up at the dusky sky even though it was impossible to tell which direction the noise was coming from. Only that it was getting louder.

'It sounds like a plane,' said Lizzy.

Taylor tried to reply but her words were drowned out. Plants started to tremble slightly at our feet. I looked around, wondering if a tidal wave was about to smash into Carousel and sweep us away to join the rest of the world.

The growling grew louder and louder. The noise was intense. Suddenly Rocky was beside me.

There was a tiny pause before a plane thundered across our dome. All grey steel and flashing lights. For a moment the giant undercarriage completely blocked the sky.

A second later it was gone and the sound hit us with its full force. We covered our ears and turned away from the direction of the hidden craft. We were facing south.

Taylor was talking but the roar was still too loud. She pressed her face close to me and I saw that the flicker was back in her eyes. I held my hand up to my ear. The rumble was gradually fading. Abruptly I got the dizzy feeling and started seeing the weird *SimCity*-style map of Carousel spreading out in front of me again. I could feel Taylor looking at me but couldn't react.

'Did you see what airline it was?' she yelled.

It was dull in my ears.

'Nox?'

'Yeah,' I replied, coming to.

'Did you see what airline it was?' Taylor asked again.

She looked at me expectantly. I shook my head and looked at Lizzy standing behind her. She was smiling. It was big and uninhibited. There were also tears spilling from her eyes. Taylor turned to look at her sister. The plane was a distant grumble now.

'What?' asked Taylor of Lizzy.

'It was Air Canada,' she replied.

'Seriously?' said Taylor. 'Do they even fly here?'

'Just to Sydney,' said Rocky and coughed.

For some reason we knew he would be right.

'What are they doing here?' said Taylor.

Lizzy shrugged and wiped away a tear. She was looking a little sheepish.

'I saw the wheels out. That means they're landing, yeah?' asked Taylor.

'They could have just taken off,' I said.

'Landing. The strip is north,' said Rocky.

The three of us looked at him and tried to process this information. Rocky coughed again. He didn't look totally stable on his feet. I walked him back to the tiki area and we sat on deckchairs.

Taylor moved over to Lizzy and looked at her as if to assess whether she required comforting. Affection was pretty rare between the Finns. Almost as if their closeness as twins made it superficial or unnecessary. Maybe not quite like hugging yourself, but something similar. Taylor placed a hand on Lizzy's shoulder and I watched them talk.

I could understand Lizzy's emotion. The plane gave her a flicker of home that she hadn't seen for a long time now.

Even if it had no further bearing on our imprisonment, it was a clear signal that things still existed. Not just the world, but maybe her and Taylor's home. I had wandered past tiny Qantas desks in foreign airports for the same feeling. A lot of the time I forgot just how far from Canada they were.

For a moment my empathy was clouded by stupid jealousy. Once again I feared the doors opening and Taylor and Lizzy leaving for Canada, having wiped Carousel and me from their memories forever. But Lizzy's reaction reminded me of how much they needed to go home, and I wanted this badly for them. And for Rocky. I had to make that feeling stronger than any other.

Taylor and Lizzy rejoined us at the deckchairs and the four of us sipped pensively on our cocktails.

'God. What does this shit mean?' asked Taylor. 'They built this place on a flight path, right. So it's kinda normal.'

She looked at me and I nodded.

'But why Air Canada. And why now?'

Lizzy and her looked at each other. Rocky was quiet.

'It's totally a sign,' said Lizzy.

Normally Taylor and I wouldn't have gone for this, but we kept quiet and considered the possibility. Taylor looked up at the hole in the dome.

'Man, I wish there was something we could shoot out of there to let them know we are here,' she said.

Lizzy and I followed her gaze.

Taylor mulled over the possibilities. Lizzy seemed happy just hanging to her momentary connection with home. Rocky had eased back on his deckchair and was looking out at the stars. I glanced at him. It was the last time he would look out of the dome.

17

Rocky's sickness was a slow-burn. It didn't reach up and snatch at him like it might have an old man or infant. Instead it took a hold in his lungs and refused to leave. His breathing took on a wheeze while he sat idle, and seemed to stop altogether when he coughed for long, horrible stretches into the night. He kept an appetite but dropped weight regardless. Except for his neck, which was puffy and swollen with overstressed glands.

We hoped it was bacterial and we could buffet him with antibiotics until one of them stuck, then nurse his stomach back to health with probiotics. But, having cycled through a series of penicillins, and having already used amoxicillin for his hand, we came to the conclusion that whatever he had must be viral. This left Rocky weak and nauseous and limited our treatment options severely.

We would make a daily soup, mixing cans with whatever vegetables we could grow. Lizzy took off on long explorations through the centre, finding multivitamins and prescriptions under counters and in staff lockers. Taylor and I made up a bedroom in a corner of JB's where he could stay warm and draught-free while we were nearby on the couches.

For all of this, Rocky wasn't able to shake it. He was quieter than normal but his moods seemed relatively stable. He still brightened with his favourite television shows, and seemed to like the sound of Taylor and Lizzy babbling away on the couch. And, as always, there was never a complaint. None of us knew a whole lot about Rocky's life before Carousel. His answers were monosyllabic and hinted of the boredom of normal teenage suburbia. Whatever his circumstances, we imagined a likeable kid who accepted his hand with the kind of quiet grace he was displaying now.

But his sickness was breaking our hearts. Without a treatment, our attention shifted to escape.

Taylor and I started working on the partially collapsed section of ceiling in the cinema. We figured that there must be a way to collapse the side that was blocking our entry, and if we did we should be able to climb up onto the roof and find daylight. So we carted a pile of useful looking tools up there from Backyard Bonanza and started chipping away at the blockage.

It was easy enough to get through the plastered ceiling and into the roof cavity. But from there we encountered a patch of thick steel framework supporting the roof.

'It's like the bend in the roof makes it harder to get through,' I said, taking a break from hacksawing.

Taylor looked up at the unimpressive hole we had made.

The twisted steel inside would need to be severed before this side of the roof might cave. We stepped away and looked at the assortment of tools we had on offer. Bonanza was a quasi backyard store that specialised in things like garden gnomes and pond decorations, not serious power tools. The best item we found was an electric hacksaw with a series of interchangeable blades. Unfortunately it seemed to bounce away from the steel rather than cut into it, and our arms were beginning to feel numb from the vibration.

Taylor took an axe and walked back over to the ceiling. Tiny beams of sweet, alluring daylight shot across her legs from the cavity above. She swung upward and brought down a shower of plasterboard. Another swing loosened the sheet above her. One more brought it down. I reached up and helped shield her face from the severed piece of plaster. We lay it on the floor behind us and looked up at the now open roof cavity. The mass of steel was intimidating.

'It's not going to happen, right?' said Taylor.

I shook my head and looked around. Taylor had brought down an impressively large sheet of plaster with just a few blows. I turned and looked behind us.

'This is Projection Booth Four, right?' I asked.

'Yeah,' said Taylor.

'So Projection Five should be next door,' I said.

'Yeah,' said Taylor.

'So that wall should be the same one as Five,' I said, nodding at the hidden wall ahead of us.

'You wanna smash through from the other side?' asked Taylor, a light in her eyes.

'You got through the plaster here pretty easy. Maybe the walls are made of the same stuff,' I said.

We trudged up the long, narrow staircase into Projection Five and found an identical room, sans the flood damage. Taylor moved straight along to the far end and started smashing at the wall with the axe. After a few blows, she tired and I took over. There was already a sizeable chunk out of the wall. I swung into this and pulled away some more plaster.

The beams inside were wooden. Timber we could get through. I smiled at Taylor and swung again. The axe head broke through. I pulled it back and waited for the flood of daylight.

It didn't come.

I sighed. Carousel was fucking with us again.

I glanced back at Taylor. She seemed confused. I looked past her to where we had entered.

'What?' she asked.

I felt like an idiot.

'We're cutting into Projection Six,' I said, and walked back past her to the entrance.

'Oh,' she said sheepishly.

We stopped at the top of the staircase and assessed the wall that really led back into Projection Four. The paint was bubbling a little. This meant there was moisture behind the wall. It was a good sign. I stepped back and cleared some room so I could swing the axe and not tumble down the stairs in the process. Taylor watched with interest.

I swung hard and plunged straight through the wet, softened plaster and into Projection Four.

Daylight swept across our shadowy figures.

'Shit. Shit!' Taylor hopped about excitedly.

I smiled at her and stepped back from the small pile of rubble I had created.

'Here,' she said, taking the axe from me.

I moved aside. Taylor had been waiting for this moment for a long time.

She swung through the plaster with a series of blows. It came away easily, either falling into the mysterious chasm inside, or pulling back with the axe to land at her feet. I started to see what was in there. Long sheets of roofing lay on a wicked slope down to a small patch of floor at the very edge of Projection Four. The walls inside were worn and damp from a winter's worth of channelling rainfall. Then there was the daylight. Not piercing or particularly bright, but still amazing and terrifying in equal doses.

Taylor was enjoying busting the wall apart. We could climb through by now but she kept at it. Chunks of plaster and timber spitting off everywhere. She was like a child tearing at the final shreds of Christmas wrapping.

The timber groaned as she jolted into a support beam. Suddenly I had a horrible thought.

'Wait!' I said.

Taylor turned reluctantly, demanding an explanation.

'It could cave in if we smash any more,' I said.

She turned back and looked at the gaping hole lined with broken and splintered beams. Her grip loosened on the axe and she put it aside.

The two of us stepped carefully through into Projection Four. I had a fleeting thought about the purity of the air we were breathing, but it was probably too late now. Plus it smelt amazing. There were clouds above us, and even a small patch of blue. The slope of the fallen roof and the wet surface made traversing upward difficult. We could have done with some rope and better shoes, but there was no way we were going back yet. Taylor went first, keeping low and holding some guttering for balance. I followed and together we edged our way out of Carousel.

The last metre or so was pretty treacherous, but then the roof sheeting flattened back to the horizontal and we were outside. The pair of us stood motionless and inhaled the heady cocktail of concrete, parkland and distant ocean that was Perth. I smiled at Taylor and she smiled back. We felt triumphant, but also a little foolish for getting outside so easily after all these months.

From our position above the cinema all we could see was roof and sky. This section seemed to be quite low relative to the surrounding buildings. No wonder it had filled so violently with rain. The sheeting also looked a lot older where we stood, compared to some of the other slopes we could see. Carousel had expanded in spurts since its opening in the seventies. The expansions seemed logical and flowing on the inside, but the roof told a different story.

We edged our way along the channel of steel that was the cinema roof. Behind us was another roof marking the end of the projection booths and the start of something higher. On our right was a long, sheer wall running maybe ten metres up to another roof. On our left were a series of massive air conditioning units fenced off with steel and jutting upward, blocking any view of what was beyond them. Several of these were weathered badly and I wondered if they were even operational, or just relics of a previous cooling system. It wasn't the sweeping vista of freedom we had expected on our escape, and we were keen to get to the end of the channel and see some horizon.

Walking along behind Taylor I had the random thought that the bowl of grey around us would make for an awesome backdrop for a Taylor & Lizzy music video. I could imagine Lizzy walking beside Taylor. Both of them singing and carrying guitars, but facing away from us as they moved toward nothing but sky. We would pace it out and roll camera so that they were a step away from the end when the song finished. The final step hidden by a cut to black and it was over. I had ideas like this all of the time. Sometimes for a novel or a screenplay. Sometimes for a video. They sprung out of nowhere and seemed like the answer to a lot of stuff, but faded and grew clichéd in my mind before I was able to tell anybody and find out if they were.

When Taylor and I did stop at the edge of the channel the view was anticlimactic. Like a couple of thirsty pilgrims in some old biblical film, we looked out on roof upon roof, a steel desert with no end. The adjoining roof was lower and did offer a flicker of horizon for us to gaze upon. It was a nondescript patch of suburbia. Tiny squares of tiled roofs. The green of some trees and parks. The snaking grey of a road. It wasn't much, but both of us stared at it wordlessly.

'Looks normal,' I said.

'Do you know where that is?' asked Taylor.

'No. I don't really even know which direction we're facing,' I replied.

We looked around for the sun but it was overcast as far as we could see. Taylor leant over the edge and looked down. It was maybe four metres to the adjoining roof. No big deal, but the real problem was what surrounded this roof. An epic platform of steel that I instinctively recognised as David Jones. It had an extra two levels on the rest of the centre. Even if we could get down onto the roof below we would be marooned by these extra floors and likely stuck on a bed of steel, neither in Carousel, nor out of it. We had come out at the worst possible section of the roof.

'Typical,' said Taylor, squinting at the wall of reflective steel.

'Maybe there's a way up with a rope or a ladder or something,' I said.

Taylor sighed and sat down on the ledge of the cinema roof. I lingered for a moment, then sat beside her. She was pensive.

'I don't think we're supposed to get out this way,' she said.

I looked at her, surprised. This was Lizzy talking, not Taylor.

I kept quiet and the two of us sat in the gentle breeze.

'I had a date marked,' she said, eventually.

I waited for her to continue.

'For when I was going to stop checking the doors.'

'When was it?' I asked.

'A week ago. Just after the plane flew over,' she said.

'But you're still going?' I said.

Taylor nodded, tossing a twig down onto the roof as if it were a lake in the forest.

'Because of Rocky?' I asked.

She nodded again. We were silent for a while.

'What were you going to do when you stopped?' I asked with a little apprehension.

Taylor shrugged.

'Just live, I guess,' she said. 'I'm tired of fighting this stupid mall.'

I felt like an arsehole.

'Sorry for not being with you on this stuff until now,' I said.

Taylor shrugged this off. 'There's no proper way of dealing with being trapped in here,' she said. 'Except being scared of getting back out.'

This stung my chest. Taylor looked at me seriously.

'But I don't think you are anymore,' she said.

I held her gaze and wanted badly to agree with her. She looked away. We sat in silence for a while.

'Lizzy says Rachel couldn't open the door because we were there with her,' I said.

Taylor didn't reply. I don't think she was ready to consider this possibility.

'Does Perth normally sound like this?' she asked.

I looked at her, not sure of what she meant.

'Like what?' I asked.

Taylor tilted her head up and listened. I followed.

We sat there for a long while, listening hard to the silence around us. I couldn't answer her question. There were the obvious absences – things we should've been hearing but weren't. Traffic. Industry. People. But I don't think Taylor was asking about those. She was asking about something else. Something bigger. The sound of a city was something you only got a sense of so often. I remembered this from when I was travelling. City after city would seem the same. Until suddenly one of them would open up for you to really hear it. Not small things like cars or church bells or beaches. But an orchestra of everything that defined the place like no sight or smell or touch ever could. In the country this would come more readily. You could pull over on a quiet stretch of road and get a place's sound right away. But cities could be complicated and secretive.

I had heard Perth only a couple of times that I could remember. Once as a teenager on my first trip up the Darling Scarp. The edge of a country-long plateau that stopped abruptly and plunged downward to hang, somewhat cautiously, over the city of Perth below. We wandered from our car to stretch out in the dense summer sun. For a moment I stood alone at the edge of the car park while Mum and Dad unpacked some chairs. I remember looking west to the ocean as a thick swirl of sound drifted up and filled my ears, resonating somewhere deep and specific.

Then again, just last year at night in the city, returning to my car after shopping for sneakers. Standing at the third level of a semi-enclosed car park overlooking the train lines and northern suburbs. I remember hesitating at the door, then walking out to the edge of the building. The city seemed to take a breath, then exhale, releasing a soothing and evocative soundscape upward to where I was standing.

'I don't know,' I said. 'It might be different.'

'I guess it's hard without the traffic and everything,' said Taylor.

I nodded.

'It still might be different,' I said.

She looked at me. I think she understood.

'You don't write as much stuff on the floor as Lizzy. Or Rocky even,' I said.

'I don't really miss stuff,' she said.

I laughed and immediately wished I hadn't. Taylor glared at me for a long second, then laughed also.

'That sounded stupid,' she said. 'I miss heaps of stuff. The internet, getting tattoos, haircuts, fresh fruit, girls.'

I nodded.

'But mostly I miss being Taylor Finn,' she said.

'Of Taylor & Lizzy?' I asked.

'No,' she said. 'Well, yeah. But everything else too. I can't be myself in this fucking mall.'

I nodded.

'Are you and Lizzy alright?' I asked, cautiously.

'Yeah. Whatever. We'll be fine,' she said and climbed back to her feet.

We took a final look at the giant obstacle that was David Jones and headed back toward the cinema.

Walking back I had a weird rush of energy or something that I hadn't felt for a while. I glanced at Taylor.

'I don't think Rocky cares how we get out of here,' I said.

Taylor looked at me.

'You want to try the dome?' she asked.

18

Taylor and I didn't mention our time on the roof to Lizzy or Rocky. It wasn't a conscious decision or a secret. It just didn't feel like there was much to tell. We had tried a door, surprisingly it had opened, but in the end it led to nowhere. Obviously there was more to it than that, and if Lizzy were to ask I felt like we would be comfortable to tell her, or take her up there. In a way we could be reassured by the freshness of the air and the lack of nuclear fallout or whatever. But even though we had breathed fresh air and felt the warmth of the sun on our faces, at no point did it feel like we had breached Carousel.

I got the feeling Lizzy would have been unenthused anyway. She probably would have looked at us like we were stupid to even try the roof option. 'Carousel won't let you just climb off the roof,' she would say. Her comments about our plans to breach the dome were similar. It started a pretty nasty argument between the Finns on things that seemed to have been simmering for a while. A lot of the stuff was old and from Canada. I didn't really have a handle on it. Lizzy accused Taylor of acting like an obsessive maniac from the moment they arrived. This upset Taylor a fair bit and she defended her actions as being driven by emotion – something that she said Lizzy used to have, but didn't anymore.

Whilst the Finns hadn't really spoken in the days since, the argument seemed to affect Rocky the most. His mood dropped for the first time that I could remember. He was sulky and rarely spoke. This worried all of us and we watched anxiously to see if the virus would take advantage.

Regardless of the compelling nature of Lizzy's argument, Taylor and I felt we had to keep trying to find a way out of Carousel. With her door-date passed, Taylor seemed keen to have a break from them but take up something similar. We were also eager to be on hand at the dome ever since the Air Canada jet had flown over. There was no guarantee that it would happen again. And even if it did there was no certainty it would have any repercussions for us. But it did suggest a rumbling of something outside of the centre. This excited us, but also put us on edge. If I hadn't built my crappy tiki enclosure we may not have seen that jet. Fate was clearly involved, and this suggested that hanging around at the dome for another plane was pretty stupid, but it still felt somehow important.

I held tightly to the bottom of a ladder and gazed up at the oval-shaped patch of sky bordered by the dome. Taylor edged her way toward the top. It was the biggest ladder we had found, but still only reached a third of the way up the enclosure. We had leant it against the wall above the sushi bar and Taylor was getting as high as she could to see if there was a ledge or anything else up there that could support a second ladder.

She stopped moving and my radio chirped.

'Okay, I'm freaking out. There are like a million spiders up here,' she said.

'Is there anywhere we could put another ladder?' I asked.

'Sure, but it's going to be swinging around in open air if it's the same size as this one,' she said.

'Right,' I said.

I felt her footsteps on the ladder. She was coming down.

We headed back out into the centre to find something bigger. Taylor took the south. I took the east. We'd already been at it all day so we didn't make a time to meet back.

I took one of Rocky's bikes from Pure 'n' Natural and coasted along slowly, looking for a store that might have need for an extension ladder. I stopped off in Best & Less which had tall aisles of discount shoes and an extended warehouse-type ceiling. There were a couple of small ladders, and one of those platforms with three or four steps and a small landing, but nothing that would help us.

I put some Chvrches on my phone and continued onward. Carousel was sunny and there were several areas where I could roll slowly through a pocket of rays spilling down from an overhead window and feel my skin momentarily warming. I searched through the chocolate bars in a newsagent and discovered the Twix still had a few months of code. I crammed two into my mouth, then took a bag from behind the counter and filled it with bars to take back to the others.

I coasted eastward for a little longer until I reached the tinted glass of Centre Management. It seemed like a long time since I'd ventured inside to search for keys and snoop on the manager's inbox. On the back of Rocky's sickness, I felt a sudden wave of panic for the guppy I'd fed last time. I abandoned the bike and paced inside.

It wasn't cold like my last visit. A gradual rise in temperature had condensed water against the glass leaving the office damp and fetid. It smelt somewhere between an airplane cabin and the inside of an old fridge. The carpet was thick and spongy beneath my shoes.

My hopes of a rescue were raised momentarily. The water in the fish tank looked relatively clean. I scanned for movement or floating fish bodies but found neither. Suddenly I realised that the tank was silent. The aerator had shut down, letting everything in the water settle calmly at the bottom. I lowered my gaze and found the guppy. No longer swollen but lifeless and solemn alongside his tankmates on the dirty garden floor.

'Shit,' I said.

I leant back on the counter while the regret swept down to my stomach. The guppy looked pretty terminal on my last visit but I had still left him there without a chance. I lingered there until the moist air made me uncomfortable and I left, deciding to never go back to the depressing beige offices.

I searched for a while longer but couldn't shake my guilt at leaving Lizzy stranded in JB's, caring for Rocky. We had shared the load pretty equally so far but today it didn't feel like it. I swung a turn outside the locksmith and powered back westward with visions of a lonely bedside vigil and the fragile beep of life support.

When I arrived back, Lizzy and Rocky were happily sipping soup and watching *Gossip Girl*. They glanced at me curiously as I caught my breath and tried to act casual about my panicked return. I wandered over to the kitchen area and drank some Mount Franklin. After a moment Lizzy joined me.

'You okay?' she asked.

'Yeah. Just hot,' I replied. 'I went to check out those management offices looking for a ladder. It's like a sauna in there.'

'What do you mean?' she asked.

'Just closed up and moist. Maybe there's something wrong with the air conditioning,' I replied.

Lizzy nodded. I finished the water and watched Rocky lying on the couch.

'Kind of smells like Rocky's old bedroom in Camping World,' I added.

'Shit,' said Lizzy after a moment.

'What?'

'I need to check something,' she replied. 'Stay here with Rocky.'

'Okay,' I replied.

Lizzy grabbed her radio and took off out the door.

I sat pensively on the couch with Rocky and waited for Lizzy to return. We watched almost a whole episode before she walked back in with Taylor by her side. They were carrying a plastic bag from the chemist. Lizzy sat beside Rocky while Taylor poured a glass of water.

'Rocky, I think you might have this thing called legionnaires' disease. It's a bacteria that hangs around leaky old ventilation systems like the one in Camping World. The good news is that antibiotics can fix this. We just have to find the right one,' said Lizzy.

I looked over to Taylor who was scanning the labels of several boxes of pills.

'I had those,' said Rocky.

'I know, Rock. We're just working that out,' replied Taylor.

She sorted through the boxes until only two remained. Lizzy read each label carefully and selected a variety called Rifampicin. She popped two pills free of the case and Rocky swallowed them without argument.

My head was spinning.

Legionnaires.

I'd heard the name on news stories and remembered Mum stressing about the hygiene of hotels I had booked for trips away to South-East Asia. Lizzy's instincts were probably right. Carousel's ventilation systems had gone more than a year now without cleaning or servicing. They were probably crawling with weird bacteria. It would be no surprise if Rocky had been exposed to some of this in that musty tent in Camping World. I couldn't remember the focus of the news stories but had a horrible feeling that they had only made the television because people were dying.

JB's felt flat in the wake of this short burst of drama. We tried to relax and remind ourselves that even the right pills would take time to work. With both Taylor and I back, Lizzy wandered off into Carousel with her guitar and some pretzels. Taylor drew up a chart to indicate when Rocky needed to take his next dose of Rifampicin and when we might consider switching to the second option. Eventually she put this aside and the three of us watched the television in silence.

After four days on Rifampicin Rocky's health seemed to spike. I came back from a morning run to find him casually sipping on a juice box and wandering through the DVD aisles. Taylor was on shift and we shared a tiny smile at his sudden improvement. A few minutes later Rocky returned with a couple of B-grade nineties horror films.

'Hey, Rock,' I said.

'Hi, Nox,' he replied.

'Rifa going okay for you?'

He nodded and knelt down at the media player.

'You here for breakfast?' asked Taylor.

'Yeah,' I replied. 'Might stick around and watch some of this stuff.'

'Cool,' she said and rose off the couch. Rocky seemed better, but there was no way we were leaving him alone yet.

'Maybe I'll go and find my mysterious sister,' she said.

'She's at the dome,' I replied.

'God. Really?' said Taylor.

I nodded and smiled a little. Lizzy had started hanging out at the dome a lot since the plane flew over. Suddenly keen on tending the gardens or getting some sun. They were pretty transparent excuses to be there in case another plane flew over. But none of us could blame her.

Taylor wandered out to find her, and Rocky and I ploughed through two pretty terrible DVDs, Katie Holmes in both of them. At the end of the second Rocky switched the TV off, leaving us in silence. This was weird. It suggested he wanted to talk properly. Something Rocky and I had done maybe twice since we met.

'Pretty crap, hey,' I said, looking at the back of the DVD case.

'Yeah,' he replied.

Rocky seemed comfortable and relaxed. I felt like the awkward teenager.

'You seen any of those Hitchcock films?' I asked.

'*Psycho* and *The Birds*,' he replied.

I nodded and put the case down.

'Do you want to see your family again?' Rocky asked, seriously.

'Yeah,' I replied. 'Of course, Rock. Don't you?'

'My mum and Grace. Danny works nights so he's usually sleeping,' he replied.

'He's at the security company, yeah?' I asked.

'Yeah,' he replied. 'My real dad is in Sydney.'

'Do you guys talk on the phone much?' I asked.

Rocky shook his head. 'Picture messages sometimes. Of his cars,' he said.

I sat in silence for a moment and thought about this.

'How many girls have you had sex with?' he asked.

'Shit. I'm not sure, Rocky,' I replied.

He smirked.

'I haven't lost count or anything. I just haven't thought about it for a while,' I replied. 'Ten maybe.'

'I had sex with Geri twice,' he said.

'That's awesome, Rock,' I said, feeling genuine but probably sounding otherwise. Rocky didn't seem to mind.

'We went down on each other the second time,' he added.

'Cool,' I replied.

We were silent for a moment.

'I got into Laneway twice and Southbound once,' he said.

'Really?' I asked.

'Yeah. Taylor and Lizzy were at Southbound,' he said. 'I was getting chips when they were playing. I haven't told them.'

I laughed. Rocky joined me, coughing.

'Good idea,' I said.

Rocky nodded. 'Do you like Lizzy best?' he asked.

'Oh no. I mean, we hang out more. But I still really like Taylor. They're just different,' I replied.

'I like them both,' he said.

It was really genuine and I got an inkling of Rocky's bond to the Finns.

'Did you like Rachel?' he joked.

'She was pretty mental,' I replied.

Rocky smiled and coughed a little. I got him a water from beneath the table.

'Hey, how come you asked her what bus she was on?' I asked.

'I take the five-oh-nine,' he replied.

'Was Rachel on the bus with you that morning?' I asked.

'Don't think so. I took the early one,' he replied. 'Sometimes me and Geri meet before work. There's a vending machine at the stairs behind Target,' he replied.

My head was spinning.

'Did you meet her that morning?' I asked.

'Played Crow and waited around,' he replied. 'Then I went inside.'

'She didn't show up?' I asked.

'Sometimes she sleeps in,' he replied.

'Did anything happen while you were outside, Rock?'

He glanced at me, eyes with a glimmer of something.

'It was really windy. Just for a second.'

I nodded and tried hard to process what I'd just been told. Having said what he needed, Rocky sat back and picked up a magazine.

19

Rocky's improvement was fleeting. The afternoon of our conversation he was back on the couch with a fever. Lizzy quickly switched him over to our last antibiotic option. This seemed to give him a slight boost. He became restless in between sleeping and we allowed him to roll around on a BMX in the adjacent corridor. During one of these sessions he disappeared for half an hour, leaving Taylor close to hysterics.

Two days later I was sitting with him when he started coughing and wasn't able to stop. I shifted him to the edge of the couch and put a bucket on the floor to catch the fluid coming up. The coughing sounded deep and raw and made me cringe, but it was his breathing that really freaked me out. There just didn't seem to be time for him to inhale any air. Crouching beside him with my hand on his back I noticed his face was mauve.

I grabbed my radio and tried hard to sound casual.

'Hey. Can you guys come back, please? Rocky has a bit of a cough and I want to get him some more water,' I said.

It was a weird thing to say and I was hoping that this

would tell the Finns that I was freaking out, without me having to say it directly.

'Yeah, Nox,' said Lizzy.

'Be there in a sec,' said Taylor.

I was still crouched beside him when they arrived back. The look on my face must have been pretty rough. Taylor replaced me quickly and put her head close to Rocky's.

'Just breathe when you can, Rock, okay,' she said, soothingly. 'I know it's hard but just suck it in when you can.'

Rocky nodded slightly. Lizzy quickly reloaded an asthmatic ventilator from the table and passed it to Taylor. She coaxed it between Rocky's lips and he inhaled a little. Rocky wasn't an asthmatic but opening up his lungs with the Ventolin was one thing we could do that sometimes helped. The presence of Taylor also seemed to calm him and the coughing eased. He raised his head and leant back against the couch again. Sweat lined the pasty, discoloured young skeleton of his face.

I glanced in the bucket and noticed the fluid was stained pink with blood. I looked up at Lizzy. She avoided my gaze.

A half-hour later Rocky was back on the couch like normal. Taylor left him and joined Lizzy and me at the kitchen table. She grabbed a couple of Twix bars and some water.

'Where are you going?' asked Lizzy.

'Back to the dome. We have to get him out of here,' she said.

I waited for Lizzy to bite, but she didn't.

'Keep your radio close,' she said.

Taylor nodded.

'You too,' Lizzy said to me, before leaving us for the couch.

I glanced apprehensively at Taylor. She put her radio in her pocket and I followed her back out into the darkening centre.

It felt like the sun had gone down outside but none of the evening lighting had kicked in yet. The corridors leading back to the dome were dull and lifeless, and the opening didn't offer its usual illumination as we approached.

'Let's forget the ladders and use a rope,' said Taylor.

'Hook it on the opening?' I asked.

Taylor looked at me and we thought it over.

'I think there are ropes with hooks in Army Depot,' I said.

I left Taylor clearing a space among the plants at the floor of the dome and raced across to Army Depot. Lights timed on and off all around me as the centre seemed to greet our twilight mission with its own instability. The array of ropes was considerable and they were graded for strength and weight with a system that was hard to understand in the torchlight. I heaped an assortment over my shoulders and powered back to the dome, taking corners dangerously close to shopfronts and stands, splitting through patches of total black with just my memory of the centre to keep me upright.

By the time I arrived Taylor had cleared a large patch of plants directly beneath the dome and rolled in the hand-operated forklift. She had it extended to full height, still leaving the top of the dome a dizzying distance above. We assessed the ropes under decent light but couldn't figure if any would be long enough on their own.

'Let's just throw one up there,' I said.

I unravelled a red climbing rope and walked out into some open space. Taylor followed. The rope had a small grappling hook attached to the end. It didn't really seem suitable for what we were attempting. But few things would be, given the smooth glass ceiling of the dome above. I positioned my hand a metre or so down from the hook, swung a few times, and let it fly upward.

The rope travelled up maybe a third of the way to the top, then fell back down amid the lettuce growing to our right.

I climbed up onto the platform of the forklift and tried again, this time aware of how much force it might take to reach up to the open edge of the dome. It got maybe halfway before it came tumbling back down and sent us ducking out of the way.

Taylor tried a few times, once getting a touch more than halfway.

Neither of us felt like we could afford disappointment. Taylor went straight over to a ladder and placed it against the wall where she had climbed before. I handed her a pile of rope and held onto the bottom while she headed upward. She stopped a step from the top and turned half around to face the open dome. She gripped the rope and threw the hook awkwardly upward.

It drifted maybe two thirds of the way up to the top before falling back down.

I kept a hold of the ladder while she quickly recoiled for another throw. I considered telling her to be careful of her balance facing outward on the ladder, but worried it would sound obvious. She swung hard and flung the hook skywards a second time.

The ladder shuddered in my hands.

I held it tight and looked up just in time to see Taylor lose her footing and slip downward. There was a clink from somewhere above as she smacked down onto the next rung and slipped out into open air. I watched in horror, still gripping the ladder as Taylor fell awkwardly, inevitably toward the floor.

The bright rope spun around her like an angry snake until suddenly it became taut.

Taylor stopped falling and swung viciously back upright. For a moment I didn't understand. Then I saw her hands gripping the rope. Her throw had landed.

We had a way out of Carousel.

I bolted away from the ladder and positioned myself beneath her in the middle of the room. She had only been five or so metres above the floor when the rope had caught her.

'Are you okay?' I yelled.

'Yeah,' said Taylor softly.

She dangled for a moment.

'Come down. It's hooked up there so just come down and rest for a sec.'

She eased her grip on the rope and slid down a fraction. I waited beneath her. She slid a little more.

There was a cracking noise above.

Before either of us could say anything there was another and the rope went slack.

Taylor fell the remaining few metres.

My arms shot out automatically but I wasn't ready for the force of her fall. She thumped into me and dropped through onto the floor. Glass crashed down beside her, then onto my shoulder and head. We crouched and waited for an avalanche to fall and shred us to pieces. The last image in my head would be the silhouette of Taylor Finn dangling beautifully from a rope in the half-light of an abandoned shopping centre.

There was a tiny tinkle, then silence.

I looked over at Taylor. She groaned a little and pulled her knees into her chest.

'You okay?' I asked.

She nodded without looking up.

'You?' she asked.

'Yeah,' I replied, checking my head for blood.

I looked warily up at the dome. We had pulled down

a square of glass with the rope, but nothing more. For a moment I wondered if we might try again. Without the jarring of Taylor's fall from the ladder maybe the dome would hold while the four of us climbed up and out.

Then I saw the cracks. Long fractures in the glass running away from the missing panel. One of these reached all the way to the top of the wall below. Others were smaller but split out into multiple fractures that spanned large sections of the glass.

I glanced across at Taylor and found her gazing upward too. We had turned the dome into a deathtrap of hanging glass.

20

The following days were a horrible, extended blur of panic and helplessness. We abandoned our attempts at escape and tried frantically to dam the swell of sickness that was swiftly engulfing Rocky. We ravaged shelves of medical books to find out more about legionnaires and locate treatments that our imprisonment could facilitate. We stripped Friendlies and the other chemists of strong painkillers, Ventolin and anything that might help him breathe. We smashed into the storage room of the dental surgery and found an oxygen machine. We messed with the gauges and tested it on ourselves before fixing the mask to Rocky and watching him rip it off, gasping for air and coughing more fluid into his buckets.

We took turns to cry away from Rocky, only returning when we were sure we could stay composed. None of us had seen sickness up close like this. It was like Rocky was collapsing from the inside and there was nothing we could do to help him.

After days of panic we eventually calmed. We let Rocky relax from his rigid upright position and bundled him with cushions, Lemsip and television. We stayed with him and filled the room with life; laughing at the TV, eating our favourite junk foods. Lizzy played covers on her guitar while Taylor and I held epic *Mario Kart* battles. All throughout, Taylor and Lizzy chatted away with a bravery that was hard to measure, offering constant comfort with the sound of their voices. They remained chirpy and funny and gave no hint of the churning lumps of grief rising deep into their throats. I loved them badly for what they gave Rocky during those days.

Deep into the night I was curled on the couch, listening to Rocky's ragged breath, hoping not to hear it stop. Straining my ears, I heard another noise. A deep rumbling that rolled toward us from somewhere north, then faded with a long sigh. I listened closely as it came again. Still mysterious and undisclosed. I looked around at the dim outline of the room. The dull grey of televisions and laptops flickered with light. Moments later another rumble rolled through.

A thunderstorm was approaching.

Lizzy watched me as I quietly sat up. She was awake beside a sleeping Taylor. I glanced at Rocky on the couch across from me. He was awake also. Once more distant lightning bounced around the walls. Rocky looked at me and I saw something in his gaze. He wanted to leave JB's. He wanted to see the storm.

I looked over at Lizzy. She hesitated, then gently nudged her sister awake.

We gave Rocky a couple of painkillers and carefully lifted him onto a mattress positioned on the manual forklift Taylor had pulled across from the dome. He winced, but made no complaint. Big grumbles of thunder reached us now. Every year Perth was battered by two, maybe three, epic summer storms. For Rocky, this one had come early.

We piled the mattress with blankets and cushions and set out toward the back entrance. I pulled it gently through the darkened corridors, its wheels and our shuffling feet echoing through the centre amid the deep, growling thunder from the north.

I checked on Rocky several times. He was pale and gaunt, but placid on the weird, hovering bed. Taylor and Lizzy Finn walked beside him like tiny elfin sentinels in some strange ceremony or vigil. Blue light bounced around us, reflecting off walls, floors and ceilings.

I rounded the corner and the large glass-paned eastern entrance came into view. It flickered wickedly with light and energy as the storm rolled closer. I glanced back at Rocky. His eyes danced with something I hadn't seen in him for a long time. They shifted from the glass to mine, and stayed there.

I pulled the platform a fraction faster. Rocky gave a tiny nod.

I banked it left and brought it around in a one-eighty so that I was pushing it now with Rocky in the lead. Taylor and Lizzy watched me but didn't speak. Thunder cracked and boomed outside.

I placed the handle in forward lock and picked up speed. Pushing it out in front of me I began to run. Rocky's hood filled with wind as he coasted through the corridors once again. Ahead of us the glass towered over, pulsing neon like a portal. There was nothing but the rush of air and rolling thunder and for a moment I forgot about Carousel and the legionnaires and the whole crazy world that had become our own.

We closed in on our reflections and I slowed us to a gradual stop. Rocky was shadowy beneath his hood but I could still see his eyes. They rose to find mine in the glass ahead. Taylor and Lizzy caught up to us, smiling and puffing and as awesome as they had ever been. Together we pulled up to watch Rocky's final storm rip across the city.

21

It was early morning on a Wednesday, or a Thursday. The Finns and I tried to do something different on weekends so that we could keep a sense of the weeks passing. But weekdays in Carousel still tended to blur. I pulled on some Asics and a hoodie and slipped silently out of JB's into the sleeping centre.

I looked for a playlist while my feet took me to Pure 'n' Natural on autopilot. The island was quiet and empty. I took an apple-berry juice box from a trolley outside and downed it while I stretched. The corridor to the east was dark and hidden. I checked the time and waited for a few seconds. There was a hum, then a flicker, and the lights timed on.

I set off eastward at a three-quarter run.

I stuck to the corridors that were lit, swinging a wide arch across the north-eastern edge of the centre, diverting under intersections where overhead vents offered fleeting wafts of cool, semi-fresh air. My legs felt sore and tight, but strong beneath me. They could carry me from one end of the centre to the other in under twenty minutes now.

Under five on a bike. Our diets had become increasingly rigid and rationed, but I felt healthier than ever before. My body stripped nutrients from my food like a machine, keeping every scrap that it needed and expelling the rest. A brutal, efficient survival machine. I gave it whatever I could and pushed it hard in return.

Together we prepared for a faceless, dateless moment.

I swung right and the eastern entrance loomed brightly at the end of the corridor. The sun hadn't risen but the clouds were rimmed with pink. I slowed to a half pace and took in the view. It was still our best window to the outside world. Mostly concrete, but also sky and a small patch of the hills. These days its sameness offered neither reassurance nor disillusionment. It was just the view from our back window.

My heart thumped a little as I walked over to the garden bed running along the base of the window. I scanned the fake wooden walls for breaches of liquid or soil. It was clean and secure. I looked cautiously over the soil inside. It was damp and fertile looking, but nothing grew in the long, rectangular expanse. I took a watering can and showered it sparingly with water from one end to the other. Last summer, we had just about drowned the plants under the dome with constant, anxious watering. Here at the back entrance it was warmer, but I still had to be careful. We couldn't afford to fail this time. We needed something to germinate.

I sat back from the garden and rolled out a yoga mat. Outside, the colours had changed, but the sun remained hidden. I ran through a simple routine I'd learnt from a DVD and let the breathing wake me properly. When the sun spilled onto my forehead I rose and jogged to Myer to start writing.

Despite now living in JB's with the Finns, I chose the third level of Myer to do my writing. For a long time I didn't venture up to the level above my previous bedroom. It was predominantly furniture and kids' toys. Taylor and I had a brief obsession with remote-controlled stuff that had us clambering breathlessly up both escalators to search the shelves for cars and trucks, but otherwise it was left alone with the other seventy percent of Carousel that we didn't enter.

Most of the desks were made of thick and heavy timber and I probably could have got the Finns to help me lug one downstairs if I wanted. But one day I sat at one with my laptop and it felt like a good place to write. Distraction was everywhere in an abandoned shopping complex. But, with its pastel lounges and dusty rows of kids' toys, Myer's upper level was mundane enough for my attention to be elsewhere.

And I was actually making some progress.

After a bunch of abandoned novellas and screenplays, I had turned my attention to shorter work. My only satisfaction, or maybe confidence, from writing so far had come from working on short stories. The stakes seemed lower and by the time a story rose up to intimidate me, it was often almost finished and I could battle through the final pages. The only thing that concerned me was that, on their own, they still felt insignificant and somehow amateur, no matter how much Lizzy would rate them. I was writing in Carousel for a lot of reasons. To fill the days, to have a focus. But also to be a writer. And a bunch of disjointed, random short stories didn't seem to offer me that. So I decided to group them together under a loose theme and produce a book. It had meant culling a few stories, and working on some new stuff, but overall I felt a lot more comfortable. The fact that any publication was entirely hypothetical didn't feel like an issue.

I chewed down an energy bar and wrote for two hours before Taylor and Lizzy fired up their amps. The final story I was working on had spilled out rapidly last week and I was currently redrafting and trying to work out if it was awesome or shit. The line seemed ridiculously fine and I was regularly unsure of its position. I reworked some sections and it felt like it might even be finished. Either way I shut down the laptop and wandered downstairs toward the fractured, alluring music.

Taylor had joined Lizzy in the Rugs a Million studio two days after Rocky died. Their musical animosity was forgotten and they began slowly, gradually putting together songs for an album. Death had a way of returning people to their most simple form of existence. I had seen it as a teenager when my nanna died. The family worked, ate and slept with a diligence that made each process significant and strangely vivid. Everything else, that which filled a life, was suspended and momentarily superfluous.

For Taylor and Lizzy Finn, existence meant music.

Initially I had left them alone in this process. What they were doing seemed precious and delicate. There was no talk of what was happening, or any tangible shift in their behaviour. They just drifted over to the studio after long, lazy breakfasts and emerged hours later; sometimes looking wired, sometimes placid and relaxed. After endless months of musical hibernation, Taylor and Lizzy were gradually waking each other and I was anxious not to get in the way.

During the first few weeks their music crept out into the centre in fleeting and broken snatches. I imagined them catching each other up on the hundreds of riffs and progressions that had been swirling through their heads since our arrival. Lizzy listening to Taylor with a weird sisterly awe as she moved from one riff to another, then another again, as if she had been preparing them in secret for months. Each one raw and fractured, but full of angst as she seemed to single out an emotion and find its truth and irony at the same time. Then Taylor, pacing about the room in a half smile as Lizzy infused it with shifting, magnetic pop from a bank of sounds she'd held secure for months, but had been strangely unable to release.

Together they would sift through these sounds with a kind of floating diligence. Always exploring, but never without direction. Finding the core of the other's work without fuss, then building, unwrapping, layering texture until it took on a new but somehow inevitable sound.

The mysteries of Taylor and Lizzy's music had become a little clearer when they asked me to come and help record some stuff on Lizzy's MacBook. I had arrived early and stood rigid at the laptop with my finger hovering nervously above record. Taylor and Lizzy glanced at one another and laughed. I felt a huge gulf of coolness open between us, the Finns on one side, me on the other.

'Nox. Relax a little, yeah. This stuff takes a while,' said Taylor.

Since then I had managed to loosen up and we developed a routine where I would turn up in the studio an hour or so after them and man the Pro Tools recording window until one of them nodded for me to hit *Record*. I'd watch as the guitar or keyboard snaked along the timeline and onto the hard drive where I labelled it and backed it up before they went again. There was some structure in the process and I focused on this and tried hard to keep the gulf narrow.

Lizzy was sipping on a juice box and watching Taylor run over some chords on her guitar when I arrived. I smiled hello and edged past Taylor to take up my position at the laptop. It was a casual looking workspace now. When

I began to understand the pace of the recording process, with its experimentation, multiple takes and long creative discussions, I brought in a bunch of magazines. I would flick through these, semi-interested, but never consumed, trying to give the Finns space for their work without seeming outright bored or uninterested. A book would be too much. As was just sitting at the screen and waiting. Recording an album seemed to require a shifting mix of focus and downtime. Taylor and Lizzy morphed into this seamlessly. For me it took some practice.

I was starting to see how a song would start out with a riff or some keys and unpack to become a skeleton for something full and complicated. Taylor and Lizzy would have me record this trigger, then play it back as they experimented with other sounds to fill it out. Once they were happy I would record the keyboard and guitar as separate tracks. At some point they would switch to vocals and play all the tracks in a rough mix through headphones whilst I recorded their voices in solitude. This gave Taylor and Lizzy a demo of the song, which they would critique and we would begin rerecording tracks until there were files and files and the Finns made a wordless decision to move on. Everything about their workflow made sense but at the same time it was like nothing I expected.

Taylor came over to sit beside me. I shifted across and she adjusted some settings on the laptop.

'How far did you run this morning?' she asked.

'Twelve k,' I replied.

'You're a machine, Nox,' she said.

I nodded and watched the screen. The program was still a bit of a mystery to me.

'You go past the back entrance?' she asked after a moment.

'Yeah,' I replied, feeling oddly guilty. 'Nothing is growing yet.'

Taylor glanced at me and nodded. Lizzy watched us from behind a keyboard across the room.

'Want to do a Coles run with me later?' she asked.

'Sure,' I replied.

She finished with the laptop and joined Lizzy at the keyboard.

We spent the afternoon recording Lizzy playing keys for a song that Taylor was calling 'Little Low'. She had written the lyrics and guitar and needed Lizzy to fill out the opening and add to the chorus. After this, the two of them had to work out what they were going to do with the drums and bass.

Even though I'd been to a bunch of Taylor & Lizzy shows and seen the rest of the band, it didn't click that recording an album without these additional musicians might be problematic. I listened through lengthy discussions over the arrangement of songs as the Finns weighed up leaving out the drums or bass, or playing something simple themselves. They tried the latter on several occasions, and I thought it sounded fine. But it was clear that Taylor and Lizzy knew otherwise. I could see their frustration as they struggled to pull sounds from instruments they didn't usually play. In these moments I wondered if this was another thing that defined them as real artists. The admission that their skills in one area, despite seeming fine to the rest of the world, were insufficient and couldn't offer the song what they knew it required. They wouldn't settle, but it was more than that. They knew.

Each song seemed such a mix of intangible elements. Even with just the two of them playing, the possibilities were terrifyingly endless. But somehow they knew when it wasn't right. And when it was. This seemed vital. Maybe the defining trait of an artist and something I had never considered.

Sitting behind that laptop, flicking through magazines and sipping on juice boxes, I was probably learning more about art than I had ever done.

Taylor and I left for Coles late into the afternoon with 'Little Low' still quite a way from being down. We took a couple of our favourite trolleys from JB's and wheeled them smoothly through the dim quiet of the southern corridors.

Our radios crackled.

'Can you guys grab some frozen corn, please?' asked Lizzy.

'We're out. There's only that pea and corn mix left,' replied Taylor.

'No cobs?' asked Lizzy.

Taylor glanced at me. I shook my head.

'Nox says no cobs,' she said.

'Dammit to hell,' said Lizzy.

We continued on toward the shops.

'There might be some out the back of Red Rooster,' I said to Taylor.

She groaned. It was a long walk with no guarantee.

'What about Red Rooster?' asked Lizzy, on cue.

Taylor and I shared a look.

'We'll check it out if we have time, yeah,' replied Taylor.

'Thanks. You're the best,' said Lizzy.

We pushed our trolleys through the abandoned checkouts of Coles and worked our way around the store.

The aisles were a strange patchwork of empty and full. We had cleared out the obvious things like canned vegetables and packet noodles pretty comprehensively, but there was still a shitload of rice and pasta. A lot of it was stale, although oddly still well in code. Our main challenge was to find additions that would offer vitamins and proteins to this stockpile of carbs and keep us from looking like a trio of pasty anaemic teenagers from the *before* segment of some reality TV show.

The confectionery aisle looked pretty ridiculous. We had gutted the place of our favourite items, leaving whole sections of shelves empty but for lonely price tags. Then there was other stuff like liquorice and peppermint chocolate that hadn't been touched and stood on sale, without a hope of being purchased. We all had our strange favourites and Rocky's death left reminders of this scattered throughout Coles. Consumption of the red curry pastes in aisle seven had ceased. As had the Tropical Sunrise shower gel. Taylor sniffed the bright pink liquid and we shared a small smile.

Rocky was all over Carousel.

His words littering the floor. His bikes scattered from one end to the other. Each one pristine and perfectly maintained. His bathroom in the back of Sports Power. A pathway of towels from the shower to the toilet, then back to the sink. Piles of surfing magazines with bikini models strewn throughout. The giant fluffy robe he found in David Jones and sometimes surfaced in at breakfast, a trail of white behind him like a wedding dress. His Nintendo controller, worn and stained by his awkward, sweaty grip. The radio that chirped with our voices for a week or so before Taylor rose abruptly from the couch to switch it off forever.

And his garden bed.

We had buried Rocky in the only place we could. The rectangular garden bed running lengthways along the windows at the eastern entrance. It was narrow but deep with soil and the only place that real plants grew, aside from the dome. We planted ornamental seeds all across the bed and hoped to hell we had done the right thing by burying him there. So far the bed had remained intact, but nothing had sprouted.

I guess one day it would stop and we wouldn't see him everywhere any longer. But then Carousel still had a lot of mystery. Now Rocky was a part of that.

Taylor and I piled our trolleys with whatever we could and wheeled out of the supermarket for the food hall. It was a bit of a walk to the south-east corner but there was still some daylight left and neither of us felt like lying to Lizzy. We passed the cleaning cupboard that marked our bizarre night with Rachel and swung left through a corridor with Baby on a Budget and The Body Shop. The hall ahead looked tired and forgotten. But for Taylor's occasional door-checking it largely was.

We had pretty much stopped cooking fast food down here since the deep-frying oils started smelling like they needed replacing. There was probably a simple way of doing this but it seemed like too much effort and Happy Meals weren't really crucial to our survival. Occasionally the storage freezers had some stuff we could use in our regular kitchen so the hall wasn't completely useless. Sometimes we would have a craving for potato and gravy from KFC, or the tiny chocolate mousse packs from Chicken Treat, and would venture down to raid the place. It was very possible that Red Rooster had a giant stockpile of frozen corncobs.

Taylor left me her trolley and wandered over to Red Rooster and Chicken Treat. They were almost identical and both had corncobs on the menu. I looked around the hall and tried to think of what else we might want.

My gaze came to rest on Curry in a Hurry.

Suddenly I needed to know what was in that storeroom. It had hung over me like a silent, breathless cloud for almost a year now. Carousel had dragged me over enough coals already. The storeroom was worth a few more.

'I'm just going to check out the curry place,' I radioed through to Taylor.

'Sure,' radioed Taylor.

'Pappadums!' radioed Lizzy.

I left the trolleys and moved over to the small, silent store.

The chubby Indian chef towered over me like a dusty relic. I edged around the counter and glanced apprehensively at the storeroom. The air smelt fine, as it did last time until I had opened the door. I knelt beneath the counter and found the key where I'd left it.

My chest started thumping like crazy. I rose and took a few breaths.

Taylor was still looking for corn. The hall was quiet and dull and looked about as dangerous as the baby store we passed on the way in. Still my heart thumped and I wanted to be out of there. But it felt like I had no choice now.

I took a small step toward the storeroom door, slid the

key inside and turned. The door swung inward.

I waited for the smell. It didn't come.

There was an odour, but it smelt similar to the musty scent we experienced all the time in Carousel. Recycled air mixed with dust and the remnants of industrial cleaner.

I stepped forward and switched on the light. It flickered, hummed black for two long seconds, then sprang to life, illuminating a normal looking storeroom with a small pile of clothing on the floor. The floor was tiled and had a square drain for mopping. There was a large basin for washing up with a small mirror positioned above. A wide storage rack covered the far wall next to the cooktops housing a bunch of spices and pastes, and some huge sacks of rice. An exhaust fan whirred slowly in the ceiling.

I stood in the middle of the room and breathed the air cautiously, as if my eyes might be lying. Maybe the room smelt a little unusual. It was hard to tell with the spices.

My eyes drifted back to the clothes. There was something odd about the way they were lying. Not balled up or folded, but kind of flattened against the floor and stretched out like they were on display.

I inhaled and my hair went rigid.

There was a bone sticking out of the jeans.

Suddenly I noticed slight bulges all over the clothing. I stepped closer and saw a deep black stain on the tiles. I traced it along as it snaked away from the clothes to the drain in the floor. My mouth was dry and tacky.

'You still in there?' radioed Taylor.

I spun around, half expecting to see her behind me.

'Yeah,' I radioed.

'Okay. Well, I have some corn. Let's get out of here,' she radioed.

'Cool,' I replied.

I quickly stepped over to the rack to grab something so I wouldn't be found out. There was a bunch of red curry pastes. I took a couple in homage to Rocky. As I pulled them away I noticed a small bundle of items on the bottom of the rack. There was a wallet, half a packet of Extra gum and a set of car keys.

I knelt down and opened the wallet. On the licence was a middle-aged Indian man named Peter Mistry. He had a couple of credit cards, a membership at Blockbuster, a loyalty card from Java Juice and zero cash.

I stared at the wallet and tried to make my brain work. What had happened in here?

'Nox?' radioed Taylor.

I pocketed the car keys, locked the door and got the hell out of there.

Taylor gave me one of her looks and we set off back to JB's. She led, I followed. As we edged back past the dome and into the last remaining daylight I took the keys from my pocket and snuck a look at them. I hadn't noticed before but there was a small label on the biggest key.

It read Ford.

22

I held onto my discovery like a silent indigestion for the rest of the week. It felt totally wrong to not spill the news to Taylor and Lizzy. I had done this before and swore it would never happen again. But something about this felt personal. Like it was for me to deal with and nobody else. And I rationalised by convincing myself I had nothing much to tell.

We found keys in Carousel all the time. They held some excitement to begin with. After all, we were trapped in a centre with a thousand locked doors. But months of failure had left them dull. There were piles of them around JB's, most probably untested, most probably useless. There were even car keys among these. Spare sets left under counters and in desk drawers. But none of us considered them significant.

The fact that someone had died in the storeroom was shocking, but also not totally unexpected. Carousel was cavernous and had been a boarded up fortress for well over a year now. So far we had survived this, but Rocky hadn't, and who is to say that others hadn't joined him, either silently away from us, or before we arrived. It was easiest to assume that the centre only existed in its current state since we found each other inside, but maybe not. Maybe it had been a gateway to some mysterious parallel dimension for years before us, and, like colonisers of a weirdo civilisation, we were only just now discovering the horrors of its past.

For all we knew there could be hundreds of bodies throughout Carousel.

These possibilities offered flickers of explanation, but nothing that would stick. I knew instinctively that the body was significant. The wallet empty of cash. The storeroom key outside of the room, rather than in with the body. The skeleton positioned conveniently above the drain. The exhaust fan silently draining the room of gas as it decomposed.

And the licence.

Peter Mistry was a middle-aged Indian man. I had never seen anybody but pasty-white teenagers working at Curry in a Hurry. It seemed way too clichéd to think that he was an employee or manager.

It sounded stupid but my main fear in telling the Finns was that it might disrupt the album. Something important was happening in that trashy rug store. I could sense it. But more importantly, in spite of their cool, experienced demeanours, I think Taylor and Lizzy could too.

None of us were any closer to knowing why we were here.

In a way the horror of Rocky's death seemed to confirm that it was all random. There could be no rationalising the slow death of a teenager from legionnaires in a modern shopping complex. But on the other hand it was terrible to think of him, and us, as simple victims of circumstance. Surely something that could result in this kind of tragedy must have a weight in the universe.

Taylor and Lizzy's album couldn't justify Rocky's death, or our imprisonment, or whatever the hell it was that was going on outside of Carousel. But unlike anything else we had done since our arrival, it felt like a part of this new world. It was born out of circumstances that didn't exist prior, and maybe would never exist again. And the music sounded different. Like it already resonated even though it was still fractured and incomplete. Like it couldn't have emerged out of any other place and circumstance but this one. Not a concept album, but somehow a concept of its own.

It had also been a saviour. In the most clichéd way that music saves a tortured artist from drugs, it had saved the Finns, and maybe me also, from a grief that may have overwhelmed us. We weren't really cut out to deal with Rocky in life, and by no means in death. Those first few days after we took him to view his last storm were like nothing I had experienced before. Living felt dangerously arbitrary and it seemed like nothing Carousel could offer would ever make things okay. In a normal world you would take on more shifts at a job. Or build a temporary obsession with something on TV. Or have sex with somebody you met at a gig and treated you like everything was normal, because you didn't tell them it wasn't. And eventually the sadness would fade into numbness, out of which other emotions could emerge. But not in Carousel. It seemed entirely possible that here we would be forced to live out the rest of our days in sadness.

But the Finns had found their music. And that had kickstarted my work on the short stories. And it seemed like their purpose would be enough for the three of us.

So long as it was protected.

There may have been deeper psychological reasons for not pulling Taylor and Lizzy into my dilemma once again. Taylor might have tied my innate secrecy to a weird fear of actually leaving Carousel. I had felt this before, quite powerfully, and in a lot of ways I still felt scared. But I think it was a different fear now. And maybe not as irrational. I could trace some of it back to logic. This gave me some comfort, and it made my decision to go back to the staff car park alone seem slightly less insane.

The Carousel ghost train was in motion again. This time I wasn't going to ride it around for days, jumping at every turn. I was getting off and turning the lights on to find out what the hell was going on.

I stayed up late on the couch with the Fiesta keys stuffed deep in my pocket. Lizzy drifted off to her corner of the room early with a book and half a glass of wine. Taylor remained with me until twelve. We watched *Drugstore Cowboy* and the start of *Teen Wolf* before she sat up and stretched, then shuffled off to bed. I stayed on the couch for the rest of the movie to ensure the Finns were asleep.

The keys felt heavy and foreign. They had an ominous feel that freaked me out.

I had packed a small bag earlier in the day with a torch and some other stuff and hid it mutinously under my bed. With this and the keys, I would venture out into the dark of the centre and seek to uncover another of Carousel's secrets.

I also had my radio. If Taylor and Lizzy caught me out, I would tell them the truth. If they didn't, I would keep silent until they finished their album.

I switched off the TV as the credits rolled and brushed my teeth at the makeshift kitchen bench like any other night. JB's was quiet. Just the soft, comforting buzz of electrical equipment and air wafting through the exposed ducts at the ceiling. I padded over to my bed and pulled on a jumper. As I knelt to reach under the bed for the backpack I heard shuffling footsteps behind me. I shot up and took a hold of the quilt, pretending to fix the bed as the footsteps approached.

Lizzy emerged out of the dark.

'Almost forgot,' she said and handed me an envelope.

It was Monday. I had forgotten.

'Thanks,' I said. 'I would have been pretty shattered.'

Lizzy sat down on the bed and wrapped herself in one of the quilts. I glanced at her and opened the envelope. There was a pair of golden retriever puppies on the front. Inside it read *Together Forever – Happy Anniversary*. Lizzy had signed her name in a crazy exaggerated fashion beneath.

'Nice one,' I said and placed it on a nearby shelf next to dozens of others. Lizzy shrugged and remained on the bed. It didn't seem like she was going anywhere. I sat beside her and covered myself in a separate quilt.

'How was *Teen Wolf*?' asked Lizzy.

'Pretty awesome,' I replied.

'What are we going to watch when we're done with the eighties?' she asked.

'The nineties,' I said with a decent amount of sarcasm.

'Oh, right,' replied Lizzy with even more. 'It was kind of a rhetorical question.'

I smiled a little and tried to relax. Peter's keys felt giant in my pocket.

'I guess we were always going to run out of movies eventually,' said Lizzy.

I nodded and thought it over. We were silent for a few moments.

'You know how your phone tells you how many days of music you have in your library, and it's always something crazy like two weeks?' I asked.

'More like six,' said Lizzy.

'Okay, sure. Six,' I said. 'But you can't ever imagine yourself just sitting there for six weeks and listening to every single song, one after the other, until they're done, right.'

Lizzy looked at me but didn't answer.

'But they still give you that figure. As if to say that, if the world ends, but you survive, you can listen to music for six weeks without repeating a song. And then never again,' I said.

Lizzy looked at me curiously.

'What?' I asked.

'I swear you weren't this weird when we first met,' she said.

'You're surprised that being trapped in a shopping complex during the end of the world has made me weird?'

Lizzy laughed quietly. I joined her.

'Do you think it's the writing?' she asked after a few moments.

'What?' I replied.

'That's changed you most,' she asked.

'Oh. I don't know. I don't really feel like I'm writing most of the time,' I replied.

'You're up there most days,' she said.

'I mean, when I'm writing up there, it doesn't really feel like I'm writing,' I said.

Lizzy looked confused.

'What does it feel like?' she asked.

'Messing around. Filling pages,' I said.

Lizzy nodded.

'But sometimes it does?' she asked.

'Yeah, maybe,' I replied.

'And what does that feel like?' she asked.

'Different. Like I'm somebody else,' I said.

Lizzy thought this over. She didn't look satisfied.

'Remember when you asked me about that kid on the bus? Why he doesn't get off when he realises he's on the wrong one? Whether he chooses to have an adventure?' I asked her.

'Yeah,' she replied.

'I don't know the answer,' I said.

Lizzy looked at me.

'Maybe I did when I was writing it. When I felt like somebody else,' I said. 'But not now.'

Lizzy shuffled about under the quilt, a little agitated.

'You've read Salinger, yeah?' she asked. 'Murakami? Cormac McCarthy?'

I nodded. She paused for a moment.

'It's not really about the answers,' she said.

Lizzy looked at me to see if I got it. I nodded without a great deal of certainty.

Eventually she rose, returned the quilt to the bed and ruffled my hair until I flashed a tiny smile.

'That wasn't really my question, anyway,' she said.

'What was your question?' I asked.

'Who it is on the bus?' she said.

I looked at her, not following.

'You or Rocky?' she asked.

Lizzy smiled goodnight and padded back to her corner. The words hung in the night like an ocean.

I sat there beneath the blanket. Keys and backpack all but forgotten.

An hour later I trudged out into the sleeping centre and headed for the car park. My conversation with Lizzy had swirled in my head for the whole of this time before I shut it away and let fear take over. It rose rapidly into my throat and sent tiny spikes of adrenaline along my skin as I traversed the silent corridors.

The path to Just Jeans was decently lit by a series of clothing stores on all-night timers. Pockets of blackness were fleeting and I didn't need to take my torch out of the backpack until I reached the corridor. I switched it on and propped it to point at the door while I knocked it open. Doing this on my own, without making a giant fucking noise, was more difficult than I had predicted. I used a balled-up t-shirt to cover the end of the crowbar and stop it from banging too sharply. It worked in deadening the sound but I couldn't wedge the door open without the sharp edge. Eventually I took it off and held my breath as a dull clink echoed through the centre and the door swung open.

I took a small dumbbell out of the backpack and placed it on the doorstep. It had been a pain to carry but the H shape slotted over the step just as I had hoped and now there were ten kilos between me and the terrifying thought of a closed door. I pulled on the backpack, took out the car keys and stepped carefully down under the tiny light of my torch.

Immediately I felt at risk.

It was jet black in the car park at night. No comforting daytime glow from downstairs. Just blackness and space. Space was at the root of most of my fears in Carousel. There was so much of it and my senses craved the confinement of the small bedrooms I'd spent my life in. The car park seemed to spread out forever. My torch struggling to catch the closest walls as I edged slowly toward the ramp and eventually felt the decline.

I shuffled cautiously down the ramp to the ground floor. I had worn canvas shoes to stay silent in the corridors but suddenly wished for something heavier and with more grip. The concrete felt dangerous beneath me. Months of dust gave it a shifting quality that threatened to kick my feet out in front of me and lay me on my back. In the darkness and the space a simple fall seemed like it would be the end of things.

I glanced over my shoulder to check the door remained propped. It was already lost from view. Just the hint of a glow emanated.

The floor levelled beneath me and I stopped. Gang of Youths' 'Poison Drum' pulsed through my head on some weird subconscious repeat. I turned and scanned the expanse of the car park for the Fiesta.

It glinted back a dull, ominous greeting.

I carefully looked over the rest of the space. It was empty but for the roller door and some wispy, floating cobwebs.

When I was right alongside the car I lit up the keys and found the central lock button. I held them out in front of me and pressed. The brake lights pulsed, sending a flash of disco-red around the car park as the locks came up with a thud.

Peter's car was open.

I stood motionless. I had expected this to happen but now I wasn't sure what to do.

I had to get inside. It looked empty and maybe there was nothing to find, but there was no point coming down here if I didn't check it out.

I opened the driver's door. A light came on inside.

The seats were grey fabric and clean, not like a new car, but one that was looked after. There were no personal items except for the sun reflector in the back. It smelt normal. The pine freshener hung from the dash omitting a stale waft of synthetic foliage. I slid my backpack from my shoulders and sat behind the wheel. It felt strange. Like I was already out of the centre.

My hands found the ignition and out of old habit I put

in the key and turned. There was a brief flicker of lights on the dash, but no sound from the engine. Not enough charge in the battery, I thought. It was a manual though, so it could be push-started.

I reached over and dropped open the glove box. There was a manual for the car and a half-empty pack of AA batteries. I closed it and scanned the space around me for anything else. There was nothing to see. Just a clean, newish Fiesta that was low on charge.

I sat back and tried to get a handle on the situation. I wanted to get the hell out of there but not before I knew as much as I could. I realised I hadn't checked the hatch.

I stepped out of the car and around to the back, trying hard not to freak out totally. I'd seen enough gangster movies to know that the boot of a car generally didn't hold any good surprises. Did the same apply to sporty hatches?

The lock clicked and the door eased itself upward. The space inside was clean. The only items were a couple of newsprint drawing pads stacked neatly on the left side. I flicked through one of them. It was full of charcoal drawings. Solemn looking abstracts of a cityscape I didn't recognise. I exhaled and gently eased the door shut. The sound still jumped around the car park like crazy.

That was it. The keys worked and the car was empty. It was big news really, but something about it felt a little deflating.

I returned to the driver's side and knelt down to put

on my backpack. I noticed something on the sun visor. A small elastic belt was wrapped around the rectangular circumference. I reached up and flicked down the visor. The belt held a remote in place. The type used to control an electronic fence as you entered your front yard.

Absently I pressed the button. Something shifted behind me.

I jumped out of the car and spun around. There was a grinding noise in the darkness. Incredibly loud and close by. I scrambled for the torch in my pocket. Suddenly I didn't need it.

A beam of cold blue light started spreading across the room. It was coming from the roller door. The moving roller door.

I looked at it hard. It was moonlight.

Panic ripped through my senses. I almost ran, but stopped myself and scrambled back into the car.

I pressed the remote again. Nothing happened.

I pressed it again.

There was a moment of silence, then a different noise.

I looked up to see the moonlight diminishing. I pulled the keys out of the car, shut the driver's door and ran.

I was heading straight for the rapidly closing roller door like in some Indiana Jones movie. I closed in and caught a waft of something outside that I couldn't place. But that wasn't my destination. I turned hard right at the base of the ramp and bolted upward. A sliver of light greeted me at the top. I bounded in its direction and pulled hard on the door back to Carousel. It swung open freely. I climbed back inside and shoved the dumbbell out of the way. The door closed with a thud.

23

Seven of the eleven songs Taylor and Lizzy were working on were ready for mastering. Of the four remaining, two were pretty much finished but for some Pro Tools texturing that Lizzy was working on. 'Little Low' needed a rerecord of a guitar track that Taylor had been tinkering with. Last I heard she was now satisfied and ready to get it down. The final track was a loud, punchy song called 'Posthumous'. Until recently I thought this was finished, but had since found out it had been effectively scrapped and the Finns were at a standstill over its direction and inclusion in the album.

For three weeks I had hovered around anxiously while the album moved achingly toward its conclusion. I eagerly gave over my days recording, archiving, locating files for Lizzy, doing whatever I could to see them finish. All the time wrapping my emotions deep beneath a façade of casual detachment while an epic battle of conscience raged inside. Without knowing it, Taylor and Lizzy controlled my destiny as much as I controlled theirs.

With my mornings swallowed, I wrote at night. Fuelled

by caffeine and anxiety I reworked old stories and created new ones. It felt mechanical and soulless but somehow the sentences leapt at me when I read them back and the collection grew large and full before my eyes. My art ran parallel to Taylor and Lizzy's and felt important as a result. Like their album, just the final step remained.

Late into the night, with my eyes set back in deepening caves within my head, I would trudge out of Myer and secretly pack supplies for our escape. Behind the counter at Army Depot was a series of plastic containers with a careful inventory of items that I would load into the back of Peter's Fiesta as soon as their album was complete. Canned food, water, tents, blankets, gas masks, jerry cans; a stockpile of props from any post-apocalyptic film. All based on rules that I assumed still existed. On a world I assumed still existed.

I would take the full brunt of Taylor and Lizzy's rage upon revealing my secret exit. It would be savage and biting and totally justified. I would listen to it all, then race them to where the containers would be waiting in trolleys with just one thing remaining. A trip to the east exit and a farewell to Rocky. We would take our time out there, my planning would allow for this. It would break our hearts but we would leave him there alone and drive out of the centre. The three of us with our lives and our art. Off to somewhere uncertain but where Taylor and Lizzy would eventually understand, and maybe forgive.

I had wiped the mystery of Peter from my mind. Escape beckoned us now. Real and tangible escape. I had smelt it as the roller door closed down on my way out of the car park. A smell different to the roof, different to the centre, different to the past. The acrid smell of the future. I didn't know why Peter had died. Why he hadn't been able or willing to get back to his car and leave the centre. Why his body was in that storeroom instead of somewhere more logical. Peter was set deep within the fabric of Carousel where I no longer had the time to delve.

Lizzy had told me it was not about the answers. She had meant something else but I clung to this like a crazed mantra as the days ground away to a Sunday somewhere deep into November.

When it ended.

Taylor was onto me.

I wasn't really surprised. She had a way of summing me up with a glance from the first day we met. Lizzy kind of had this also, but with Taylor you knew that she knew. She held your gaze just a moment longer as if to say 'Okay, I get it, you're not actually tired, just sick of talking', or 'I know you're not scared of this so why are you acting like you are?' It was kind of alluring and intimidating at the same time.

We were gardening beneath the dome. Lizzy was working away on Pro Tools and Taylor had needed to get 'the hell away from these musty rugs'. She asked me to help her out with some planting and I had grudgingly agreed. My head swirled with a hundred things I needed to do but I found myself turning soil and planting seeds for vegetables I would never eat.

It was time to put in a summer garden. The sun swept in long, slow arcs above the dome in the afternoons, drying the filmy bacteria gathered on tiles and peppering our strange population of pots with warmth. We gathered together the remnants of the winter plants, a scattering of rocket and lettuce, some button mushrooms, a few stunted zucchini, and prepared the soil for new seeds. The winter's gardening had been a bit mishmash but it had confirmed to us that we could grow food if we tried. Taylor was ambitious about summer and had collected seeds for tomatoes, capsicum and sweet corn, determined to do a decent job of feeding us for once.

I worked hard to clear my mind and focus on the gardening. Edging my way methodically from pot to pot, churning up the soil, adding water and a shake of fertilising pellets so Taylor could come behind me with the seeds. Eventually the process calmed me and my thoughts drifted beyond the current chaos to the distant warmth of girls and travel and beaches.

When we stopped for a drink, the Fiesta was back in the recesses of my mind.

'What's happening, Nox?' asked Taylor, as we sipped on

a couple of tropical juice boxes and dangled our legs from the forklift. The fractured glass dome hung precariously above.

I glanced at her to gauge the question.

'Just gardening and stuff,' I replied.

'You're pretty into it,' said Taylor.

'Are you serious?' I asked.

'Yeah,' she said.

I nodded, not sure of her angle.

'It will be good to have some decent veggies this summer,' I said.

It sounded pretty fake. Taylor looked at me and nodded.

'Thanks for all of your help with the recording,' she said.

'No problem,' I said. 'Seems like you guys are almost done.'

'Yeah, maybe. It can drag out a little at the end,' she said. 'But you can take off and get back to your writing whenever you want.'

I nodded. There was a bit of silence.

'You don't get creeped out walking back from Myer in the middle of the night?' she asked.

'No. I'm over it,' I said.

'What's the secret?' she asked.

'What secret?' I asked.

'To not being creeped out?' she said.

'Oh. Booze, maybe,' I joked.

Taylor smiled a little but she didn't buy it. She hopped

down and stretched. I sucked at the last drops of my juice and joined her.

We resumed gardening as the sun dipped away. Taylor was stabbing into darkness but she knew it was a small space, and that me and my secrets were in there somewhere.

Later that night I left the Finns deep into season two of *Girls* and coasted over to Myer on a jet-black mountain bike. I wrote for just on an hour before getting edgy and heading down a level to pack up some things from my previous bedroom. It was strange hanging out there now. Like a shrine, static and preserved.

A lot of Carousel felt different now that I knew we would be leaving. I had always thought cities changed as soon as you were on your way to the airport. No longer insular, but a part of the world. A name on a departure screen alongside countless others. Now that was how I felt. I started thinking about the world, having trained myself to ignore it.

I tried to gauge whether I knew intuitively if my friends or family were alive, like in some disaster film, but again I came up numb. I might have sold this as just a result of time had I not felt the same since we arrived. My strongest feelings were for random things like the pretty blonde girl who had just started work in the café near home. Or the roster at work with my name surrounded by a revolving series of others like Sophie, Dave and Misha. And the lawn at my parents' place that I knew would be perfect to lie on in the afternoon sun, but had never tried.

I wondered about sex, unsure if my time in Carousel proved that I could live without it, or that I definitely couldn't. It seemed a distant and arbitrary part of my former life. I made imaginary line-ups of the girls I had slept with and searched them for emotion or resonance. Their faces were blank and gave away nothing. Even Michelle and Heather, who I'd fallen for pretty hard. I decided that I needed to have sex quickly once we were out, not because I felt desperate or lonely, but so I could remember how I felt about it.

Mainly I worried about whether I would be different to the person I was when I arrived. This seemed crucial and drove small decisions like what clothes I was packing, but also huge ones like keeping Peter's skeleton a secret. I didn't feel like I arrived with an identity crisis, but Carousel had sure as hell helped me develop one. I looked at my time inside like it was some kind of Buddhist retreat or volunteer abroad program. Something to be ground-out because the results would be profound and life would open up afterwards. And like some warped Contiki tour, I was determined to make my final night a big one so that the resumption of my regular life wouldn't suck, at least for a week or two.

During the recording of their previous album Taylor and Lizzy uploaded a video blog where they were filmed from the seaside studio talking on speakerphone to distant friends and family about their day. I imagined them sitting there telling somebody in Canada about me and the bizarro thoughts I was having, as if they knew everything that came into my head.

'Nox lines up all the girls he slept with and stares at them like every second day,' said Lizzy.

'Oh my god!' said the listener. 'What else does he think about?'

'It's so random,' said Taylor. 'One minute he'll be looking at his roster at work, then he'll be volunteering in Africa somewhere. Then he's wondering whether an Indian guy's skeleton looks different to a white guy.'

'So fucking weird,' said the listener.

'I know, right,' said Taylor.

'How is the recording going?' asked the listener.

'It's okay. Kinda different to our normal stuff,' replied Lizzy.

I felt increasingly mental.

I put some music on and skirted around the edges of the room tossing things on the bed where I could decide if they should be taken or left. We had become accustomed to not owning clothes, just wearing them. Now it was hard to determine where my wardrobe started and finished. There was a weird progression evident. The hoodies and jeans of my initial months had morphed into slim chinos and dark pullovers. I liked that I could notice this and carefully selected items to take in the Fiesta that reflected the way I now dressed.

At eleven thirty I got a wave of sleepiness that curled me up on my old bed for an intense twenty-minute sleep. I woke to an imaginary thump at the back of my head and sat up amid the piles of clothing. My radio was beeping. I had rolled over on it and pressed a bunch of buttons. I switched them off and clicked back toward our regular channel five. At channel two I hit the voices of Taylor and Lizzy.

I stopped and listened. There was a pause, then talking.

'Mum uses that treatment,' said Lizzy.

'Really? Okay,' said Taylor.

I checked the channel again. I was definitely on channel two. I had stumbled across their private conversation.

'Is there any left here?' asked Taylor.

'I don't know. Probably somewhere,' said Lizzy.

'What do you think she's doing?' asked Taylor.

There was a long pause, as Lizzy seemed to be deciding whether to answer. I watched the radio and waited.

'It's like eleven in the morning over there, right?' asked Lizzy.

'Yeah,' said Taylor.

'She's still in her gym clothes from earlier in the morning. But she's chewing on a muffin at home now. One of those big blueberry ones,' said Lizzy.

'I'd kill for one of those,' said Taylor.

'The drier is on, and she's run the sink to do the dishes but forgotten about them now that she's online,' said Lizzy.

'What is she looking at?' asked Taylor and sniffed.

She sounded fragile.

'Our site. Reading your blog. Checking the tour dates. Working out when she can call,' said Lizzy.

Taylor sighed a little in response. There was a long pause and I wondered if that was the end of their conversation.

'You know what he did today?' asked Taylor.

'What?' Lizzy sighed.

'Missed like seven pots with the fertiliser,' said Taylor.

'Wow. That's totally insane, Taylor,' said Lizzy.

'He doesn't care if anything grows. You don't think that's a little alarming?' asked Taylor.

'I don't know what's alarming in this place. Why do you always try to attach logic to stuff? It doesn't work here,' said Lizzy.

'I just don't get why he is so fixated on us finishing the album,' said Taylor.

'He's a fan, remember?' said Lizzy.

'I'm not attacking him. I'm concerned,' said Taylor.

'So am I,' said Lizzy. 'But he's still Nox.'

Taylor was silent for a bit. I stared at the radio behind big, stupid tears. The Finns were silent for a moment.

'Do you still think mum could have been on that flight?' asked Taylor.

'I don't know,' said Lizzy. 'I don't want to talk about it.'

More silence.

I felt gutted for them. I turned the volume down to zero and climbed back beneath the covers. Had I returned to JB's then I would have hugged them hard and raced them down to the Fiesta and away from Carousel forever. But instead I lay frozen and still, and drifted into broken, shifting sleep.

24

The following morning I helped Taylor record the final guitar section for 'Little Low' and Lizzy began mixing, having finished the other two songs she had been working on. By midafternoon it was done and only 'Posthumous' remained. I watched the two of them as Lizzy shared her news and they confirmed that the album was almost ready. They seemed relieved but a little underwhelmed. I listened hard for any mention of 'Posthumous' but it didn't come up. Instead Taylor pulled out a box of expensive looking wines from Liquor Central.

Before long they were open and we started sipping and chewing down snacks. Taylor drifted over to play DJ in the JB's music library and Lizzy and I fired up *Mario Kart*. Eventually the wine took the edge off my anxiety and I let myself relax for the first time in weeks.

By the time it was dark the three of us were drunk.

'Come on. You guys said you would take me up there whenever I wanted,' said Lizzy.

She wanted to go up onto the cinema roof and look at the stars. Taylor and I had wandered back up there a few times since busting it open. Initially just to make sure we hadn't missed some obvious way to get down. Then to feel the sun and breathe the air and convince ourselves that we could smell the ocean. Lizzy knew about the roof, but up until now she hadn't been interested. When I asked Taylor about this she told me Lizzy had been a closet acrophobic from age six when she stranded herself on the roof of their Montreal row house.

Taylor and I shared a glance. Both of us seemed to think that going up there at night was a bad idea.

'You can see stars from the dome,' I said.

'What like five,' replied Lizzy. 'I want to look around. See what's out there.'

Taylor looked at her sister and they shared a glance.

'Alright, fuck it. Let's go,' said Taylor.

She looked at me to see if I would object. I felt warm and a little woozy. My head swirled with emotions but no arguments surfaced. Lizzy grabbed a three-quarter-full bottle of wine and we chose bikes and set out once again into the dark-filled centre.

The Finns wove in and out of shadow like a pair of wraiths, ambivalent to both good and evil. Behind them I pedalled gently, focusing hard to keep upright and make the turns as we rolled though the centre toward the dome and the cinema. The air was cool on my face and I sobered up just a little.

The dome opened up in front of us. The blue flicker of

fluoros merged with the bounce of moonlight from the floor to create a glow that was otherworldly. The Finns fanned out playfully and swung right to circle the garden and gaze upward at the sky. Like kids let out of the house, their faces beamed with energy.

I followed, not keen to slow too much for fear of falling sideways. I looked at the pots and remembered what Taylor had said yesterday about me not caring if anything grew. It wasn't true. Even though we were leaving, I wanted them to grow badly. The thought of closing the door and leaving Rocky with a lifeless, empty centre got me lower than anything.

We left the bikes at the edge of the dome and trudged up the escalators to the cinema. The foyer was dry now but evidence of the hole in the roof and the winter rains was all over the carpet. We had propped open the office door after our first visit to stop any build-up of water in the event of a heavy downpour. Since then moisture had seeped down and out, slowly turning the floors from red to a deep brown, teeming with bacteria. We took light, wavering steps through to the candy bar and led Lizzy upstairs to Projection Five.

We struggled our way up the slippery, collapsed roof until it levelled and Lizzy stopped to gaze upward. Taylor and I followed. If the view from the roof in daylight was unimpressive, at night it was anything but.

The sky was giant and imposing.

There were scatterings of stars and a half moon, but it was the blackness that struck us most. Inside Carousel our sky was a constant shade of dirty white. When Taylor and I had ventured outside previously the overcast skies had mirrored this. But not now. The vacuum of our inebriation sucked in an immense sweep of southern sky and we all remembered that we were part of the universe. Yes, we were tiny and insignificant. But we were also a part of something.

Lizzy sighed and smiled a little. Taylor and I joined her.

We moved carefully along the sunken cinema roof to find the edge where we could look out upon the small vista we had seen previously. Lights greeted us as we approached.

'Wow,' said Lizzy.

Suburban Perth was vast and black as it spread silently away to the west. Yet amid the darkness there were small scatterings of light. The warm glow of a hidden porch. Blue light from a petrol station or car yard. An intersection with traffic lights shifting from green to red, awaiting cars that never arrive. The pockets seemed random. Some clustered together, others distant and lonely. Carousel wasn't the only place that was somehow still on the grid.

'Total zombie apocalypse,' I said.

'Shut up, Nox,' said Taylor and swigged back some wine.

Lizzy laughed and grabbed the bottle. Taylor and I laughed too. For a moment the three of us were in hysterics.

'Oh my god. Stop it,' said Taylor. 'There's a fucking ledge here somewhere.'

We settled and I took out a small packet of expensive cigars I'd found in Liquor Central. I'd cut the end off a couple a while back and shuffled through until I found one that was ready to smoke. I lit it up and inhaled too much.

'Seriously though,' I said with a cough. 'What the fuck is going on out there?'

Taylor and Lizzy glanced at me, then each other, and burst out laughing. Lizzy took the cigar from me and tried it out.

'Mystery, Nox. A city full of mystery,' said Lizzy.

I looked at her, wondering what she meant.

'I bet Rachel is out there somewhere,' said Taylor. 'Drinking pre-mix bourbon and watching reality TV reruns.'

'She'll outlive us all,' I said.

We passed around the wine and cigar in muddled circles, unsure which was ruining the taste of which. I felt bold and stupid and like nothing was off limits.

'Are you guys stuck on "Posthumous"?' I said.

The Finns shared a glance and seemed to decide that it was okay to answer.

'You know what it's about, yeah?' asked Lizzy.

I shook my head and felt like an idiot.

'Someone who is waiting to get famous posthumously, but it never happens because everyone else is dead too,' said Taylor.

Her big, beautiful eyes glazed importantly in the distant lights. Lizzy looked at her sister.

'Oh,' I mumbled.

'It has a tricky structure that we're trying to figure out,' said Lizzy.

We stood in silence for a moment and finished the wine.

'Where is the airport from here?' asked Lizzy, after a while.

I looked up at the sky and tried to get some bearing. The stars blurred and I closed my eyes tightly.

'Over there,' said Taylor, pointing to our right. 'Past David Jones. I think.'

Lizzy gazed in the direction of the distant, blocky building. It seemed like something Taylor had already thought about. I watched them both and remembered the conversation I'd stumbled into. Their longing for the jet plane and their mother.

I felt drunk and low and on the edge of something big. I stared hard at the floor and swallowed it down without knowing what it was.

I turned and moved back toward the glowing hole of light in the cinema roof.

'Careful, Nox,' said Taylor.

I waved a hand to say that I'd heard. The Finns chatted away behind me as I edged reluctantly back down into Carousel.

Back in the cinema staff room I splashed water on my

face in the kitchenette for what felt like ages. I cupped some awkwardly in my hand and swallowed it. My mouth felt numb and furry as it passed over. The spike of cold woke me slightly and I wandered back out into the foyer to wait for the Finns. A tacky gold railing bordered the area and I looked down upon the entrance below. Our garden looked small and sad from a distance. A broken-down relic of our failed society.

I stepped away and slumped into the console of the *Devil Driver* game in the foyer. The screen looped with clips of players making turns and driving over cliff-faces. My head started to spin. I turned away and stared at the floor.

Something was written on the tiles beside me.

I tried to focus my gaze. The writing was stumpy and familiar.

It spelled out ROCKY.

He had written it himself. Adding his name to all the other things we missed and scrawled out on the floor. Sometime before he died. Before he knew he would die.

I tried to swallow but my mouth was dry. If I had gone into the storeroom earlier we would have had a door to get him out. And a car to take him somewhere. I tried again and started to cry.

The Finns found me a little while later. Bundled up in the console. Inconsolable and mumbling about a garage door. Eventually I calmed enough to spill my secrets.

I told them about the terrible smell in the storeroom. About how I had chickened out and left it for months and months, wiping it from my mind before finally going back to discover Peter's skeleton on the floor. I told them about the wallet and the keys and the Fiesta with nothing in the hatch but some charcoal drawings. And finally I told them about the remote control.

The three of us headed straight to the car park.

It was hard to know whether Taylor and Lizzy really expected the garage door to open. My revelation in the *Devil Driver* console was drunken and confused. I remember their faces close to mine, staring at me seriously as they tried to pull the logic from my ramblings. I must have convinced them enough to try and the tone of our evening altered irrevocably.

Their faces had brightened when I fumbled my way into the Fiesta with Peter's keys and showed them the controller. Taylor reached across and pressed it quickly. Then tried again. I told her to wait and held it down deliberately like I had some special touch. Each time we stared at the black void across the car park and waited for the door to open. Each time it stayed silent and closed.

I dashed back up the ramp and brought down a stack of new batteries. Taylor and Lizzy sat in the Fiesta and waited. The hope already drifting from their tired, drunken eyes. We opened the controller and replaced the battery with a fresh one. Nothing changed. We searched the glove box for another controller but there was none. I took it off the visor and walked it over to the door. Pressing the button over and over until I saw the Finns step out of the car and head back toward the ramp.

I had waited too long. Once again Carousel had found a way to keep us inside. Taylor and Lizzy turned away from me and trudged up the ramp. I followed them back into Carousel and the three of us slept for the best part of a week.

25

I felt flat and lifeless without the trajectory of my secret escape plan. Time went from a delicate, tension-filled entity to something vague and unimportant. I stopped writing and skulked about the centre beneath hoods and sunglasses, doing chores that would help out the Finns but not look like shallow attempts to apologise or regain their trust.

Summer spread across Carousel like an uncomfortable blanket. The garden sprang to life in random clusters of manic vegetables. They shot upward rapidly before developing patches of stunted fruit and foliage. The air lost its damp and started to smell differently. Not fresher, but without the dankness of the cold concrete enclosure we had become used to in the wet months. Occasionally tiny wafts of the outside would drift past our noses bringing trees, flowers and soil all the way from the hills above the city.

Taylor and Lizzy finished 'Posthumous' and completed their album. Their seventh since starting out as teenagers playing at colleges and cafes. Sometimes they still met in

Rugs a Million to listen through the final mixes or discuss how the songs could be played live. But the journey of the album was over.

I hung out with them in small snatches over breakfasts and television. There was no real grudge or animosity about the Fiesta and our failed escape. Our relationship had drifted beyond that kind of thing to something more permanent. Lizzy and I still exchanged cards on Sundays and Mondays but they lacked the spark they once had. We would read them in private, then file them away like a postcard from the place where you already lived.

From a distance I watched the Finns carefully and they seemed neither broken nor complete. The album had been important but it seemed like they knew that a void would exist once it ended. Lizzy kept a small grip on the music, toying with the mixes and playing the arrangements out loud. She filled the remaining time with books, reading constantly and widely across Carousel's selection. I imagined her photographed for some boutique design magazine while she read in sunshine on deckchairs beneath the dome. On stools over coffee and biscuits at Pure 'n' Natural. In her giant, awesome bed at the back of JB's.

After the album Taylor stopped trying to open the doors. Instead she turned to gardening. She pulled out every book and magazine she could find on the subject and built a reference library in milk crates at the entrance to the dome. She cultivated lumps of steaming compost in black rubbish bags and turned it through soil to infuse it with nutrients and offer fuel to struggling plants. Our diets improved significantly with foods like cherry tomato and eggplant that we hadn't eaten fresh forever. But Taylor didn't just grow vegetables. She grew flowers and succulents and weird looking plants I'd never seen before. She wasn't just gardening to keep us alive. The dome was a place of life now and Taylor gravitated there whenever she could.

The summer also brought life to Rocky's garden bed at the east entrance. His bed was now covered in a scattering of ground covers. Some areas were dense and vibrant, others were wispy and gentle. Taylor carefully planted other things in there too. Pockets of colour and life. It was my favourite place to sit now. I would wander down after breakfast for long yoga sessions before the heat of the day reached in at us from outside. Or to listen to one of my iPhones. Each one packed with music I had painstakingly loaded via CDs from JB's. A lot of stuff I hadn't heard before. I took the time to lie down there and discover new artists, occasionally stumbling onto a band like Camera Obscura or The Mountain Goats that I couldn't imagine having lived all these years without.

I also listened to Taylor & Lizzy. The new album that had yet to be named, heard or played, but which Lizzy gave to me casually one afternoon a few weeks back. It was dense and moody but jumped into my ears with a vibrancy that floored me over and over again.

I was lying on my back listening to 'Little Low' when Lizzy emerged into the sunshine of the eastern end. I sat up and hit *Pause* like I'd been caught doing something I shouldn't.

'Hey,' she said.

'Hi. What's up?' I replied.

Lizzy shrugged and sat down next to me on the couch.

'What are you listening to?' she asked.

I hesitated for a moment, but couldn't lie to her.

'Taylor & Lizzy,' I confessed.

'Finally,' she said.

I smiled, but quickly realised she was serious.

'I listen to you guys all the time,' I said.

'Really?' Lizzy asked. 'Whenever I ask you it's always something else.'

I thought about this and realised it was true.

'I think I was just embarrassed,' I said.

Lizzy sighed and shook her head.

'Sorry,' I said. 'I didn't realise you cared.'

'That our last remaining fan has stopped listening to us?' she said.

'Oh, okay. I get it,' I said.

We sat in silence for a bit.

'The new stuff is pretty amazing. I think,' I said carefully.

'Really?' asked Lizzy, and looked at me.

'Yeah. I don't really know how to explain it,' I said. 'It's like nothing I've heard before. But it also kind of feels like it's been in my head forever. Like some distant childhood memory that resurfaced to tell me something important.'

Lizzy smiled and looked away.

'We could totally write that on the cover,' she said.

I smiled and looked at her.

'Does it feel weird having finished it?' I asked.

Lizzy took a breath, then shrugged.

'Until it's played somewhere, or listened to by people, it's just a bunch of files on a computer,' she said.

I nodded and kept quiet to see if she wanted to say anything else. She didn't.

We stared at Rocky's garden in calm, slow-moving silence.

'Taylor's gardening is fucking spectacular,' I said.

'Yep,' said Lizzy.

We stayed there for a while until an idea swirled out of the soupy mush of my brain.

26

In order to broadcast something on an AM radio frequency you need several things. A power source, a transformer to modulate the electrical signal, a tiny square thing called an oscillator to turn the modulated signal into radio waves, and preferably somewhere high to send them out via an antenna. And of course, some audio.

It took me just a morning to establish that Carousel had all of these elements.

Like television, mobile networks and the internet, radio didn't reach us in Carousel. It was just static on both AM and FM. Not the type of random messy static that if you listened to carefully you might discover some distant voice. This was a constant shower that matched the snow on our TVs and made it clear that nothing was getting through.

I flicked through a couple of tech mags in the news-agent and discovered that there were a few things that could block radio waves, but none seemed to be present in Carousel. I also read that a radio signal could pass through some pretty crazy shit such as a fully-grown elephant and a nuclear submarine. It seemed more likely that radio waves were no longer being broadcast in Perth or Australia, rather than being blocked from Carousel specifically.

This should have been pretty alarming, but all I was thinking was that it seemed fairly possible that I could broadcast Taylor and Lizzy's new album.

Rather than fill them with false hope, I set about testing this out in private. There weren't really any useful books on amateur broadcasting in Carousel. Radio was old technology and the books I found just focused on podcasting. But without the internet this wasn't an option. I had to go old-school and the best reference I could find was *Future Scientist Magazine*.

It was a pretty cheesy mag aimed at geeky teenage science nuts. A lot of the content was internet based but I lucked out and stumbled across an edition with a feature on a bunch of kids who built a radio transmitter out of an old motorbike as part of a grade six science experiment. I didn't have a motorbike, but I had all kinds of other stuff, and without too much trouble I'd gathered all the required elements in Projection Five.

The hole in the cinema roof offered a perfect spot for a broadcast antenna. From what I'd learnt from the grade sixers, the surrounding buildings shouldn't affect the broadcast, but large land masses might. Carousel was the tallest building in a big, sprawling swampland on the eastern edge of the city. If I could work out how to get a signal out it should be receivable all the way to the hills in the east, and to the Indian Ocean and beyond in the west.

Taylor and Lizzy took my sudden and secretive venture with a deal of caution. And rightly so. I felt like I'd been messing around behind somebody's back ever since I arrived in Carousel and I hated the idea that they thought I was doing it again. But this could be a great surprise and Christmas was only a week or so away. Our last Christmas sucked and we sheltered away from it with movie marathons and junk food. But if I could get my shit together and resemble the awesomeness of the sixth graders in just a small way, maybe I could give Taylor and Lizzy something decent for a present and give this long, chaotic year some sense of closure. But I resigned myself to not lying. If they asked me what I was doing I would tell them up-front. The surprise was a luxury.

But they didn't.

They just seemed to watch me silently, probably crossing their fingers that their last remaining housemate wasn't losing his shit as surely one day we all would.

Late into a warm December afternoon I was ready for a test. I had taped an antenna to the top of one of the old air conditioning units on the roof. From here I ran a wire back down into Projection Four, and across to Five where I had set up a small desk with a transformer, oscillator, computer and microphone. The mic was an afterthought and I didn't really plan on starting some crappy breakfast program, but the setup didn't seem complete without it. I ran some power to a separate radio and set the dial to the 87.2 where I was about to broadcast. I put on a song by Radiohead, turned the computer volume to zero and ran the transmission.

The static on the radio drew a tiny breath, then morphed into beautiful nineties alt-rock. I smiled properly for the first time in ages.

'You're not going to tell the zombies where we're hiding, are you?' said Taylor.

I jumped up and spun around. Taylor was standing in the doorway with an expression I couldn't place.

'Hadn't planned on it,' I said, after a moment.

Taylor nodded.

'Radiohead,' she said.

'Yeah. It's kind of obvious. But still classic,' I said.

She looked around at my setup.

'Sorry to ruin your secret,' she said.

'Yeah, well, there goes Christmas,' I replied.

'What do you mean?' she asked.

'I was going to broadcast your album. If you wanted me to,' I said.

'Oh,' she replied. 'To who?'

I shrugged honestly.

'Sorry. Tough question,' she said.

We stood there and listened to the song for a bit.

'So is it working?' asked Taylor.

'Yeah. I guess so,' I answered. 'This radio picks it up so there's no reason others couldn't.'

'How far away?' asked Taylor.

'I don't know really. Most of the city,' I replied.

Taylor nodded. The song finished. I switched off the equipment. Taylor wandered around the space.

'Christmas,' said Taylor, and shook her head.

'Yeah, I know,' I replied.

'I hate New Year's here the most,' said Taylor.

I nodded, understanding why.

'Easter is pretty shit,' I said.

Taylor laughed.

'What's wrong with Easter?' she asked. 'Aside from having no eggs.'

'I don't know. Perth is like a ghost town at Easter,' I said.

'Yeah,' said Taylor, sarcastically.

'No, I mean, like a different ghost town. Everyone in Perth goes away for Easter. The city is deserted. So I drive up to the hills and hang around at Mum and Dad's for the weekend,' I said. 'It's so boring. Me and Danni drive each other crazy.'

I was going to keep going and try to explain why I missed that, but Taylor was already nodding.

'I miss fighting with people too,' she said. 'Not really fighting, just arguing about something. Having it out. Even with Lizzy.'

'You guys fight a little,' I said.

'Not properly. You can't in this place, right? It's too hard already,' she said.

I nodded.

'It's like you swallow it down a little bit each day. Then eventually you stop needing to. Because in here nothing really matters,' she said.

'You should have torn shreds off me for the roller door,' I said. 'I mean, I expected you to.'

Taylor didn't look at me.

'All I could think of was Rocky,' she said.

I sucked in a shallow breath.

'But you didn't have the key in time for him. Right?' she asked.

I shook my head. Taylor exhaled a little.

'Plus this stupid mall probably wouldn't have let him out. Like it didn't with us,' she said. 'Lizzy has been right all along.'

I nodded.

'The door opened for you. But you didn't leave. You came back for us,' she said, dead serious.

'I think I just freaked out,' I said.

Taylor ignored me. 'I watched you packing in Army Depot for weeks. All that stuff. Tiny bottles of my shampoo. Those crappy socks Lizzy likes. Rocky's hacky sack,' said Taylor.

'You didn't say anything,' I said.

'I didn't think you had a fucking key,' she said and we

both smiled. 'I just figured it was something you needed to do.'

I felt beat up inside and stared hard at the dirty red carpet.

'You drive me crazy, Nox. But it doesn't bother me,' she said.

I smiled and we both focused on the carpet for a while.

'Maybe we'll never get out of this place,' said Taylor. 'And maybe we're lucky because there's a life in here for us. A pretty weird one, but it's still a life, and none of us knows whether anything better exists somewhere else.'

I looked up at her. She seemed relaxed but her gaze held an intensity, as always.

'But if we do get out, the Nox you are in here, with the writing and the haircuts and the leather jackets, that Nox doesn't need to stay here. It's not determined by this place, or by me or Lizzy, or anything else. If that's you, then that's you, Nox. The apocalypse is irrelevant,' she said.

I nodded and took a breath. Taylor smiled at me and looked up at the small window of sky above us.

'Carousel does a decent summer. All things considered,' she said.

She stepped across to ruffle my hair and wandered back toward the stairs. I watched her go. With the album done and the doors left alone, the tension had finally left her shoulders. Taylor Finn was calm and stable, and for better or worse had found a place in Carousel. She stopped and turned around.

'You should do it, by the way,' she said.

'What?' I asked.

'Broadcast it. Lizzy will totally lose her shit,' she said.

'Seriously?' I asked.

Taylor nodded, and smiled magnanimously.

27

Christmas morning was awkward. We'd put up a plastic tree in our lounge area and covered it with some lights and a scattering of decorations from a discount stand in David Jones. In the days prior, a few presents appeared underneath as one of us made a wordless decision to gift something and the other two followed. We wandered over after breakfast and unwrapped them to flickers of surprise and guesses over which shop each item was from.

Taylor gave me a pretty awesome writing pad she'd found down the back of a newsagent. Lizzy gave me a t-shirt from Myer that I somehow hadn't seen despite walking past for over a year. It was navy and had a small pocket stitched into the front. I liked it straight away. I gave Taylor a book on hydroponic gardening I found when I was looking for radio information. I don't think she'd considered this before and she seemed at least a little excited by the idea. To Lizzy I gave a small radio from Dick Smith. She was confused but I told her I would explain later. Taylor and Lizzy gave each other a trolley full of carefully selected clothes for a special Christmas edition of trolley shopping.

The whole thing was fine but over in a matter of minutes, leaving a giant Christmas vacuum to fill for the remainder of the day. We strolled east to see Rocky's garden and ended up sitting down there for a while talking about all the foods we missed.

On the way back I sat through a few hours of trolley shopping in the corridor next to David Jones. It actually wasn't so bad. Lizzy had baked some muffins and made a playlist of some great artists like Elvis and Bright Eyes doing Christmas songs. I flicked through some magazines and watched the Finns circle from trolley to change room in a kind of Zen state that seemed pretty comforting.

Eventually we returned to JB's and watched the *Home Alone* box set up until halfway through the third one where I conveniently suggested that we head up onto the roof with a few drinks and catch some afternoon sun. I told Lizzy to bring the radio. She gave Taylor a glance but to her credit she didn't give anything back. My surprise remained intact.

I had draped a sheet over my broadcast setup and Lizzy didn't seem to notice it as we edged outside into what was a stunning Perth day. The sea breeze had probably rippled across Fremantle an hour or so ago and it reached us in cooling wafts of freshness as our skin sucked in the sunshine and thawed out what was beneath. The sky in Perth could be crazy blue. At the start of summer, before the first bushfire of the season, it regularly looked liked somebody had photoshopped the hell out of it. Even for me, it was hard not to stare at it when I ventured outside. Taylor and Lizzy dipped their eyes behind another pair of Wayfarers and gazed up with wonder as we made our way to the edge of the roof.

We spread out a blanket and some cushions and cracked open some Beck's from the rapidly diminishing shelves of Liquor Central. Soon we would be onto liqueurs and fortified wines. Facing a long, hot summer with just Tawny Port or Tia Maria for refreshment was a pretty depressing thought.

'So?' asked Lizzy and looked at me.

'Yeah. Okay,' I said. 'I'm a little terrified about this so try not to lose your shit too much.'

Lizzy looked at Taylor. She shrugged. I stood up.

'You'll need to turn that radio on and tune to 87.2 AM,' I said.

Lizzy looked at me pensively and nodded. I headed back to the projection booth.

I pulled off the sheet and turned on my equipment in what now felt like a fairly routine procedure. I loaded up the new Taylor & Lizzy album and hesitated for a second. I think if Taylor hadn't already have caught me out and told me it was a good idea I might have gone back out and checked with Lizzy first. But she had, and they were out there waiting now. So I hit *Play* and listened.

From a distance I heard the first few chords of track

one on Lizzy's new radio. I grabbed my beer and headed sheepishly back outside to catch her reaction. She and Taylor were talking as I approached. I couldn't hear what they were saying but at one point Lizzy flashed a smile and looked out over the horizon. It was a good sign.

I reached them and sat down and the three of us listened until the first song faded.

Lizzy looked over at me.

'Thanks, Nox. This is pretty awesome,' she said.

I went to tell her she was welcome. And that the album was awesome. And it would be a fucking beacon of hope for anyone listening. And that if anything about Carousel was worthwhile it was this album. And that when we got out, she and Taylor could go back to their lives in Canada and forget me and I would be okay, or better even.

But the second song started and Lizzy turned back to face her horizon of hidden listeners. Instead, Taylor gave me a little smile that reminded me that she knew pretty much everything I didn't say, and if she knew, Lizzy probably did also.

So I sat back and enjoyed the music and the beer like I don't remember ever enjoying them. I thought of that great scene from *The Shawshank Redemption* where Red and co get an hour or so to drink some beers on the roof of the prison and bask in the momentary freedom. Maybe our circumstances weren't quite as poetic, but in another way, maybe they were.

28

On Boxing Day, Taylor was gardening in the dome when she heard someone knock on the front entrance. She told us how she was wrist-deep, turning a stack of compost and humming the tune of Wilco's 'Heavy Metal Drummer' when she heard three distinctive bangs.

'I stopped and looked straight at the front doors. You know when your eyes automatically go to where your ears have heard something. Like there's no doubt in between your senses,' she told us.

'Did you go over there straight away?' asked Lizzy.

Taylor shook her head ruefully.

'I just knelt there like an idiot, waiting to hear it again,' she replied.

'But you didn't?' I asked.

Taylor shook her head.

'So eventually I stood up and walked over. I was right over the other side at the lettuces so it took me maybe twenty or thirty seconds to get there,' she said.

Lizzy and I nodded.

The main entrance of the dome had a frosted glass

partition running in an arch just inside the door. When Carousel was open for regular business you came in through the outside doors and then swung either left or right to get into the actual entrance, and the dome. Whether it was filtering pedestrian traffic or sheltering the quasi-tranquillity of the dome from the car park outside, it made exiting the centre a clumsy process.

'When I got to the doors there was nobody there. I mean, you can only see out to that little wall at the edge of the car park so they could have been just around the corner. But they didn't come back,' said Taylor.

'Did you try the door?' I asked.

Taylor looked at me a little strangely and shook her head.

Lizzy and I were pensive.

'God, I don't know. Maybe it was just a bird flying into the glass or the wind or something,' said Taylor.

Lizzy looked at her carefully.

'But it wasn't,' she said.

Taylor met her gaze. I watched the two of them as information and emotion flew across the private Finn highway.

Taylor shook her head.

'When I got to the door I felt them,' she said. 'Like when you go into a room somebody has just left. I used to be pretty crap at that but this place sharpens you up. You're alone so fucking much you really feel when somebody else is around.'

Lizzy gave Taylor a tiny, reassuring smile and started thinking it over.

I had a stupid thought that I didn't want to share, but felt like I should.

'Do you guys have big post-Christmas department store sales in Canada?' I asked.

Taylor and Lizzy shared a strange expression.

'Yeah. I guess so,' said Taylor.

'They're a pretty big deal over here. Some people totally lose their shit. Lining up at the doors for hours until they open. Trampling over each other to get to the sale racks,' I said.

The Finns were quickly impatient.

'It starts on Boxing Day,' I said.

'Holy shit,' said Lizzy.

'Really?' asked Taylor.

I shrugged.

'Why not?' said Lizzy.

'Someone out there still thinks there's a stocktake sale even though the world is crumbling down?' said Taylor.

'It's about as nuts as a cleaner coming in to do the unused toilets every week,' said Lizzy.

Taylor sighed and looked up at the ceiling.

'Fuck. This place,' she said tiredly.

We were silent for a moment or two.

'It's like some people just didn't get the memo,' I said.

'Yeah,' said Lizzy, nodding seriously.

'What do you mean?' asked Taylor.

'This massive thing went down in the world, and some people: us, Rocky, Rachel, Peter, Stocktake Sale Lady, just didn't get the memo,' I said.

'And now we're just wandering around, trying to find hobbies while we figure out if we were lucky or unlucky,' said Lizzy.

Taylor looked at her, and then back out at the entrance. Her brain was ticking over.

'Nox, you know how you said Peter had those drawings in the back of his car,' she said.

Lizzy and I didn't follow.

'He must have been some kind of illustrator,' said Taylor. 'Nox is a writer. We're musicians,' said Taylor.

Lizzy looked at her sister carefully.

'It's like, the people that didn't get the memo are all artists,' said Taylor.

'Rachel? Rocky?' I asked.

Lizzy shrugged as if to say, *they could be*. Taylor didn't have an answer. She looked at Lizzy and the two of them tried to work out whether it could be true. That instead of politicians, scientists or doctors, it was artists that had been saved from the apocalypse.

I joined them in pensive silence. Quietly wondering about my place within this exclusive, fantasy demographic.

29

It was a week or so into the new year when we started hearing other noises outside. For a while I racked my brain to remember whether there were normally fireworks or celebrations at the start of January that might have offered an explanation. But I couldn't think of anything. Plus these didn't really sound like fireworks. They were lower. Maybe not underground, like I imagined an earthquake would sound, but definitely somewhere around street level. They were bassy and without a real echo.

The Finns and I ran through the lists of things we thought we had heard outside Carousel since our arrival. There were trucks or large car sounds that would drift in from somewhere distant, maybe the hills, maybe the city, before quickly fading away again into silence. Sometimes we thought we heard a dog barking somewhere deep in suburbia where his owners would presumably silence him for fear of discovery. Then there were random things like church bells, a football siren, a Mr Whippy van, guitars tuning, a ship leaving the port. One morning Lizzy swore she could hear a Britney Spears album playing somewhere to the west of us.

Nothing could be confirmed or denied. Every sound was fleeting and uncertain. Maybe Perth was still alive, but she was keeping things close to her chest.

Until the noises started.

The Finns and I listened carefully from various vantage points around the centre. We tried to place them geographically but the source was shifting. We watched the sky for the yellow tinge of smoke, but it remained brilliant and blue.

Eventually we grew used to them.

However, the noises had a kind of unspoken legacy. They reminded us that, despite our diminishing food stocks, the risks of illness and the constant battle to stay sane, being outside Carousel was not necessarily safer than being trapped inside. We understood the strange parameters of our centre, whereas outside remained a dark and sketchy mystery. We had never considered staying or going as a choice, and maybe we would never have to, but the noises seemed to raise the stakes either way.

Late into a windy summer afternoon Lizzy and I were watching TV, waiting for Taylor to return from the dome with some vegetables for dinner. We reached the end of season four of *Mad Men* and got through two episodes of season five before Lizzy paused the disc and looked at me curiously. I gazed out the doorway.

The daylight had left all but the highest sections of

Carousel. The rest of the centre hung in dark limbo. Taylor should have been back a while ago. I lifted a radio to my lips when the echo of boots drifted into JB's. Lizzy and I glanced at each other and listened as they grew louder. Taylor surfaced out of the shadows and joined us on the couch. Lizzy and I sat up and watched her carefully. Her head was full of something.

'I found a video of when we arrived,' she said.

'What do you mean?' asked Lizzy.

'The security cameras. They're recording everything to hard drives.'

Taylor had been unable to shake the Boxing Day experience from her mind. Something about the knock on the door had resonated with her and wouldn't let go. That morning while gardening she had a brainwave that maybe she could somehow access archived security footage of the entrance and find out who the hell it was out there.

As she led us back to the security office she told us how she had spent most of the afternoon screwing around with the computers up there trying to find footage of the entrance when she stumbled across a file that showed us dragging Lizzy's bed into Dymocks a year and a half ago. When she realised how old the footage was she quickly skipped back further. Half an hour later she found a file named S032011 that revealed our entrance into Carousel.

The three of us huddled around a computer as Taylor reopened the file, skipped past some footage and pressed pause. We looked at her. It was tense as all hell in there. She hit *Play*.

It was an odd angle. A ceiling camera somewhere in the east end. Not focused on a major entrance, but a nondescript door beside some cleaning closets. It made no sense that anyone would arrive through it. We watched the static, empty space for a few moments, before the door shifted slightly, then opened inward and Taylor and Lizzy entered.

'Holy shit,' whispered Lizzy.

The Finns stepped inside. They looked a little confused at where they had entered and Taylor turned to look back at the door. It had already closed behind them.

They lingered for a second until Lizzy pointed out something down the hall. She took a step toward it but Taylor said something that stopped her. The two of them looked around at the dead-empty corridor. Eventually Lizzy shrugged and walked out of frame.

Taylor paused the clip.

'We go down the hall to the chocolate store,' she said.

Lizzy and I looked at her, still processing the vision.

'What about Nox?' asked Lizzy.

Taylor reached across and scrolled forward around twenty minutes.

'Keep watching,' she said.

We refocused on the door. A moment later it opened again and I stepped through into Carousel. The emptiness struck me quicker than it had the Finns. I looked confused and turned back to catch the door as it was closing. Taylor paused the clip with the door still a foot or so open.

'There's the cab,' she said.

Lizzy and I leant in close to the screen. It was true. Through the gap between door and doorway was the pearly white of a Perth taxi. Taylor resumed the video and the door closed before I could stop it. We watched as I tried to open it again, but found it locked. I paced around the corridor for a few moments, clearly confused by the emptiness and the door. Eventually I left in the same direction as Taylor and Lizzy, and most likely the bookstore.

'It's weird that you took a cab, yeah?' asked Lizzy.

'Yeah,' I said. 'I mean, my car is shit, so it does break down a bit. But it was weird that the driver stopped at the bus stop and picked me up like he did. And dropped me at Carousel.'

'At that same door,' said Taylor.

'You don't remember what he looked like?' asked Lizzy.

I shook my head. We'd spoken about this a bunch of times already.

'Sorry. I was half asleep and screwing around on my phone. I just remember a normal looking dude,' I said.

Lizzy held in a sigh.

'Ready for what's next?' asked Taylor.

We nodded. She closed the file and opened another that offered a pretty wide angle on the dome and front entrance. Lizzy and I watched for several long minutes. Nothing appeared to happen.

Taylor stopped the clip and looked at us. We shrugged. She flicked back and replayed from a point near the start.

'Watch the doors,' she said.

Lizzy and I leant in close. A few seconds passed. Lizzy opened her mouth and was about to ask 'what' when both of us saw it.

The doors shuddered and the light outside went black. As if somebody hit the switch on some giant vacuum. It was over in a second, but resonated right down to our bones. Even Taylor, who had seemingly watched this a few times over, seemed a little shaken.

'What the hell was that?' asked Lizzy.

'It's the same right through the centre. Six fifty-two am,' said Taylor.

My legs were jittery. We had known something had happened in the world for a long time now. But this tiny flicker of footage had finally made it real.

'God,' said Lizzy, blinking through some tears.

Taylor put a hand on her sister's shoulder.

'Where was Rocky when that happened?' asked Lizzy.

'Outside,' I replied.

Taylor looked at me. 'What did he tell you?'

'Said he was waiting for Geri. There was a spot just outside Target where they would hang out before work sometimes,' I replied.

'Was she there with him?' asked Taylor.

'She didn't show,' I replied.

Taylor's brain was running in overdrive while she stared hard at the floor.

'Did he see anything out there?' she asked.

'He just said it was really windy for a moment,' I replied.

'I don't understand how he survived,' she said.

'It was Carousel,' whispered Lizzy.

The three of us were silent for a moment.

'You didn't find him entering?' I asked Taylor.

She shook her head. 'Just inside Target. A little later.'

Taylor took us through a series of files. I was pretty impressed at how quickly she'd been able to locate the footage. Taylor would often do things like that and shrug as if you were the weird one when you complimented her efficiency. On a file taken not long after the door shudder we watched Rocky emerge from somewhere within Target. He was wearing his uniform and looked generally normal. He paced the store for signs of anyone else, then stood at the entrance for a moment looking out on the empty corridors. After this he simply walked over to the camping section, took a mat from the shelves and set up a bed within the PJ aisle nearby.

Nothing about any of this seemed too unusual for Rocky. If he had been hysterical or energetic that might have been alarming. But he seemed, at least from the distant, elevated camera, to be his normal self.

He did lie still for quite a long time. Taylor skipped through a lot of footage and Rocky remained pretty much motionless on the mattress throughout. He wasn't asleep. His eyes remained open. The camera was too far away to assess his expression, even in a close-up this was difficult with Rocky. But I couldn't help but think he was processing whatever had just happened outside. We'd seen a second of it on a computer screen and had been rocked backward. Rocky had been out there and somehow survived. I started to think that his week-long hibernation in Target was pretty understandable.

'I looked through a lot of files and can't find anybody else show up,' said Taylor. 'Until Rachel arrives for her shift about a week later.'

'Did you see Peter anywhere?' I asked.

Taylor shook her head.

'There's so much of this stuff,' she said, scrolling through file after file in just one of countless folders.

'It doesn't matter anyway,' said Lizzy.

Taylor and I looked at her. She was probably right. Whatever had happened, happened. The fact that we entered through the same door was the most interesting discovery. We had always suspected this; it was the first place Taylor really started checking doors. But there were a lot of doors down there and, as with the taxi driver, our recollections were cloudy.

Now we had proof. This footage confirmed that this

was where the taxis, or taxi, as Lizzy would have it, had dropped us both. Not at the front or the back, or even one of the minor entrances running to car parks. Places that would no doubt have been locked.

Lizzy was right, it didn't seem arbitrary.

'So we got here just before the shudder, and Rocky pretty much just after, and then nobody shows for a week or so,' I said.

Taylor watched me and ran it over in her head.

'I didn't go back any further,' she said.

'What do you mean?' I asked.

'Before we got here,' she said.

Lizzy and I watched as she leant across and scrolled through to find a random file well above S032011. She opened it and the three of us watched. It showed a corridor full of shoppers.

'Oh god,' said Lizzy and turned away from the screen.

'Sorry,' said Taylor.

She quickly closed down the window. It was way too weird to see all of those people in Carousel, knowing what we knew.

Lizzy paced the room in anxious circles. Taylor looked at me as if to ask if she should continue. I shrugged, then had a thought.

'Maybe just look a week back from when you first saw Rachel arrive,' I suggested.

Taylor nodded and scanned through the files in a folder

named Centre East Corridor. She found what she was after and before long we saw Rachel emerge from her cleaning door with a Redbull and what looked like a nasty hangover.

'Chipper as always,' said Lizzy, watching from over my shoulder.

'This is not long before the door shudder, right?' I asked.

'Yep,' replied Taylor.

We watched as Rachel cleaned the gnome-free bathrooms and completely missed the flash of dark outside. She left through the door in the east end an hour or so later, hesitating only briefly after stepping back outside.

We ran through a lot of footage that night, carefully examining the days right after our arrival, in case there were others. We watched as an Indian man surfaced a few days after us and decided it must be Peter. We couldn't find footage of his entrance but it was in the vicinity of the staff car park. He shuffled about anxiously for the best part of a day, narrowly missing Taylor at the dome before eventually making his way to the food court. It was pretty harrowing to watch. The guy seemed erratic, and was clearly distressed by whatever he had witnessed outside. He huddled in the corner of the Travelex for long stints in between gorging on random foods and gathering together top-line electrical items. It seemed like he knew the Travelex store and Taylor suggested that maybe he had a job there. Late in the day he spent several long and ominous minutes with a bottle of water in Friendlies Chemist before slipping into the food court toilets, where he remained indefinitely. We stopped the video and decided we had uncovered enough of Peter's mystery. None of us needed to see Rachel make the discovery. Or shift him to the storeroom.

Lizzy left us in thick, heavy silence. It was a lot to take in about a world we had wiped from our minds. I stared hard at the desktop and tried to find a word for how I felt.

'Did you find Stocktake Sale Lady?' I asked, to break the silence.

Taylor looked at me and nodded.

'Seriously?'

She nodded again. There was a tiny flicker of something in her gaze.

'Well?' I asked.

Taylor opened another folder and located the file. She skipped through a half-hour of empty footage on the front entrance. Until a figure came into view.

She was in her twenties and pretty, from what the grainy footage suggested. She was wearing jeans and a black top and carrying a kind of chunky retro handbag. There was something odd about her clothing. Taylor noticed me straining to see and paused the clip. I looked closer.

'Is that paint?' I asked.

Taylor nodded.

The mystery shopper had paint all over her clothing. Not the heavy white splatter of a tradesman, but the random palette of a painter.

She lingered at the door for a few moments, knocked gently, then waited a few moments longer. Another couple of seconds passed before she turned and left the frame, her shoulders dropping a little with disappointment. She looked a touch edgy maybe, but hardly like someone fearful of zombies or nuclear fallout.

'Artists,' said Taylor, and closed the video.

I looked at her and suddenly remembered something. I shook my head and almost laughed.

'What?' asked Taylor.

'Rachel said something to me that night we were drinking,' I replied.

Taylor looked at me curiously.

'She asked me if we were artists,' I said. 'But it was kind of like she already knew that we were.'

'Because we were alive,' said Taylor. 'Protected.'

I looked at her and tried to process everything that had happened to us.

'Who would do that?' I asked.

Taylor stared at the static screen. She didn't have an answer.

'Come on. We better go find Lizzy,' she said.

30

Following Taylor's discovery I set some goals for my writing and was pretty keen to at least get through January before letting them slide. We had delved too deeply into the murky and sombre Carousel past. Digging it up had left us fragile and revealed little that was of use. Somehow the centre had protected us from a kind of apocalyptic vacuum. This protection had been enough for Rocky as he waited outside Target, while Rachel had been fatefully inside already. How Peter arrived was still a mystery, but seemed innately connected to the drawings in his Fiesta.

From there the six of us adapted to our new environment in the best ways we could. None of us wanted to judge Peter's decision. Or Rachel's upon finding his body. The security footage held its own silent judgement on each of us, and that was enough.

The only thing I chose to hang onto was the idea that my arrival here wasn't arbitrary. That there was a reason I was alive and in Carousel. I let this drive my writing goals.

The first one was just to finish the book of short stories and move on to something new. It had been all but done for months now but I had to decide on whether I wanted to include the 'Boy on the Bus' story or leave it alone and forgotten.

If I was straight with myself I knew the story had to be included; in a way, it was the one from which all of the others had stemmed. It was more a matter of whether I knew what the hell it was about. And if I didn't know, and couldn't figure it out, deciding whether this actually mattered.

Lizzy had asked me something important about the story that I felt I needed to get straight. It was important for the writing, but also for me personally. Rocky's death was a weight on my shoulders that I don't think he would have wanted. Taylor had tried to lift this, telling me it was Carousel that decided if and when we could leave, and whether we lived or died, not a remote control in a dead man's Fiesta. But the weight had remained.

Somehow I knew that the boy on the bus was Rocky. But I didn't know what he decided by staying aboard the wrong bus. If I could work this out and finish the story, maybe things would become clear and the weight would lift.

I danced around the story for weeks, sometimes sitting down and reading it carefully, line by line, as if the answer was available to the focused eye. I tried typing it out on my laptop and shuffling things around. Digging like a child in a sandpit, manically shifting the surface, but never going deep. And I would walk the corridors with the writing pad in my pocket. The story bobbing in my head as I kept myself moving and willed it to surface.

On a Thursday I set out southward where the corridors were long and wide and I could wander for hours before passing the same stores. I skirted east around the dome and left Taylor to herself with the gardening. I would see her and Lizzy at dinner and my best chance of an answer seemed to be in solitude. I passed Woolworths, the music shop and the bubble tea outlets and continued onward. This was the edge of my neighbourhood and I gazed around as my memory ebbed and flowed ahead of my vision. I was moving faster than I normally did. For once not so aimless.

Before long I found myself standing in front of Target.

I stared up at the huge red logo. The checkouts stood below like lonely, silent pillars.

I hadn't been to Target since Lizzy started building her studio. Since I went in to get us a Vitamin Water and ended up staring at the place where we found Rocky. The realisation ripped across my skin like an icy southern wind.

I got the dizzy feeling on auto dial. The loss of my feet. My head towering above my body. The spread of the centre like a complex, 3D map. My eyes searching through a mass of doors, narrowing and narrowing, before I was tilted too far over to know the ceiling from the floor and I jolted back awake.

I caught myself on a checkout and sucked in some air. It felt like hours had passed but I knew this wasn't the case. This dizzy sensation had plagued me ever since my last visit to Target. Suddenly being back at the store didn't feel so accidental.

My feet returned and I stood upright and tested myself against gravity. I steadied, then pushed through the checkout and into the store. Rocky's first bed was tucked away at the back and I weaved toward it without hesitation.

Within moments, his tiny dwelling was before me. A thin rubber mat rolled out to sleep on. A small, battery-powered lamp. Empty bottles of Sprite and Pepsi. Chocolate wrappers. A pile of clothes for a pillow. I knelt and looked over the sombre arrangement and wondered if I was going to break down. For a moment I wavered, before I noticed a glint of silver within the clothes.

Rocky had pulled down a bunch of shirts from a nearby rack to form his pillow. They had remained there, dusty and unmoved since we found him all those days ago. But within this mass was something else. I shifted the shirts away. A set of keys lay beneath.

Nothing for a car or bike. Just a couple of regular keys with a cord to a security card.

They were Rocky's.

With a horrible, unexpected jolt I knew what happened at the bus stop. What the boy really decided. What Rocky had decided.

I grabbed the keys and radioed Taylor and Lizzy.

'Should we bring anything?' asked Taylor.

'Just your album,' I replied.

'And meet you at Target?' asked Lizzy.

'Yeah. Please,' I said. 'Just leave everything but the album and come straight over.'

'Alright. We'll be there soon,' said Taylor.

It was hard to gauge their voices over the radio. But they were coming, that was what mattered.

I left the bed and skirted the long left side of Target. I reached the end, then turned along the back wall, but still didn't find what I was after. I moved past manchester, into electronics and eventually toward camping supplies. Then, in the back right corner, beside the fishing rods and eskies, I found the door.

Just a regular grey door with a small sign saying *Staff Only*.

Beside it was a tagging mechanism like the one we had seen Rachel use. A steady red light emanated from the front. I lifted Rocky's card to the sensor.

The light turned green.

I stood there for a moment and took a breath. I didn't push the door open. Instead I sat down and took out the small writing pad Taylor had given me at Christmas. My original 'Boy on the Bus' story was folded and worn inside. I lifted it out and read it again.

Everything made sense. The boy's reluctance to go

home. The mystique of the wrong bus. Strange comings and goings of the passengers. Friendships built out of the darkness. The moment where he realises what's happening, but does nothing. The inevitability of his destination.

The story was finished. Had been for a long time now.

In trying to make my own decision I had written about Rocky's. I had only ever considered staying in Carousel as cowardice, but somehow Rocky had made it brave and defining, like so many things.

I closed the pad and felt Rocky resonate somewhere deep, below the numbness. Tears streamed from my eyes but the air I breathed felt fresh and vital in my lungs.

'Nox? Where are you?' radioed Taylor.

'At the back,' I answered.

Their footsteps echoed closer until they swung into view and found me.

'Shit. Are you okay?' asked Lizzy.

I looked at them both as they knelt down beside me. Hair all choppy. Oversized black shirts rolled up at the sleeves. Big, luminous eyes staring right into me.

About as Taylor & Lizzy as you get.

'Yeah,' I said. 'Sorry.'

Taylor looked around.

'What are you doing here?' she asked.

I handed her Rocky's keys. She and Lizzy looked at me carefully.

'They're Rocky's,' I said.

Taylor glanced at the door, then stared at me hard. I nodded and climbed to my feet.

Taylor and Lizzy looked at each other.

'Did you bring your album?' I asked.

They nodded.

I stood by the door and waited. Taylor edged forward and held out the card. She waited a moment, then lifted it to the sensor. The light turned green.

She placed her hands on the door, looked at me, and pushed.

31

For a long time we just sat outside on the concrete, breathing in the air and trying to work out how we felt.

We had exited Carousel onto a small concrete ramp that led away from Target toward some staff parking. At a turn in the ramp was a platform sheltered by the cornering walls and an overhang in the roof. Central in this platform was a dusty vending machine.

It seemed like we were on the southwest corner of the centre as the sun was edging away from us toward the horizon.

The horizon.

It was messy, flat and suburban, like any other day I had seen in Perth.

The three of us stared at it across the vacant car park. An empty highway divided the centre from the brick and tiles of the surrounding suburbs. Everything looked quiet and gentle.

'You don't think he forgot?' asked Taylor, after a while.

I looked at her and shook my head. She turned away and bit her lip as she cried.

Lizzy held her sister's head against her chest.

'He wanted to stay,' said Lizzy softly. 'Didn't he, Nox?'

I looked at her and nodded. A familiar rumble reached us from somewhere in the suburbs. Suddenly it didn't sound so distant.

Taylor sniffed and we all looked out at the horizon once again.

'All that stuff you packed,' Taylor reminded me.

I looked at her, then Lizzy.

'We can't go back,' said Lizzy.

Taylor and I nodded. The rumbling came again. We looked up at the sky. It was clear and cloudless.

'I think I can get us to the airport,' I said.

The Finns glanced at each other. Lizzy nodded and Taylor pulled herself up off the concrete. Lizzy and I joined her and the three of us edged down to the base of the ramp. We shared a nervous smile and set off across the long, windswept car park.

About the Author

Brendan Ritchie is a novelist and academic from the south coast of WA. He was the winner of the 2022 Dorothy Hewett Award for an unpublished manuscript, and is the author of novels including *Carousel* (2015), *Beyond Carousel* (2016) and *Eta Draconis* (2023). Brendan has a PhD in Creative Writing and has also published poetry and non-fiction in several notable journals and collections. He lives on Wadandi land with his wife and two young daughters.

Acknowledgements

Large and overdue thanks to Marcella Polain for her longstanding belief and support on so many writing journeys. I'm not sure that books can happen without people like you. Thanks to everyone at Fremantle Press. Particularly Cate, for a phone call that won't be forgotten, and Naama, for getting *Carousel* and guiding me back through its web. Thanks to Edith Cowan University for opening its arms to creative research. Thanks always to Claire for her love, support and honesty, and for reading first while I hovered, feigning confidence. Thanks to Ange for reading second and inhaling where I'd hoped people one day might. Thanks to Mum and Dad for reading third, sharing the final pages by the fire in Karridale. I'll remember that story. And thanks to my twin sisters. Maybe even to twin sisters everywhere.